The Ballad of LLewellynn

2012

Robert Rowen

Text Copyright © 2012 Robert Rowen
All rights reserved

To Mary for all your support, encouragement, love and faith that made doing this possible

Prologue

Britain, 473 AD

The great room was quiet at last. A once blazing fire dwindled to embers in a hearth large enough that two men could lay head to toe within it. Servants bustled back and forth between the great room and the kitchen to clear away the evening's feast. They carried off the platters that had been laden with meats and cheeses, breads and vegetables, and threw the scraps to the dogs.

The lady of the house wore a fine gown of light blue cotton, cinched at the waist with a dark blue sash and gathered at the shoulder with a silver brooch. She called out to an empty handed worker. "You there! If you've nothing to do, take a broom to this floor." As the girl in a frock made of brown home spun wool did as she was told, her mistress turned her attention to the manse's main doorway. The heavy oak door had been barred properly after the departure of the last of their guest. All was secure.

Her husband came up behind her, his beard neatly trimmed, wearing robes reminiscent of those of a Roman general. He was tall and lean, his muscles well defined. The dimming light hid all but the most recent scars of battle. He put his hands on her waist and gave her a squeeze. The woman gently took his hand away and turned to face him. "Wait until they're done," she said, kissing him lightly, then went to the tables where the last of the food was being carted off. The girl finished sweeping the crumbs to the fireplace and returned the broom to its niche by the front door.

A toddler entered the room wearing robes just like his father's. He crossed the flagstone floor to a wolf hound nearly twice his height that was gnawing on a bone by the dying fire. "Puppy," he said, reaching out to pet the dog behind his ears. The dog rumbled a warning to the boy, took the bone in his teeth and moved to another spot at the other side of the fire. The action caught his father's eye.

The man scooped the child up in his arms and held him, sitting in the crook of his elbow. "What are you doing up, little man? I thought you went to bed hours ago."

"Couldn't sleep."

The lady joined them, cupping the back of the little boy's head with one hand and putting the other arm round her husband's waist. "I think we need to try again. It's late."

"Don't want to." The boy squirmed, trying to free himself from his father's grip. "Want to play." The man put him down, lest he lose his grip and let the boy fall.

"One game," his father relented, "then it's off to bed." He bent over, putting himself eye to eye with his son. "You go find yourself a place to hide, and make it a good one." The man put his forearm up over his eyes.

The little boy trotted off with glee. "You no look either, Mommy." He scurried off to the kitchen and found a nook among the shelves where he could fit.

"That's not a good place for you tonight, young master," said one of the cook's helpers. The boy climbed out reluctantly to make way for a pair of earthenware jugs and went to find another place to hide. He avoided the bedrooms. That was the point after all. At the end of the hall, he went down a stairway to the storerooms.

His favorite hiding place was in a room paneled in aromatic cedar. He always paused for a deep breath when he entered. In one corner, a section of the paneling opened into a passage barely taller than he was. It was long, dark and full of spiders. It led to the bakery at the foot of the hill his house sat atop. He used it from time to time when he felt in need of a treat. He stepped into the passage, pulled the door nearly closed and listened for his pursuers.

Standing in the dark, looking through the crack of the door, the grogginess crept back but he fought it off. There was not a sound. At first, he felt proud of his hiding spot, then the pride turned to annoyance at his parents. *Were they even looking for him?* He crept out, crossed the storage area and climbed the stairs. He heard smacking noises, a giggle from his mother and a few vague *mmm*'s. Peering over the top step, he saw his mother leaning with her back to the wall with her arms around his father's neck.

He stood to go up the remaining stairs just as the front door burst open. The heavy oaken door slammed hard against the stone wall. He noticed the board used to bar it was missing. Men streamed in, brandishing swords. He thought he'd seen them earlier, enjoying his father's hospitality at the feast. They hadn't been wearing armor then.

The boy ducked back down out of sight. He was afraid to look up, but the sounds told the story. He heard the wolfhound's snarling barks, only to be cut off with a yelp and a whimper. His mother screamed. Metal clanged against metal. Harsh voices spoke words he didn't understand. "Arrrgh." It was his father's voice.

Metal clattered on the floor amid sounds of things falling, thudding. "No!" his mother screamed, sobbing.

"Where's the boy?" An angry voice demanded.

"Leave my son alone. He's done nothing. He's just a baby." More sounds of violence, another short scream from his mother and then quiet. Even the sobbing had stopped.

"Mommy?" The boy whimpered. He ran down the steps to the store room and pulled the hidden door fully closed behind him. He felt a warm wetness run down his robes and over his feet. The muffled sounds of furniture being overturned continued. The sounds grew closer. He could hear them in the storage room, rummaging through the goods there. The little boy stood quivering in the dark until they faded.

When things had been quiet for a time, he ventured into the store room again. Through a vent to the outside echoed the sound of horse's hooves clattering down the stone road that wound down the hill. Still, he didn't dare go up into the house. Tears flowed down his cheeks as he made his way, sniffling down the pitch black passage way to a place he knew he would find comfort.

Table of contents

Prologue

Table of contents

Chapter 1 - The Machine

Chapter 2 - Found

Chapter 3 – Living in the Past

Chapter 4 – Cub Scout Projects

Chapter 5 – The Apprentice

Chapter 6 – Trymme

Chapter 7 – Alarm

Chapter 8 – Attack

Chapter 9 – The Minstrel

Chapter 10 – The Ballad

Chapter 11 – Call To Arms

Chapter 12 – The Battle

Chapter 13 – The Castle

Epilogue

Chapter 1 - The Machine

Gamertsfelder Hall
Ohio University, Athens Ohio

Jeff Warren sat hunched over his project, sleeves of his plain flannel shirt rolled back to the elbows. A four foot square piece of hardboard lay across the two battered metal desks in his dorm room. The side he was working on was a maze of wires covered in black plastic insulation that snaked their way across the board, seemingly at random, the ends twisted around and soldered to metal posts pushed through from the other side.

Jeff held a hot soldering iron to one of the connections and brought the tip of a coil of solder to touch the hot metal. The soft lead instantly liquefied and flowed into the nooks and crannies between the twisted wires and the post. A wisp of the resin flux that helped the molten lead flow vaporized in a puff of smoke that flared his nostrils. He blew on the join to cool it and pulled the wire to be sure it was tight. He repeated the procedure at the other end of the wire and then put the iron down in its cradle while he checked to see if any of the other joins were loose.

"What are you trying to do, burn the place down?"

Jeff pushed the clear plastic safety glasses up, out of the way and turned to the open doorway. The speaker was Tom Parker, a Junior who lived down the hall. "Trying not to," Jeff said, smiling. "Putting the finishing touches on my Circuits project." He flipped the board over to check it over from the other side.

In contrast to the back, this side was meticulously laid out. A dozen or so electronic components a nine volt battery and a small speaker, each carefully labeled, were mounted evenly about the space. In place of the rats nest of wiring, color coded lines were drawn perfectly straight with ninety degree corners laying out the diagram of the circuit.

"Looks good," Tom said. "What have you got there?"

"Check it out," Jeff said.

He connected the battery, making the speaker crackle. It crackled louder as he moved a contact along a coil of bare copper wire until he found the spot he needed, then the crackle became a voice. "… basement of Gamertsfelder Hall, this is WGAM the radio voice of the East Green of Ohio University."

"Nice!" said Tom. "You're a regular Marconi."

"Yeah, right," said Jeff. "Except Marconi didn't have a text book, a couple of lectures and the guy at Radio Shack to tell him what to do."

"Or even let him know what he was doing was even possible." Tom laughed. "Still, not a bad job. Maybe you're ready to jump over to electrical engineering now."

Jeff unplugged the soldering iron and set the project aside. "No, I think I'll stick to mechanical. I always wanted to design cars."

"Too bad. I came down to tell you, my dad got me a job in his company for the summer. If you went electrical, I thought I might be able to get you in, too."

"That would have been great, except I've already got a job lined up lifeguarding by my parents' house in New Jersey," Jeff said. "It's kind of late to back out. They're counting on me."

"It's not like it was up to me, anyway," Tom said.

"It would have been a tough decision, a dead end job full of sun, sand and bikinis at the beach or a good career move at a lab in The-Middle-of-Nowhere, Pennsylvania."

"That's the best part," Tom said. "My dad got transferred to the office in England. I'm going to spend my whole summer over there."

"Now you tell me," Jeff said. "I'm going over there for ten days. I thought that was good. The whole summer, that's awesome."

"Where are you going to be?"

"My mom's cousin lives in London. I'm going to stay with her," Jeff said.

"I'll be on the West coast. Not far from the Welsh border, but it's still only a few hours away," Tom said. "Maybe you can get over there. I'll show you what we're working on. It sounds really cool. When do you get there?"

"The 8th. I get done lifeguarding on Labor Day, then time for one Yankee game before my flight," Jeff said. "They're playing the Marlins, should be a romp."

"You and your Yankees," Tom said. "I'll bet you they blow it."

"I'll take that bet," Jeff aid. "If I win, you wear a Yankee shirt for a week."

"Sounds fair. I'll pack a Marlins shirt for you," Tom said. "Email me when you get there. I'll give you directions."

"You're on," Jeff said, picking up his guitar. The battered old acoustic went everywhere he did. Playing it was how he relaxed whenever he had to think. Exam time was near. He was going to need it.

ST&C Labs
Western England, near the Severn Channel

"Here's what we've been working on." Harry Parker explained to his son. Tom would run the digital video camera to record the experiment. Harry held out his hand, showing him a small violet gemstone. "These Crystals were discovered a year ago on the Arctic sea floor." He placed the stone in a receptacle in the machine and secured it there. When we pass an electrical current through one of these, what comes out is a signal we call the fingerprint. Every crystal's is unique. The machine generates a harmonic of the fingerprint, which we amplify and send back through the crystal like this." Harry made a few adjustments on the laptop controlling the machine and the crystal began to glow.

The crystal gave off a purple light which was focused onto another DVC camera which had been placed in line with the beam. It was recording also. Harry hit another button on the laptop. "We turn it up a bit more and…" There was a loud pop and the recorder disappeared.

"Holy sh-." Tom hesitated, remembering he wasn't in college now. "Holy crap. It's gone."

"Gone is right Tom. Not just invisible, it isn't there. We think it might be something like the transporters on Star Trek."

"Where'd it go?"

"That's the problem. We don't know. We need to figure that out if we're ever going to be able to control it. Last time we tried a GPS tracker, but the whole time it was gone, we lost the signal. Either there is some kind of interference or it's going someplace beyond the range of the satellites."

Tom ran his hand through the space where the camera had been.

"Don't!" His father nudged the hand back. "I don't know what would happen if it comes back with your hand in the way and I don't want to find out."

Another loud snap announced the camera's return. Tom rubbed his hand as if in pain.

"Total time, thirty seven seconds," Steve Evans, a software engineer on the team called out. The other technicians, Bill Dougherty and Chris Rutledge, jotted the time into their notes.

Harry picked up the DVC. "Let's see what's on this thing. Maybe it'll give us a clue." He played the video back on the monitor. The haze of purple grew in intensity, then stopped abruptly but the scene didn't change. "That's odd," he said. He uploaded both videos into the computer and ran them side by side and frame by frame. They synched up perfectly except that the subject camera's video was twenty two seconds shorter, exactly the time the subject was gone on the other one. It was as though the subject didn't exist in the time it was gone.

"What do you think happened?" Tom asked.

"That's what we have to figure out."

ST&C Labs

Mr. Parker started the day as he always did, with what he called "a two minute meeting". It was a recap of the progress so far, the stumbling blocks they've encountered lately, and finally the plan for the day. "All summer we've been looking into where the subjects are going and we still don't have a clue. So, today we're going to put direction on the back burner and go another avenue entirely."

"We're going to try it with a live subject to see if it can survive. Any volunteers?" Harry asked. As the only member of the team without a degree, it usually fell on Tom to do the odd jobs like picking up take-out food or going for supplies when needed. His hand started to go up automatically before it occurred to him what was being asked. He pulled it back down even quicker. "Of course not!" Mr. Parker continued with a smile, and the rest of the team laughed along with him. "I've ordered some mice for advanced tests. They'll be in later in the week. So, we're going to use what are readily available, ants. I mainly want to know if any living thing can survive the process. So they'll be a good start." He handed a small container to his son. "Tom, this is a job for you. They've been harassing us all summer, so I'm sure you can find a few subjects."

Tom spent a good part of the morning crawling around the lab looking for the insects. At times they had been a downright nuisance and it had been his job to deal with them between visits from the exterminator. Today it was all he could do to find one. Finally, just before breaking for lunch they were able to run the experiment. Three ants in a plastic container were set in front of the machine. Power was brought up until a purple light shone on the subject and then *SNAP!* The ants were gone, container and all. Not just invisible but gone without a trace. Five minutes later, without warning, there was another *SNAP!* and they were back, crawling around inside the container as if nothing had happened.

ST&C Labs

"Good morning," Harry Parker began the meeting, "We learned some interesting stuff yesterday. The ants survived the night, so we know the process is not necessarily fatal. Which is a long way from saying it is safe, but it appears to be benign."

"Up to now the subjects we've been working with have been robust. We went from a coin to a paperweight to electronic devices. They've all come through unscathed, but these items are not exactly delicate. The electronics are undamaged, but recorded nothing at all during the process. Today we're going to try something a bit more perishable, so meet our subject." Harry presented, for their approval, a piece of butter crumb coffee cake.

"Hey! That was gonna be my breakfast!" Tom complained.

"I thought you already had breakfast," his father said, more amused than annoyed.

"I did, but I could still eat, and that looks good."

"No problem, we only need a little bit. Cut off about a pair of two inch pieces and I want them weighed and measured, then you can eat whatever is left." Harry added another thought. "Let's run this one in reverse polarity while we're at it."

"Harry," Steve Evans jumped in. "We've tried reverse polarity three times and always got nothing."

"True, but all three were very low power. I want to make sure we don't overlook anything. I'll make you all a deal though. Set it up and if we get nothing, then write up your notes and we'll break early this afternoon."

"That'd be cool!" Said Tom. "My friend Jeff from OU is coming out this afternoon. We're gonna go down to Merlin's and make a few pints disappear."

"Then I guess we'd better get to it!"

With that, the meeting broke up, everyone went about their tasks, and Steve began to ready the machine. "ANTS!" He said. "We've got ants! The machine is crawling with them, looks like they decided to make it their nest." The rest of the group rushed over to see.

"It took me two hours to catch three of them yesterday, and now there're hundreds of them," Tom said.

"Looks like we've got our work cut out for us," Harry said. "Tom, give Steve a hand there. They've got to be cleaned out before we try to use it."

Tom usually got the job of exterminating when the ants showed up. His favored method was to pour a pot of hot water from the coffee machine over them. It was effective and didn't leave fumes, but he couldn't pour water on the machine, so Tom and Steve spent the next hour sweeping, blowing and picking the ants out of the machine.

By the time the ants were cleared out, everyone else was ready as well. The cake was set in the receiver and the experiment began. The violet light shone on the cake, the power was increased, and *SNAP* the cake was gone.

"It worked," said Steve, "I stand corrected."

"So much for leaving early," moaned Tom.

"Let's keep an eye on this one, folks," Harry said. "Since we didn't know for sure it would work, there's no telling when it might return."

Glastonbury, England

When Jeff got to England in September, he avoided the guided tours most people take, preferring to wander alone and at his own pace. His cousins even loaned him an old MGB sports car for excursions outside the city.

He did a little shopping and checked out a few nights spots but he spent most of his time immersing himself in History. That was one of his passions, the older the better. When the history was uncertain, its realities more speculative, that was better still. It made him wonder what things had really been like, once upon a time.

One of his favorites was King Arthur. With a few hours to kill before meeting Tom Parker, he made a visit to Glastonbury cathedral, the purported burial place of the legendary monarch. Now it is a ruin with only a few sections of the outer walls still standing, yet those walls spoke to him of the world they had once seen. Jeff wandered around the stonework in awe and wonder.

He climbed the seven-fold path to the height of Glastonbury Tor, a hilltop shrine that dated back to the druids. He walked the path as it meandered along, spiraling its way to the summit. All the while thinking, "What was this place like in Arthur's time? Did Arthur even exist? Or Merlin? Where does history end and myth begin?" He wondered what it had been like then. Would he find it the idyllic life of the myths and legends he imagined, or would the harsh realities of a primitive time, cut off from the comforts he was so used to, be too much.

At the top of the hill he rested, pulled up his guitar, and looked back down to the village and the ruined church. He played an old guitar instrumental called Greensleeves. Then another song came to mind. He sang...

    Guinnevere... Had green eyes
    Like yours Milady, like yours......

He lost himself in the music, the place, and the moment. He felt like he could stay here for days, but instead he checked his watch. He hadn't needed to know what time it was since his arrival in England. It was always "vacation time", but today he had somewhere to be at four o'clock. The hours have a way of shooting past at times like this, and it was much later than he had thought. Reluctantly, he started back down the hill to the car, dropped the convertible roof, and sped off.

ST&C Labs
Late in the afternoon, Bill was working at his station, when an ant crept by on the floor. Annoyed, he stomped it and went back to his work. Then, in his peripheral vision, he spotted

another. He was about to step on that one too, but hesitated and bent down for a closer look.

The ant was scurrying along with a heavy load. It never ceased to amaze him, the loads these tiny insects could carry. Other ants followed along behind it, each with a similar load, all of them heading for a gap in the cabinets under his lab table. They weren't heading toward the machine. They were heading away from it.

Each ant carried a large piece of food over its head. Most of the burdens were yellowish, but others were a light brown. The crumb cake! But the scientists had been very careful not to leave any crumbs behind this morning, and besides, the ants were swarming the machine an hour before the experiment. They had to have been attracted to the machine hours before that. Then it hit him. "I know where it went!" Bill shouted.

"What?" came a scattered chorus from around the room.

"I know where the cake went. And it's not coming back," Bill said.

"What do you mean?" Harry asked.

"All this time we've been trying to figure out where the machine is sending things, and it's not a where, it's a when. The machine's not transporting things, it's shifting time."

"But that's impossible." The lead scientist was incredulous.

"I'd say so too, except it's the only thing that makes sense. It's why the GPS didn't record any other location. It's why the video recorder didn't skip a frame. We were sending things into the future until today with the cake. It probably popped back in around midnight last night, plenty of time for the ants to find it and send for reinforcements."

"You may be right," Harry mused, as improbable as it sounded, it did make sense, "and if you are, this is huge. I mean, the transporter thing would have been big, but this. Wow! But we ran reverse polarity before. Why didn't we see it then?"

"Because, with the low power settings, we only sent things back a short time. The objects had already been placed in the receiver, so when they went back, they were already there. It's confusing, but it follows."

"I wonder how far we can send things," Steve said, thinking out loud.

"With the bigger crystals and max power, years, maybe hundreds of years. Who knows?" Bill responded.

"We have to find out," Steve said.

"Absolutely!" Harry agreed. "Just know that if we send something forward in time, we then have to wait a year, two years, who knows, before it returns. By the time we have our result, we probably will have long since had the answers. And we'll look into that too, eventually. First though, we need to send something back. Far back!"

"Now here's the problem with that. This building is only a year and a half old." Harry pondered that dilemma. "Anything we send back before that will have been scooped up by the bulldozers. So we have to go outside, and we have to go big enough to be sure that we can find it, and we have to go back far enough that the age will show clearly. I think I know just the thing. Pack up, we're going out to the plaza.

Along the Severn Channel coast

Jeff ran the MG through the gears as he cruised his way along the little country road. The road wound its way along the coast occasionally giving glimpses of the sea, silver in the late afternoon sun, whenever the road crested a hill. Here, an arm of the sea narrowed to become the Severn channel. Jeff caught glimpses of the Welsh coast on the other side. Set back on the right behind a whitewashed fence there was a restaurant, The Llewellynn Farms Inn. He knew he was getting close.

Thoroughly enjoying himself, he wound out third gear as he crested a rise, went into fourth coming out of a turn, and was about to flip the switch to kick in the overdrive when he saw the sign VILLAGE OF LLEWELLYNN. He quickly braked and downshifted, then rounded a curve and was glad to have slowed. The blacktop road gave way to cobblestone and narrowed, winding between little shops and stalls of a quaint seaside village.

The little sports car bumped its way gingerly over the stones and rolled to a stop at a traffic light. To Jeff's left was a tavern. A hand painted sign hanging over the doorway read, MERLIN'S. The place looked so old it could have hosted the magician himself. Alongside the old inn was a single-lane alley leading to a wharf-side dead end. Across the road on the right side was a stone church just as ancient as the inn. It was the landmark Jeff was looking for. When the light changed, he turned right, heading back out of town. After the last little shop, the road became blacktop again and skirted a little hill.

When a sign announced, AVALON OFFICE PARK, he turned into the drive, passed a large granite monument, and found a parking spot near the first building. He fumbled with the car's convertible top, wrestling it toward the frame of the windshield. After two attempts to line it up, he gave up and let it fall back. He grabbed his guitar off the passenger seat, slung the strap over his shoulder, walked inside and made his way to the second floor lab.

Several men were busy at a table covered in electronic gear, disconnecting and packing things up. The youngest of the bunch looked up as Jeff came in. "Hey, Jeff! You made it!" Tom said, putting down his load and coming over to welcome him. "Glad to see ya. What's with the guitar?"

"I'm driving my cousin's convertible, I didn't want to leave it in the car with the top down, and putting the top up is more trouble than it's worth. Besides you never know when you're going to need music." One corner of Jeff's mouth worked up into a wry grin.

"Well. In case it gets cool with that top down, I've got just the thing." Tom pulled a T-shirt up off a counter nearby and held it up for Jeff. It had a big blue fish and the word MARLINS on it.

"I was hoping you forgot," Jeff said as he pulled it over his flannel shirt. "Are you ready to go?"

"We've got a bit to do here yet, but then you and I can go down to the inn in town for a few beers. It's a great old place. Local legend says it's where Merlin first met the young King Arthur." Tom led Jeff over to the group and introduced him around. "Come on and meet everyone. This is Steve, Chris and Bill, and of course, my dad."

"Nice to meet you all." Jeff greeted the scientists, and turned to Tom's father, "Mr. Parker."

"Call me Harry, "said Tom's father." I hear you're an engineering student too. Would you like to help out?"

"I don't know how much help I can be, but what can I do?"

"Even a mechanical engineer can carry a box. Grab that one, and follow me," said Tom, picking up a load of his own. "I'll get you caught up on the way outside." As they carried their boxes out of the lab and down the stairs, he went on. "We're running a little late. Hope you don't mind waiting, but this is really big."

"It all started about a year ago. The lab was testing a newly discovered crystal and made a discovery. With the crystals, this machine we can make things disappear for a time. We were thinking it might be like the transporter on Star Trek but today that changed. It's looking like what we have is a time machine."

Jeff stopped dead in his tracks, not sure he had heard correctly. His eyes widened. "You can't be serious!"

"I'm absolutely serious," Tom said. "We're just not sure."

The stairwell let out at the rear entrance to the building. Outside the doors there was a patio used by employees at lunch time, beyond that a brick walkway led to the monument Jeff had seen on the way in. They put the boxes in a growing pile near the monument and went back for more.

"...So now we're running it again, only we have to move outside. And we have to send it far enough that it will show the time. We have one really large crystal, so we're going to send something big just as far back as we can. We want to send it back far enough so that it shows the wear, a hundred years or more. And you get to help. Think of it, you may be a part of history."

A part of history. *I like the sound of that*, he thought as he left the box with the others. Aside from running an extension cord or other simple task he knew he couldn't screw up, Jeff stayed out of the way as the scientists set up their equipment.

"You should have some great stories when you get back to school." Jeff said.

"Yeah, about that," Tom said. "I'll be taking a semester or so off."

"But, you're set to graduate next spring. Are you sure you want to mess with that?"

"I talked it over with my dad. This is so big, it's more important. If I go back to school, I can get my degree, go on to grad school, and in two or three years I'll be studying the stuff I'm DOING now. Or I can stay here and be in on the cutting edge. Even if I don't end up working at ST&C, this will be huge on a resume."

"Good point." Jeff accepted the logic, it's not like he was taking time off to go backpacking. "I'll say hi to everybody for you when I get back."

The monument was a pink granite obelisk set on a gray granite base. It stood by itself in a circle of wood chips and low shrubs at the center of the paver plaza. On it was a polished brass plaque that read, "DEDICATED TO THE MEMORY OF OUR FOUNDER - ADRIAN STERLING."

The plaza was at the crest of the hill overlooking the entrance to the office park. From it, Jeff could see the tops of the taller buildings in the village he had come through. In the distance, he could make out a river on its way to the Channel.

An assortment of monitoring equipment was spread out on folding tables. Extension cords wound their way back to the building, a video camera was setup on a tripod, and the machine itself was positioned near the monument. Each of the scientists took up a station by a monitor. Mr. Parker was at the control on a laptop computer, and Tom operated the camera to record the experiment. Jeff stood off to one side where he should be out of the way, but still able to watch the action.

Mr. Parker keyed a command into the laptop and called out to the group, "Everything up and running?"

One by one each of the men called out "Check." Then, Tom at the camcorder called out, "Camera is recording."

Mr. Parker keyed in another command. "Power coming up," he made a few adjustments, "fine tuning signal."

Jeff stood by, transfixed by the enormity of what they would see if it worked. The machine began producing a beam of light, focused on the monument. It was very pale at first, but gradually increased until it bathed the monument in a purple glow. The intensity of the light built and the polished stone of the monument shimmered. Jeff stood well back, farther from the subject than any of the scientists. Even from that distance he worried about being in the way and he stepped back further still. From his new perspective, the brass plaque shone more brightly than the stone. His hand instinctively reached for the sunglasses in his shirt pocket. It never got there. The light became a brilliant flash and everything went black.

Chapter 2 - Found

The blacksmith and his apprentice pulled their cart along the trail that led down out of the wooded hills toward the little town. They had spent the day gathering wood for the forge and the cart was piled high. The smith, head down, wordlessly pulled the cart along the familiar track past fields of grass and clover, conserving his strength in the bright, late summer sun. Eldric was a big man, powerfully built, barrel-chested and broad in the shoulders. He was still the strongest man in the village even if he was past his prime.

The apprentice on the other hand, had all the energy of youth. He was young, not yet fully a man, but tall for his age, almost gangly, though working the forge was beginning to show its effects. He was full of questions. "What will we be making when we get back to the forge, Eldric?"

"The inn keeper needs a new hinge for his door," replied the smith with a sigh. They'd had this conversation before. "And probably some tools the farmers will need for the coming harvest. In between we'll make some nails. We never seem to have enough nails."

"But when are we going to make a sword? Or a breastplate? Even a helmet?" Arthwyr rolled his eyes, bored with the repetitive nature of daily routine.

"I know it's not exciting lad, but we make what people need."

"But what if the raiders come again? Some say we are overdue. Shouldn't we be ready?" The youth persisted.

"I don't disagree it might be a good idea to have a few weapons around if we should need them, but unless someone comes to me and wants to buy it, a sword just takes too much time and steel to make. Besides, when the raiders do come there are always too many of them. Unless the entire village stood up to them, one man with a sword would probably just get himself killed."

As they rounded the base of a small hill, the boy went on, "I just think we ought to be prepared."

"You have a point...." the smith was cut off mid-sentence by a lightning strike not fifty yards away. The flash immediately drew their attention to the top of the hill and the tall grey stone. "That was close!" Eldric exclaimed, instinctively ducking. He composed himself. "I've never seen lightning without either clouds or rain before."

"Too close. I've never seen that before either," said the youth, pointing to the granite monument.

"It must be new." "I didn't see it this morning going the other way."

"Maybe we just didn't notice."

"Maybe." The apprentice stopped abruptly. "Is that someone on the ground there?" The boy let go of the cart, which immediately teetered back. Eldric had to wrestle with it to keep from dumping its load. Arthwyr bounded up the hill to the body that lay sprawled face down in the grass. "Eldric come quickly! It's a man."

The blacksmith steadied the cart down and followed the boy up the hill. "Is he alive? Who is it?"

"I've never seen him before, and he's dressed very strangely." The boy turned the man over. He pointed to the monument and asked, "Do you think he put that here?"

"Not likely. I couldn't budge that thing myself. I'm not sure four of me could. No. He'd have to be a giant to put that there. Or a wizard. And he's definitely no giant." The victim appeared to be a young man, wearing a plaid flannel shirt, sneakers, and blue jeans, none of which either man had ever seen before. Over the flannel shirt was a t-shirt emblazoned with a large fish and the word MARLIN. Where the shirt hung over the big Smith & Wesson belt buckle, the energy had apparently focused and burned a small hole where the "S" had been. There was a guitar slung over one shoulder. "He must be a minstrel or a jester."

"Yes." The smith agreed. "I'd say so, too. He certainly is dressed strangely."

"That's some kind of fish on his tunic," The younger man said, pointing to the T-shirt. "Do you suppose he's a fisherman?"

"I never met a fisherman who didn't smell of fish." Eldric read the t-shirt "Hmm, Marlin. Do you suppose that's his name?"

"I didn't know you could read."

"There's a lot you don't know," retorted the blacksmith as he bent down over the stricken form, saw that the man was breathing, and tried to revive him, gently shaking him. "Are you all right? Can you hear me? Son?" No response. He looked him over to see if he was hurt in any other way, and not finding any clear signs of injury, picked him up. "We've got to get him into the village. Come on, give me a hand."

They carried the unconscious man down the hillside to their cart, rearranged the load to make him as comfortable as possible and eased him on top. It was slow going to negotiate the ruts in the dirt track and not jostle the man or overturn the top heavy load.

Over the next rise, the village of Llewellynn came into view. Most of the buildings were crude little houses with thatched roofs common throughout the British Isles. The larger buildings were of Roman design. There was the church, an inn, a mill, even a roman bath all built of stone with slate roofs. Beyond the little wooden bridge over the millstream was the ruin of the old barracks that served the small garrison, which had protected this outpost.

As smith and apprentice crested the hill, their charge began to speak. They stopped to check on him. He didn't seem to be awake yet and was gibbering unintelligibly, speaking a language neither had ever heard. "That babbling can't be a good sign," said Eldric, taking up his load again.

Burkellynn had run the inn all his life. He helped out as a child when his parents ran things. As a young man, he'd taken over the operation with his wife. His daughter Mairwen had been a child when his wife died, but she stepped in to take up a share of the work. Now, at an age when other girls were off and married, she continued. There was no shortage of suitors. She was a pretty girl and young men frequented the inn in hopes of catching her eye. She brushed them all off with a smile. Her father worked so hard as it was, she feared that if she were gone he would work himself to an early grave.

The innkeeper straightened and wiped tables in a last rush to get ready for the evening crowd. There were only a few fishermen hanging around now, but as the sun turned from gold to red, that would change very soon. In his haste, he almost knocked the broom out of Timothy's hand.

Timothy certainly didn't see him coming. He'd been born with poor eyesight and it had gotten progressively worse from there. For all his efforts, he didn't so much clean the floor, as rearrange the dust. When he finished, Burkellynn would give him a plate of food and Timothy could at least feel he'd earned it.

"Do a good job for me, Timothy," said the innkeeper. Burkellynn brushed the wavy silver hair back off his forehead as his brow began to sweat. At forty, he was considered old but was not nearly ready to admit it. Being on his feet all day and most of the night kept him in good shape, despite the beer belly that he wore like a badge of honor. "Mairwen! How's that soup coming?" he called out.

"Nearly ready." The innkeeper's daughter stirred the soup then checked on a fowl that was roasting on a spit. The evening's fare was nearly finished, and so she attended to her own readiness. She straightened her wool skirt and brushed her linen blouse, then tied her light blonde hair back with a pale blue ribbon that exactly matched her eyes.

Mairwen spotted an empty plate left behind in favor of the dartboard and went out to clear the table. Her path took her past two of the younger fishermen and a hand reached out to circle her waist. She swiveled her hips to shrug off the embrace and swatted the hand away playfully. "Daffyd, behave!" Daffyd feigned embarrassment at the rebuke, turning his head and averting his eyes in his best impression of a child being scolded. His friends all laughed.

"You wouldn't want me to tell my father you've had too much now, would you?" It was an empty threat. As long as the customer was willing to pay, Burkellyn was happy to pour.

"No, no," Daffyd waved his hands to fend off the threat, laughing as he did. "No need for that." It was far too early to take that chance.

The laughter was broken up by the sound of the door banging open, its worn hinge shrieking in protest. In came an excited Arthwyr. "Come quick!" he said. "There's a man here and he's hurt! I think he was hit by lightning." The innkeeper came running, followed by his daughter and Timothy. Timothy held the door as the others carried the unconscious young man inside. "Should we put him on a table?"

"No, he'll be more comfortable on a bed in the back room," replied Mairwen. "Besides, it'll be quieter when it gets busy later. Who is he?"

"I think his name might be Marlin. At least that's what it says on his shirt," said the blacksmith. "Probably a traveling minstrel," Eldric placed the guitar alongside the young man's bed, "he had this."

"I've never seen such clothing, even on a musician." The girl said, feeling the cotton of his t-shirt between his fingers. "It's such fine material."

"He could be a wizard," Arthwyr added. "He was lying next to a great shiny stone that just appeared out of nowhere."

Mairwen ignored the talk of wizards and went for a pail of warm water. She began wiping the young man's face as the blacksmith went on. "He woke up a couple of times coming into town, but he just babbled and I didn't understand a word. The letters on his shirt are Roman so I thought his language might be Latin, but I'm not so sure. It sounds different. Still, we should get the priest." Without being asked, Timothy took off for the church.

By the time Timothy returned with Father Ewan the others had undressed the young man and put him in the bed. Burkellynn and Mairwen left to attend to the first patrons of the evening. Mairwen checked back on him when she could.

"Hello, Father, I hope you can help," greeted Eldric, "He spoke a few times, but I couldn't understand him. He may just have been babbling."

"Thank you Eldric," Father Ewan said as he sat by the bedside. "Hello, Marlin." he approached the young man then tried in Latin. "Abyssus. I am Father Ewan. Ego sum Abbas Ewan."

The man on the bed roused slightly, but didn't answer. His eyes opened somewhat but didn't focus. The priest sat back and said a silent prayer then turned to the others. "When he wakes we'll try again. In the meantime keep him as comfortable as possible and let him rest."

Jeff Warren faded in and out of consciousness. The last thing that he remembered clearly was standing around the science team as they ramped up the experiment, the purple light from the machine, the reflection off the brass plate and then blackness and pain, after that only bits and pieces from the haze. Two bearded men were leaning over him. Paramedics? They weren't in uniform. In fact, they looked like they just stepped out of a Christmas pageant. And their accents! They sounded like Welshmen, or maybe Irish, but the accents were so thick he couldn't understand a word.

There had been a long bumpy ride, then he was carried into a building, not a hospital, the only light was a flickering oil lamp that hung from the rafters. It was a rustic old building, like a hunting lodge perhaps, and there were more people. Two more bearded men, and a pretty young girl, then later a priest by the cross around his neck, and he spoke Latin. Jeff couldn't understand the Latin either, but he definitely recognized it as such. A few of the words sounded like English words so he picked up a little.

Through the night he awoke several times and always someone was there. Most times, it was the young girl. *Mairwen?* And that was fine with him. She wiped his face with a warm towel, made sure the blanket covered him, or just sat and held his hand. It was a comfort to wake up and see her there. Later the one they called Timothy took over. He wasn't nearly as nice to have around as Mairwen, but late in the night when it came time to relieve himself, he was glad to be saved the embarrassment of having the girl attend to it.

Jeff came to again, but this time he felt different, better, his head less fuzzy. He noticed Timothy. "Where am I?" he asked. Timothy didn't respond. Didn't seem even to understand. He muttered something and left the room. It was brighter now, the lantern was out, but the shuttered window was open, letting sunlight and fresh air stream in. He had slept away an entire day. His cousins would be worried. He should have been back by now. He reached for the cell phone in his pocket and realized he wasn't wearing pants. He saw them folded over a stool across the room but, before he could try to get up, Timothy was back with Mairwen and the priest.

"I need my cell phone," said Jeff, but they all just stood there dumbfounded. "Doesn't anybody here speak English?" Jeff saw confusion in their faces and softened his tone. "My phone?" he repeated, but still no one responded. He pointed at his blue jeans and that got through. Father Ewan handed over the pants.

Jeff retrieved the cell phone and flipped it open, the display lighting his face in the dimly lit room. The others recoiled at the sight of it, eyes widened. Jeff brought up his cousin's number and hit send with no response. He checked the display, no service. There was still some charge left, but no signal. He dialed again anyway, still nothing. "Do you have a phone that works? A land line?" Again, they didn't seem to understand. Jeff made the universal sign for telephone holding his hand to his ear. "Is there a telephone?" Still, none of the three moved. The phone call would have to wait.

Jeff's building panic turned to anger. This couldn't be real. But if not, someone had gone to great lengths to perpetrate such an elaborate hoax. Could Tom be behind it? "Tom!" Jeff called out, loud enough to be heard in the next room or beyond. "This has gone far enough, Tom." He stood to get up. "Tom!" he yelled again. The exertion made his head swim again and he sat down hard on the bed. He had expected Tom and the rest of the engineers on Mr. Parker's team to come in laughing. All he saw were horrified looks from the girl and the priest, fearful of his outburst. "Sorry," he said, letting the anger dissipate again into despair. Maybe it was real.

When Mairwen left the room, Jeff got dressed. He stood to put on his pants and sat back down on the bed again. His head swam. He felt deflated. No phone. No electricity. No indoor plumbing. These people obviously didn't understand English. He felt like he had stepped into The Canterbury Tales. It was beginning to dawn on him that the machine with the purple light had done a lot more to him than give him a headache. He fought off the panic that was building again.

He turned to the priest, searching his mind for the Latin words. He studied it for a semester in High School years ago. "Quist annus est is?" *What year is it?* He hoped he was at least close.

"Anno Domini, Quattuor Centum Octogentum quinque." *485 AD.* Jeff let that sink in.

Timothy led him into the inn's main room. The blacksmith and his apprentice were there, installing new hardware in the door. Mairwen had set out a meal, a bowl of stew, a large hunk of bread, and a mug of ale. Jeff dug in with relish.

When he finished his meal, he tried again to communicate with the girl. She tried, but the language barrier was not easily crossed. Eventually, they established a combination of gestures and the occasional word that sounded similar in both languages and managed to introduce each other. When Burkellynn came in Jeff did his best to convey his thanks for their hospitality. The innkeeper responded by going into the other room, returning with Jeff's guitar. The meaning of that gesture came through loud and clear. Jeff would have to sing for his supper.

He made his way to a stool by the hearth and slung the guitar over his neck. He looked out at the crowd that was developing. Bearded men in homespun clothing, not exactly the audience he was accustomed to. He closed his eyes and played his guitar. It was the first thing since he awoke that felt normal. An obvious starting point came to mind.

"Yesterday. All my troubles seemed so far away......" He sang the old Beatles tune, thinking about the changes the last twenty four hours or so had brought, then went on through his favorite golden oldies. The audience appreciated everything he played, but their faces showed not a hint of recognition no matter how popular the song. He couldn't remember the last time he played any of those tunes that someone hadn't joined in.

No one in the crowd understood a single word of lyric but it made no difference. The music itself was a universal language and Jeff was comforted that at least at some level they were communicating. Jeff noticed the crowd beginning to thin. He was getting tired and was about to wrap up when he noticed Mairwen watching him from across the room. He sang one last tune, watching Mairwen watching him and, in turn, a pair of young fishermen at the dartboard watching her. When he finished, he acknowledged the crowd one last time as he hung the guitar on a peg. When he stood, the fatigue hit him hard. He made his way to the back room and collapsed on the bed. Within seconds, he was sound asleep.

Jeff awoke, hoping that the events of the day before had been a dream, a hallucination. He decided quickly that it was not. He went out into the main room of the inn and found Mairwen, asleep on a bench. He stood there a moment thinking how pretty she looked. It occurred to him that the bed he'd been sleeping in was probably hers. He went out the door as quietly as he could, thankful for Eldric and the new hinge.

Standing outside the inn in the early morning chill, Jeff tried to get his bearings. The sign over the door was missing and the shuttered windows had no glass, but the old inn looked otherwise the same as it had when he'd driven by. The trendy little shops were gone along with all the newer buildings, that is, any that were built in the last thousand years. The traffic light was missing and there were no vehicles, or power lines, no sign of anything modern at all. It was very different from the little seaside village he had driven through, and yet, the cobblestone street, the lay of the land, and most of all, the old roman church were unmistakable. He tried the cell again, still nothing. Fighting off panic, he decided to have a look around while he figured out what had happened, and more importantly, what he could do about it.

If this was, indeed, the corner he turned at yesterday, then there was one place he had to go. He crossed the street and followed the route he had taken in the car. After the last shop, the cobblestones gave way to a dirt track that curved around a grassy hill. At the top was the stone monument. He left the road for a closer look.

The granite monument stood alone and out of place on the hilltop. There was no brick plaza surrounding it, no parking lot below, no sign at all of the ST&C building. But, above the trees bordering the field he saw the bell tower and roof of the church just as he had before. There was no doubt in his mind that this was the same stone. The sunlight reflected off the plaque like a mirror, so bright he could feel its warmth. He stepped back just a few inches and he was out of its focus. The beam from the machine must have caught him in just the same way.

Jeff fell to his knees as the understanding hit him like a crushing weight. This was real. It was not a dream and it was not a theme park. He had traveled back in time hundreds of years, to a place as alien to him as any distant planet. He had no money, no home, no family or friends. His lifetime of education provided not a single skill that could be used here. He couldn't even speak the language. The English he spoke would not exist for centuries to come.

"Well, I can sit here all day feeling sorry for myself," he finally said out loud, "or I can face the situation head on." *If the scientists can perfect the machine, they might come and rescue him*, he thought, but there wasn't much he could do to make that happen. In the meantime he had to survive. He walked back down the hill and into town. The first thing he needed to do was learn his way around.

He returned to the intersection of the two main streets. Directly across from the inn was a butcher shop. On the third corner was the church. The fourth corner was left vacant, affording the church a commanding view down the hill past half a dozen fish monger stalls and out to the river.

At the bottom of the hill the street dwindled to a narrow trail as it twisted its way out a spit of land bordered by marshes on either side, ending finally at the wharf. The wharf was little more than a reinforced embankment of the river where it met the millstream. Above the wharf, the stream split. Only the shallowest draft boats could venture further. Jeff could make out the last of the fishing boats, barely visible as it went out on the morning tide, the top of its mast peeking over the reeds.

Jeff walked along the main street checking out the shops that lined it. There were several different craftsmen, a cabinetmaker, a potter, a candle maker, a weaver, and finally, a bakery sitting next to the mill.

Over the bridge that spanned the millrun was the ruin of an old Roman barracks. There was not much left of the building but a few crumbling stone walls, all overgrown, some as tall as a man, others, little more than knee high. Jeff's curiosity and sense of history took over and he decided to investigate. Creeping around the rubble, he was surprised to find the blacksmith's apprentice, sitting on a large stone with an iron poker at his side. The younger man seemed lost in thought and unaware of Jeff's presence as he nibbled on a piece of fruit. Jeff decided not to bother him and backed out of the old ruin.

Opposite the mill was a roman bath, built for the soldiers who manned the barracks and still enjoyed by the inhabitants of the village. It was fed by a spring that entered the millstream where it met the marsh. Jeff noticed a hint of sulfur in the air. The building was quiet at the moment and appeared empty, but a faint wisp of smoke trailing off the chimney suggested otherwise.

At the edge of town, the cobblestones ended and the street blurred to the double groove of a wagon track. Jeff could see it winding past farms and fields before cresting a rise as it ran southwest along the coast. It was no longer paved, but it was the road he drove in on. *Was it two days ago or a thousand years from now?*

He continued his tour of the village, back up the main road and past the inn. The smell of wood smoke mixed with the scent of fresh bread from the bakery piqued his appetite. As hungry as he was, he didn't feel right asking for another free meal at the inn.

The street beyond the church was devoted primarily to private residences until, at the edge of town, he came to a stable, a glassblower, and the blacksmith's forge with smoke billowing from the chimney., Beyond the forge the road wound through an orchard before fording the river on its way northeast along the coast. Jeff rounded up a few apples on the ground and found a spot to sit under a tree.

When he'd finished his meal, he picked up and strummed his guitar. A part of him wanted desperately for this all to be some sort of elaborate theme park, but as he walked around the village, it became clearer and clearer that this just could not be the case. The attention to detail was just too complete, there was not a single concession to the comfort of the visitors, no electricity, no telephones, no restrooms, no gift shops or cash registers. He hadn't seen or heard a single aircraft in the sky or powerboat in the water. He was obviously the only person in the village who spoke anything like modern English. He tried the cell phone one last time, still nothing, and turned it off to preserve the battery.

He had awoken in early Middle Ages Britain, and if he was going to survive here, he was going to have to do so on Middle Ages terms. He would have to learn to live the way people had for thousands of years before machines were invented. He would have to learn to speak the local language. He would have to earn his way.

The first thing he was going to need was a place to stay. With no money, and the five and ten pound notes in his pocket had no value here, he couldn't stay at the inn. He got up, slung the guitar over his shoulder and went looking for the one person he knew who might be in a position to help.

The blacksmith's forge was a short walk back up the street. In nice weather like this, the workshop was open to allow in the breeze. From the street, Jeff could see Eldric the smith busily wielding the hammer in one hand while holding a piece of iron, glowing red from the fire with tongs as well as working the bellows. Performing this juggling act, he was clearly in need of another pair of hands. The apprentice was still nowhere in sight.

Jeff hung his guitar on a peg and manned the bellows. The smith looked up and saw who was helping and without a word, gave a nod. They worked together for some time in a silence broken only when the smith needed something. "Tlu" the smith said pointing to the tongs. Jeff handed the tool over. Eldric made himself known via gestures always following with the appropriate word. Each time, when Jeff complied, he repeated the word to show his understanding.

Jeff concentrated intently on the smith so that he might anticipate what the man needed him to do and particularly on the fire itself, in order to learn how to tend it so that he could maintain the desired heat level. They had been working for perhaps an hour, when Jeff saw Arthwyr return. Not wanting to create any ill will with the younger man, Jeff immediately stepped away from the bellows and let Arthwyr take over.

Throughout the afternoon, Jeff helped out where he could. He swept the floor, fetched things and stepped in to help, especially where the strength of an extra set of hands seemed a welcome addition. All the while, he deferred to Arthwyr's seniority.

When Eldric took a short break for a drink of cool water, Jeff pantomimed sleeping to the smith, who nodded and pointed to the storage loft. After shaking the man's hand in thanks, Jeff climbed the ladder for a look. About half the loft was covered by a pile of straw and rolled up in a corner was a blanket and a few personal items. Apparently, he would share the space with the apprentice. Jeff was used to having a roommate.

Eldric returned to his project, his hammer ringing as he pounded the iron. To Jeff it sounded as though the note echoed across the forge. When Eldric paused to turn the piece he heard it too, the church bell. The smith dropped the iron hissing into the quenching water, hurriedly banked the fire and raced out into the street with Jeff and Arthwyr on his heels. By the time they reached the church, a large crowd had gathered with more coming in from every direction

A heavy man in a butcher's apron presided over the mob. Jeff couldn't understand any of what was said but he recognized looks of fear and voices laced with stress and anxiety. From gestures and pointing he sensed there was some danger in the river or beyond it. The cacophony of voices trailed off as some accord was reached and the crowd began streaming up the road out of town.

Little time was taken to gather belongings. Those living close by grabbed some food and blankets. One man came back with a wagon for an old woman too frail to walk and another with two infant children. Everyone else took only the clothes on their backs. Jeff buttoned up his flannel shirt, eyeing a sky turned gloomy.

By the time they reached the woods, the weather had taken another turn for the worse. It started to rain and the Northeast wind blew in gusts that chilled to the bone. People huddled together or found what shelter they could. Jeff was still trying to make sense of it all. He spotted the priest.

"Father!" he said. "What's going on?"

"Hibernian Incursios." Father Ewan did his best to find words the newcomer would understand. "Pirates."

"Pirates." Jeff repeated. That was a word he knew, even through the heavily accented Latin. It wasn't enough that he was stranded in this primitive world, the quiet little village was threatened by pirates. With the entire village huddled around him to share in his misery, Jeff had never felt so alone. He stood in the shelter of a pine tree shared with three other souls all clustered together. They eyed him warily and kept their distance. He shivered through the night until the church bell rang all clear at the first morning light.

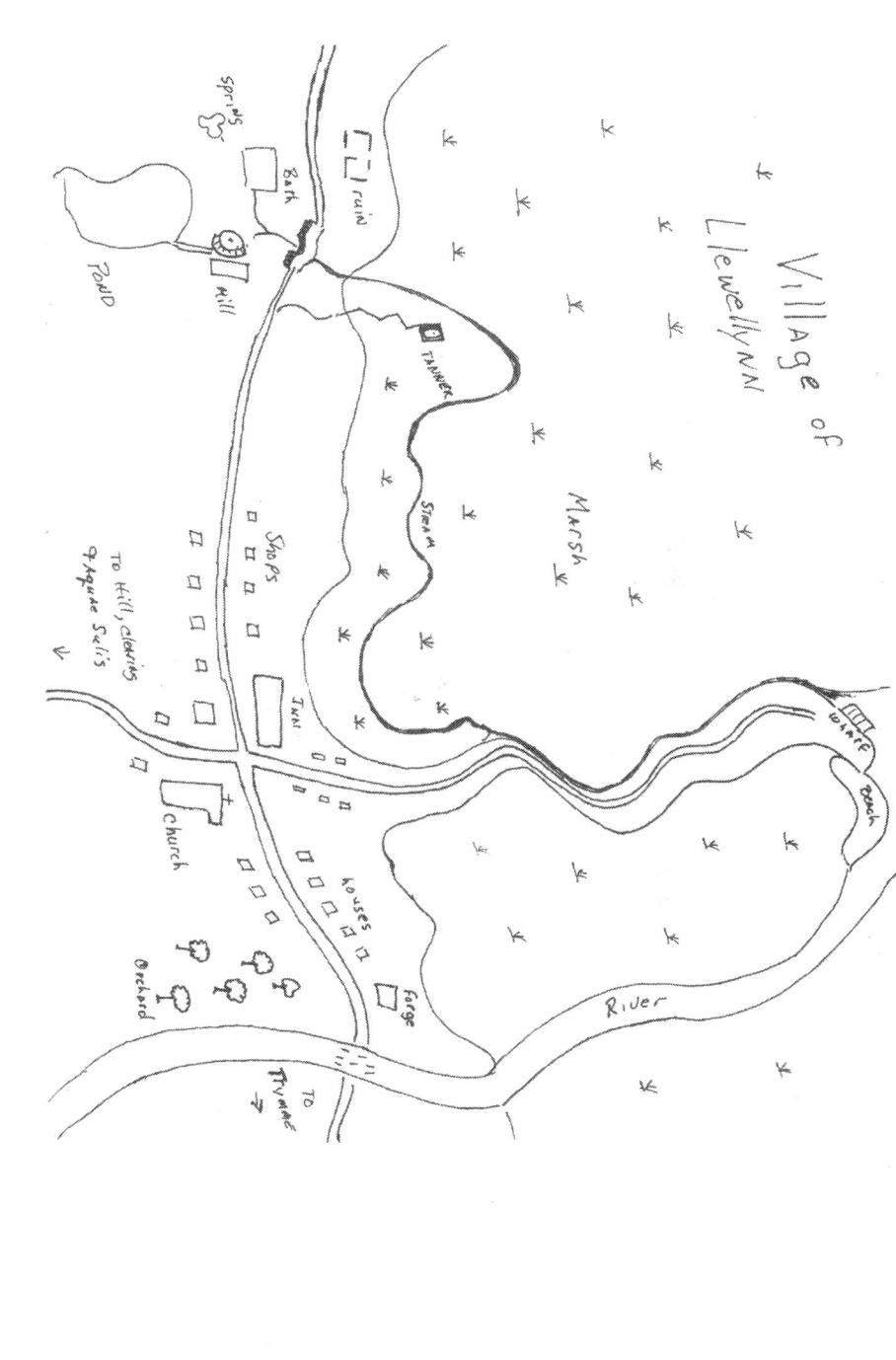

Chapter 3 – Living in the Past

After the cold, miserable night in the woods, Jeff returned to work at the forge. He was exhausted, barely awake. The heat of the forge was a godsend. Eldric never let on that he was affected but his pace was markedly less than the day before. When it came time to break for the noonday meal, Eldric instead just called it a day.

Jeff took his guitar from its peg, planning to go back to the inn, then he hesitated. He went back and grabbed a hammer and chisel. There was something he needed to do first. He walked out of town to the monument. On a clean face of the granite, he carved his name and the date, AD 485. It was crude work, but deep enough to stand the test of time. The Arabic numerals were a message in themselves. He knew the scientists would look for the stone to prove their experiment worked. If there was any hope they would come for him, they had to know when to look. He hoped rescue would come soon.

He made his way back to the inn where he found Burkelynn. He strummed a chord on the guitar and pantomimed eating. The innkeeper nodded agreement. Jeff was sitting head down, exhausted, when his meal arrived. A plate of turnips, a slice of mutton, and a cup of ale clanked onto the table in front of him. He looked up to thank the innkeeper and saw that it was Mairwen who brought the meal. She bent to lay the plate before him and their eyes met. Her eyes were a bright blue, the color of the sky on a bright sunny day, edged in a darker hue, the color of the sea. Jeff smiled and looked deep into them. Mairwen returned the smile for a moment then lowered her gaze, but before she could go away, Jeff pointed to the meat and said "Baaaa?"

Mairwen stifled a laughed at his impression of a sheep then replied in confirmation, "Mutton."

Her laughter nearly melted his heart. "Mutton." Jeff repeated. He continued the process with "turnips", "plate"," knife" etc. He took a bite of the meat and smiled again at the girl. She smiled back and left him to eat.

When he finished she returned to take his plate. Jeff

rubbed his belly and said, "Yummm."

"Tasty," she gave him the word. Every night, the lessons continued.

Jeff worked hard to learn the language as quickly as he could. Over the next few weeks his hope for a return to the life he knew faded. All such thoughts were pushed aside in favor of the far more pressing need to survive. Work in the forge provided his space in the loft and he was fortunate enough to have arrived just in time for the harvest and the income that provided. He spent his evenings at the inn singing for his meal and learning the language. Being near Mairwen was an added bonus.

The green of late summer turned to umber and gold. As the weather cooled, Eldric's wife, Bryggyd had given Jeff one of Eldric's old cloaks. Jeff and Eldric were about the same height, which kept the hem of the garment off the ground, but Eldric was much broader in both the chest and shoulders, and so the cloak draped across him loosely. Jeff found the look rather satisfying, a little bit mysterious. The weeks without disposable razors or shaving cream had given him a light beard. He was looking more and more like the villagers, at least until you noticed his blue jeans and Marlins t-shirt.

With two helpers now, Eldric could work undisturbed while the young men handled tasks that didn't require his expertise. When it came time to restock the supply of wood, it was Jeff and Arthwyr that made the trip to the forest. They pulled the empty cart up the street in the early morning. The village was quiet as people were just beginning their day and few were out and about yet, save the fishermen who had gone out at first light. The only soul they saw as they made their way up the street was Timothy, sitting on the steps of the church, a tin bowl at his feet.

Arthwyr let down the cart for a moment and walked over to put a coin in Timothy's bowl. It dropped in with a clink. Timothy reached in and picked up the coin. He brought it very close to his eyes and squinted, then smiled. "Thank you, sir," he said. But for the ringing of the coin in the bowl, Arthwyr hadn't made a sound. Timothy probably didn't even know who his benefactor had been.

Jeff was touched by the thoughtfulness of the gesture that seemed almost out of character for the brash youth. Recalling his help in the first days after he was found, Jeff felt affection for the blind man. He had to smile as they brought the cart around the corner and onto the road that led into the hills. In the few short weeks since his arrival, Jeff had picked up an amazing amount of the language.

It was incredible how quickly you could learn a language if there was no other choice. Still, it was a work in progress. He spoke slowly and deliberately, he listened intently, and whenever possible he let others do most of the talking. With Arthwyr, there really was no other option.

Given a few simple questions, Arthwyr would take it from there. One idea would lead to another. Often he would go on wild tangents. It seemed aimless, and yet it was not all nonsense. Here and there, hidden among the rambling were bits of wisdom and insight. You could learn a lot if you paid close enough attention, and Jeff did.

Working their way up the road, Arthwyr kept up a monologue. The road wound past the spot where Jeff had made his entrance, the granite monument still guarding the hilltop. Jeff paused for a moment looking at the stone. When he had first carved his name in its surface, it had given him hope. Now, with each day that passed without a rescue, it seemed to mock him.

"That's where we found you, up on that hilltop," Arthwyr said. "We were coming back with the wood cart, just like today, and BANG a bolt of lightning right out of the blue. Not a cloud in the sky, but lightning. Eldric thought you must be a wizard. I think he still does a little, 'cause it had to be magic.

"I had just been asking Eldric about making a sword. He just wants to make the things people are asking for, boring stuff, tools. You know. But if the raiders come back we're going to need weapons to fight 'em off."

"Raiders?" Jeff asked.

"Yeah, I guess you don't know about the raiders, eh. Well, they come by boat, from Ireland maybe, and they hit the little towns along the coast. They take anything that's worth anything. They kill the men and take the women and young boys as slaves. Sometimes if there isn't enough loot it makes them angry and they burn the place.

"You don't usually get much warning. People try to run for the hills, but there isn't always time. Haven't hit us here for a while. Came close the day you arrived, though."

The memory of a night spent shivering in the woods sent a chill down Jeff's spine. "I remember," he said. "That was a miserable night."

"Yes it was," Arthwyr agreed. "But that's probably what spared us. That chill Northeast wind blew them back down the channel. We heard they hit a village southwest of here a few days later."

"I don't need to spend another night like that," Jeff said.

"Neither do I." Arthwyr's tone became more defiant. "That night I vowed I would never hide from them again." He was clearly agitated. "I hate them. They killed my parents."

"I'm sorry."

"Thanks. That's how I ended up in Llewellynn. I was about two or three, but I can still remember. I used to play all kinds of games with my dad, but my favorite was hide and seek. Sometimes I would want to play with my dad, but he would be paying more attention to my mom, hugging and kissing and all. That's when he would suggest we play hide and seek.

"I would go hide and my parents would look for me. If I hid real good, when they found me I'd get a treat, like something sweet, a piece of cake or cookies. We lived in a big house and I was really small so hiding was easy. Sometimes it seemed it took hours for them to find me." Jeff chuckled at the thought of what might have taken so long.

"That night I hid in one of my favorite hiding places. There was a secret door in a storeroom. It opened into a passage to the cook's house and I used to sneak there and get treats from the cook. I had only been hiding for a little while when I heard noises. A door was smashed in and men came in, yelling and screaming. I heard things breaking, and metal hitting metal, like in a sword fight. It got quiet except for the sound of the horses' hooves clattering away. I'll never forget that sound.

"I was afraid to go out into the house so I went to Cook's instead. She took me to the church and eventually they brought me to Llewellynn and that's how I ended up with Eldric and Bryggyd. They took care of me and when I was old enough, made me his apprentice.

"Most people want to hide when the raiders come, but not me. I want to be ready and fight them, beat them so that they never come back! Hiding was fine when I was a child, but I'm not a child anymore."

As Arthwyr recounted his tale, his face had reddened. Although the cart they pulled was empty, Jeff noticed the hand Arthwyr held it by was white knuckled. "That must have been terrible. You were so young. To go through all that and lose your parents…" Jeff's voice trailed off as he thought about the horror, that such a story could happen to a real person, especially one as well meaning as Arthwyr. He decided to change the subject. "You've been smithing all your life then?" Jeff asked.

"Pretty much. Since I was little. Probably wasn't much help at first. Then again, I'm not always that much help now. It's not like I don't care. I mean Eldric's been great, Bryggyd too. Took me in. Took care of me all my life. Gave me a trade. Taught me all about smithing. I want to be as helpful as I can. Just, I don't know if a blacksmith is what I'm meant to be."

By the time Arthwyr finished relating his tale, they had reached their destination. It was a little clearing in the woods with a small shed. A pile of logs was off to one side. Jeff pointed to the shed and asked "Who lives there?"

Arthwyr responded, "We use that for shelter if the weather changes too quickly to get back to town. Never stayed there overnight though. Not sure I'd want to. Eldric says there are wild men living in caves out there." He pointed off into the hills. "Never seen one, but I've seen the caves. They're not far."

Leaving the cart in the clearing, Arthwyr explained, "These logs are seasoned and ready to burn, but we always cut new ones to replace what we'll take. Then we cut the seasoned logs and split them to take back in the cart. But first, we'll need our strength." He produced the lunch that Bryggyd had made for them and they sat to devour it.

It was a crisp autumn morning, bright and clear with the season's first frost on the ground, and Jeff had a day to himself. He decided to explore his new environment. Eldric's loose fitting cloak left plenty of room in its folds for Jeff to stuff the bread, cheese and fruit he brought for lunch.

He pulled the belt tight at his waist to fend off the chill as he followed the road into the hills. A group of woodsmen were already hard at work felling trees. One of the men leaning on his axe as he took a brief break waved to Jeff and Jeff waved back.

At midday, he came upon a stream that gurgled off the rocks into a shallow pool before it spread across a gravel bed creating a natural ford which the road crossed, a perfect spot for a picnic. Using one large rock as a table, he stretched out on another even larger one and soaked up the sunshine as he ate his lunch. The babbling brook, the soft breeze in the trees and the occasional bird were the only sounds.

The quiet was one of the things he loved most about being here, but, at times it just served to remind him of his fate. He would strain to hear just one airplane going overhead. He hadn't thought he would ever miss the sound of cars, trucks and motorcycles. Even the hundred car freight trains that passed his dormitory at night would have been a comfort.

When Jeff finished his meal, he left the path to follow the stream toward its source. The gentle hillside became a rocky cliff with the stream issuing from its base. Jeff looked up expecting to see the water dripping down the cliff's face, but the rocks were dry. Where the water emerged between two huge boulders, he discovered an opening. It was a small cave, barely as tall as a man, though it did seem to extend deep into the hill. The walls were coated in a white crystalline substance and the floor was covered in a muck. There was a feral, musky odor that said something lived here, *probably bats* he thought. The only foot prints were the distinctive pattern of Jeff's own sneakers. He hoped it would fossilize. *Let some future archaeologist figure that one out*, he thought with a grin. While the cave did appear to be deep it was clearly too small for humans.

When he left the cave, Jeff followed down the stream past the road. It flowed out of the hills to where it left the woods, crossed a meadow and then met the river. Jeff walked along the muddy banks of the river among the willow trees, working his way downstream. When he skirted a small marsh and rejoined the river, he saw a gaggle of geese and they saw him. As one, the geese turned and took to the air, rising over the marsh. From the edge of the marsh an arrow shot into the air piercing the last of the geese, dropping it onto the riverbank.

A portion of the edge of the marsh detached itself and floated toward the goose. What looked like a clump of grass and reeds turned out to be a boat, camouflaged to make it indistinguishable from the wetlands that lined this part of the river. A man stood at its stern and used a pole to push off the shallow river bottom propelling himself to the bank. When he reached land, the man jumped out to retrieve his prize. He grabbed the bird by its limp neck and stuffed it into a burlap sack where it was clearly not alone. He acknowledged Jeff with a wave and called out, "Hello, traveler."

Jeff, still startled by the man's appearance out of nowhere, approached him and thrust out his hand. "I hope I didn't cause you a problem here. I had no idea you were there. I'm Jeff."

"Well met, Jeff. I'm called Wahlgren and no, you didn't disturb anything. In fact your timing could not have been better. Flushed them right over me." Wahlgren hefted the bag to his shoulder and carried it back to the little boat.

"Are there others about? Do you hunt alone?" Jeff asked the man.

"That depends. There are a group of us. We usually work together when we go after larger game, but when I go for fowl I like to work by myself. My friends probably aren't far off, but if they are lying in wait, even I can't always spot them," the hunter responded. "I don't see many travelers this far off the road. Where are you going?"

"No place in particular, I'm just exploring the area," Jeff replied, "but eventually, the village of Llewellynn."

"Well then, that goose was my last for today. I'd planned to take them to Llewellynn anyway. Can I give you a lift?" The hunter offered, gesturing to the watercraft.

"I'd be much obliged," Jeff beamed, stepped into the boat, sat cross-legged in the bottom, and steadied himself as the man pushed off with the pole.

The boat was a flat bottomed punt, just large enough for the two men and their gear. Its shallow draft made it ideal for a stream like this, which varied from a few feet in depth to only a few inches. The craft moved along with ease as Wahlgren repeatedly pushed off then brought the pole back up in one smooth motion.

As they made their way downstream through the calm waters, the countryside opened up. More streams joined the flow and while it remained shallow, it became wider and the wetlands grew larger and more abundant. In the absence of a road Jeff was appreciative of the opportunity to ride rather than work his way through and around those marshes, all the more when they finally arrived in the village with nightfall not far behind.

When the harvest was finished and the fall worked its way toward winter, the leaves blew off the trees and the warmer days were replaced by cold rain. Four consecutive rainy days brought the little village and the forge almost to a standstill.

Eldric, Arthwyr and Jeff did what they could to stay busy. They finished up the jobs they had before them. They stocked up on nails, wedges and other small items that were likely to be needed soon. They tried to anticipate other needs that might arise. They cleaned and maintained the forge and all their tools and equipment. By the end of the third day, there really was nothing left to do.

On the morning of the fourth day of rain, Eldric met his apprentices and made an announcement. "I think today we say well enough to the forge and instead, take care of some maintenance of a more personal nature. We'll spend the morning at the baths."

When the deluge ebbed to a lull, the trio made their way up the street to the bath. The run-off from the rain rushed along the gutters at the side of the cobbled street in little rivulets, leaving the street itself high and dry, but for a few scattered puddles. Arthwyr still managed to hit every puddle along the way as the others dodged his splashes. They reached the bath house and entered, shaking the rain from their clothes, just as Timothy disappeared down a flight of steps carrying an armload of wood.

The bath house was a vestige of the Roman occupation, built of local stone, more utilitarian than decorative, with a slate roof. Small, compared to baths in larger cities, it was built to accommodate the dozen or so soldiers that were stationed there at any one time. The building sat alongside a natural warm spring whose waters were diverted underground. Further heat was provided by a small furnace downstairs.

Jeff disrobed eagerly and rushed into the water. He was long overdue for a bath but it was wisps of steam rising from the water that beckoned him. Stepping down into the chest-deep water, he knelt down so that the water was up to his neck, then ducked under letting the warm water rush over him. He held his breath to stay under as long as he could, leaning back as he surfaced, luxuriating in the warmth. It was funny, he thought, that only when you get warm, do you realize just how cold you had been. The cold damp weather had a way of penetrating to the bone.

Jeff was in his own little world as he soaked in the warm pool. He floated with his head back and his eyes closed, the echoing sounds in the building reduced to a dull murmur. When water splashed in his face he straightened up, opening his eyes to see Eldric looking at him. He shook the water out of his ears.

They had been joined in the pool by several men, all having come to the same conclusion, more or less, that this was the best way to make use of the day. The bath was becoming crowded with men spread about, three of them congregating in a corner with Eldric. Two of the men he had seen before, but neither frequented the inn. A third he recognized as the butcher.

The blacksmith began his introduction. "Gentlemen, this is Jeff, the young man I've been telling you about. He arrived out of the blue some weeks ago, and seems to have adopted our little town as his own."

Jeff made his way toward them across the pool as Eldric presented the men. "The guy with the red face is Ferrell. He is our glass maker. You've seen his shop right up the street from the forge, no doubt." A smallish man thrust out his hand. He had a ruddy complexion and, in the warm pool water, his face resembled a ripe tomato.

"Pleased to meet you." Jeff greeted the man as they shook hands.

Next to Ferrell was an older man named Arvel, who merely nodded when introduced. He was a carpenter, with a shop at the end of town opposite the forge. He seldom spoke, preferring to listen instead. He may have been strong once, but age had withered him. His knobby shoulders protruding from the water told the story.

Finally Eldric got around to introducing the butcher. "I believe you've met Caradog, our mayor."

Caradog was a heavy man, barely past the age of the blacksmith though he looked much older, between the double chins and a balding head. He huffed and puffed his way about, breaking into a sweat when he ventured out around the village. While Jeff had met him, he hadn't known about his status, though it did explain seeing him bustling about despite the difficulty of doing so.

The mayor had been crouched in the water as much for the buoyancy as to absorb its therapeutic effects. He straightened and stepped forward, hand outstretched. "Welcome to Llewellynn," he said as he pumped Jeff's hand. "Eldric's been telling us how much of a help you've been to him, and of course, I've seen you at the inn. Such an enterprising young man is certainly a welcome addition to our village."

"Thank you." Jeff was a little embarrassed by the praise. "Everyone has been so helpful ever since I got here. It's the least I can do to pull my own weight."

Caradog nodded his understanding. "How do you like our little piece of paradise?"

"I like it a lot. The people are very friendly. They've made me feel at home here. The town is charming, like something out of the stories I heard as a child, and it's so peaceful."

"So I guess there is some advantage to being small, insignificant, and far from the beaten path," Ferrell said. "If you keep to yourself, you get left alone."

"Not exactly the way I'd put it," said the mayor, "but true enough. Even the Irish raiders have mostly left us alone."

"I've heard about them." Jeff said.

"They're a bad lot." Ferrell said. "They did come here once, when I was a boy. Fortunately, they were seen coming and the tide kept them in the river 'til we could get into the hills. They stole anything of value, killed livestock whether they could eat it or not, burned a few houses."

"Since then, they've kept mostly farther north, harassing the Picts." Caradog said. "When they have come south, they seldom come this far up the channel. Probably don't like the idea of being cut off from the sea. Anyway, if they continue to leave us alone, it'll stay quiet."

"At least until the Saxons get here." Ferrell said.

"The Saxons?" Jeff was eager to fill in the gaps in his knowledge of history. The History classes he took mentioned the migrations of Germanic tribes after the fall of Rome, but it was little more than a footnote.

"The Saxons are the real threat," said Ferrell. "The Irish only want what they can carry. The Saxons want everything, the valuables, the women, the land. When they come, they stay."

"Ah yes, the Saxons. They are another thing altogether." Caradog, like any politician, loved having an audience. He leaned back against the side of the bath, stretching his arms out along the ledge, and relaxed as he related what he knew of the Saxons for Jeff. "They started coming soon after the Romans left, only a few at first, then more. As their numbers swelled so did their power and they took more and more land, most of it by force."

"Finally, we rose up. We had a leader named Uther, a Celtic king. He united all the lesser kings in Celtic Britain, all the way south to land's end and west to the Irish sea." The mayor went on proudly, "Men came from far and wide until we had an army that could stand up to the Saxon onslaught. He led them, defeating the Saxons in battle after battle until they either gave up or went in other directions. Either way, they left us alone."

"So what happened?" Jeff asked.

"In a word," Caradog replied with disgust, "treachery! What an army couldn't accomplish on a battlefield, an assassin could in the night." The mayor scooped some water in his hand and let it run down his face. "A band of men burst into Pendragon's house one night and killed him and his family. Without a king, the resistance is sparse if at all and the Saxons take Celtic lands and slaves almost at will."

"Some say the son survived, but I doubt it." Arvel added. "Too bad, too. When the Saxons come this way, and they will, it's only a matter of time, it would be good to have a king."

"That it would," said Ferrell. "My father brought us here when I was just a boy, trying to stay ahead of the Saxon advance, just as his grandfather had before him. If they came here, I don't know what I'd do. There's precious little island left beyond here."

Jeff spotted Arthwyr running along the side of the pool. The youth leapt out over the water, tucking himself into a ball with his arms wrapped around his knees. Jeff held his breath just in time as the boy hit with a whump, drenching the men.

"I hope you'll excuse me gentlemen," Jeff spluttered as he shook the water out of his face, "but someone is in need of a lesson in manners." With that Jeff swam off after the retreating apprentice.

Jeff awoke to a November morning that dawned gray as so many of them did. Overcast and cool was perfect sleeping weather and Jeff fell right back out. The next thing he knew he was being shaken and he heard Eldric's voice.

"Marlin!" Eldric always called him Marlin. Maybe because that was the first name he knew him by. Maybe because he thought it suited him better. Maybe just to be contrary. He was still wearing the t-shirt. He didn't have much choice. "Wake up. Come on. You can't sleep all day. We've got a lot of work to do."

With the coming winter weather it was important that they completely stock up on charcoal. Arthwyr and Jeff made repeated trips to the clearing to get wood and today they were going to convert it all to charcoal.

Groggy, Jeff dragged himself out of the loft. He shook off the cobwebs and mused, "What I wouldn't give for a cup of coffee or a Red Bull right now."

"A red bull? I've never seen one that was red, but what good would a bull do you anyway?" asked Arthwyr. "We're building a fire not carting the wood."

"Never mind, it doesn't exist." Jeff admitted as the three walked out to the fire pit, Arthwyr with a quizzical look on his face. The pit had been dug the day before at a safe distance behind the forge. They all set to work stacking the wood. When it was done, the pile was nearly as tall as a man, twice that in width, and some thirty feet long.

Eldric lit the fire and together they spread the flames out along the pile. Once it was burning well, they began to throw dirt on it, not to put it out, but just enough to smother the flames, allowing enough heat so that the wood blackened but was not consumed. All day the trio tended the fire until all the wood was charred as completely as possible.

While they worked the wind, light as it was, shifted. Cooler air met moisture along the coast and turned to fog. Slowly, the fog built until it was so thick they could barely see their own shoes. The three men were oblivious, their concentration focused on the needs of the fire. Heat kept the fog at bay, while smoke and fog became indistinguishable.

They worked well past sunset as the fire dwindled. Eventually, when they found themselves doing more watching than working, Eldric spoke up. "I can handle this from here. You go on. Get yourselves some dinner." Jeff didn't need to be told twice. He went up to the loft to get his guitar, put on the oversized cloak and walked up the street to the inn. It was cold and damp so he pulled the cloak tighter as he walked, noticing the fog for the first time.

Arriving at the inn much later than usual, he expected to find it bustling. Instead it was deserted. "Burkellynn?" he called out, but got no answer. "Mairwen?" He looked into the kitchen area thinking she might be concentrating on some cooking, but the kitchen was empty and the hearth was cold. He went out the back door to the root cellar, but that was empty too. He noticed for the first time, a glow in the direction of the waterfront, so he headed down that way. He walked down the hill and out the winding trail to the wharf, following the light to its source and soon all his questions were answered.

When he arrived at the wharf he found a bonfire on the careening beach. Most of the village was here. Many carried candles. All brought a piece of wood for the fire. The latecomers left their pieces on a pile that would be used to keep the fire burning brightly through the night.

Jeff worked his way through the crowd until he found a familiar face. "What's going on?" He asked a farmer he'd seen at the inn a few times.

"The fishermen should have been back hours ago. In the fog the boats are stranded. Any that are close enough to see the fire can follow it home, but frankly tonight it's so thick, all they can do is sit tight and hope they're not blown out to sea."

Jeff was speechless. Severe cold and blowing winds he understood as dangerous, but the fog had always seemed just a benign nuisance. He took a deep breath and stood with the crowd in silence.

Caradog stepped forward. "Friends, on behalf of the men and their families, I just want to say thank you for this outpouring of love and support. We stand here tonight in support of those whose husbands, and sons, and fathers and brothers are on the sea tonight. We are here not only as a village, but as a family, as those men are brothers to us all." He then stepped back and waved forward the priest. "Now, Father Ewan will lead us in prayer, Father."

Bible in one hand and crucifix in the other, Father Ewan stepped up and bowed his head. "Let us pray. Dear Lord, we pray for Siorus. Watch over him and keep him safe that he may be delivered. Lord, hear our prayer."

"Lord, hear our prayer," the villagers responded.

"Dear lord, we pray for Daffyd. Watch over him and keep him safe that he may be delivered. Lord, hear our prayer." One by one he prayed for each of the missing men. When he was done the crowd stood again in silence. Jeff stayed well into the night, gripped by both the concern and fear and by the resignation to the inevitability of events like this.

One by one, people began leaving until only those closest to the missing men were left, and of course, Father Ewan. Some huddled together by the fire, gaining strength from each other, others stood stoically alone. One woman, both husband and son among the missing, stood apart from the others, away from the warmth of the fire. She stood like a statue, her eyes locked on that spot beyond the haze where she expected to first spot the masthead of a returning boat.

Father Ewan circulated among the families offering prayers and encouragement, sometimes just a warm handshake when silence seemed most appropriate. He stopped when he got to Jeff. "It's good of you to come."

"Thank you, Father." Jeff greeted the priest with a handshake, "I didn't know what was going on. When I found out, I couldn't leave. It's not an easy life they have."

"No, it isn't. Your support is appreciated. It's easy to see that you care about your adopted town." With a nod, the priest moved on.

Jeff stayed a while longer, and then went back to the forge. Eldric was still tending the charcoal. Jeff took the shovel from his hand. "Eldric, why don't you get some rest? I'm used to being up late. You're not."

"If you don't mind." Eldric handed over the shovel and plodded home.

Jeff sat down on a rock and strummed his guitar. He couldn't have slept anyway. He thought about the men. About how hard life was for these people. About how much he had taken for granted in his former life. The warm glow of the fire was comforting, but just served to bring him back to the men and what it must be like out in the boats, cold, damp, and dark, unsure they'd ever see home or loved ones again. Lost in thought, he didn't notice Eldric's return until he was standing next to him.

"I've come to relieve you." said the older man. "Go get some sleep."

"Is it morning already?"

"Almost."

Jeff looked to the East and realized two things, that the sky was beginning to lighten and that the fog had begun to dissipate, and then a third, he heard the church bell ringing. Tired as he was, he walked down to the waterfront in time to see the first of the boats returning. The men were met joyously by their families and friends who had manned the fire all night. With his spirits raised, Jeff walked back to the loft and got some much needed sleep.

It was late in the afternoon before Jeff dragged himself out of the loft. The fire pit was deserted and the fire out. Nothing to do here until it all cooled down. Eldric was probably home resting.

He'd been up all night save for the few hours Jeff had taken over. Arthwyr was off wherever it was that Arthwyr went.

The fish stalls were bustling when he got there, the townspeople showing their support for the fishermen. Most of the stalls were already closing, having sold all they had. Daffyd manned the last one displaying a lone, but fair sized cod. Though he was a regular at the inn, Jeff hardly knew him. He was never openly hostile, but treated Jeff coolly, even avoided him when he could. "I'm not sure what I did to earn your ire, Daffyd, but maybe we could start over," Jeff said. Jeff looked the fish over, "That's too much for me, but I'll tell you what. I'll take it if you'll come back to the inn and split it with me."

"A bargain it is," Daffyd grinned as he handed over the last of the catch and put away the money. He shuttered the stall and the two strode up the street to the inn.

Once inside, Jeff handed the fish over to Mairwen to be cleaned and prepared, and ordered two cups of ale. The inn traditionally offered its own fare to patrons, but they were also happy to give hunters and fishermen the option of bringing in their catch to be prepared for a small fee, sales of ale always being a separate issue. Today the latter was the rule rather than the exception. Jeff found room for the two of them in a corner and they settled in. He handed a cup of ale to the fisherman and raised his own. "Here's to a safe return," He toasted and then took a large swallow.

"Here, here" was Daffyd's hearty reply with echoes around the room, "and a free dinner to boot." He also took a large swallow and continued. "Thank you for that, it really wasn't necessary."

"It's the least I could do. I can't afford to feed the entire fleet so you'll have to eat for all of them. It's just good to have you back. So, how are you doing? Long night, eh?"

"Good to be back, but it could have been worse." Daffyd said, "It was damp and cold but not frigid. The sea was calm, not too choppy. The worst part is not knowing where you are."

"How's that?"

"When the fog comes in you're completely at the mercy of the sea. You drift where the tide takes you. You don't dare move."

"Afraid you'll end up on the rocks?" Jeff queried, wondering if perhaps his education could provide a solution. "Would it help if we put together charts of the area?"

"No, that's not it at all." corrected the fisherman. "When the sea is calm like that you could row in slowly. We know every rock on this coastline, if we could find the rocks we'd be home in no time at all, but when that fog rolls in the only directions you can be sure of are sea, sky, and fog. The real fear is to go out, thinking you are coming in. You could end up in a current that took you to Ireland, or worse yet, miss Ireland entirely."

Mairwen approached with a platter piled with pieces of cod fillet that had been dipped in batter and fried, with a measure of vinegar to be poured over them to taste. "Here comes our dinner," he cheered.

"Here we go boys," Mairwen said, standing just a little bit closer to Jeff than was necessary.

Daffyd flirted with her, "Mairwen you area sight to behold. This looks wonderful."

Jeff took a piece of the fillet and brought it up to savor the aroma. "Now, if you could just get your hands on a potato, I can only imagine what fish and chips you would have. This is fantastic. Thank you."

Jeff and Daffyd attacked the pile of fish as only young men can. Out of the corner of his eye Jeff saw Father Ewan enter and work his way about the room, greeting people, letting the fishermen know that the villagers' prayers were with them.

The young men were finishing the last pieces of the fish when a call rang out from the vicinity of the dartboard. "Daffyd!" It was Gorloch, Daffyd's boat mate. "I've accepted a wager and I need a partner." Daffyd was renowned for his steady hand and so Gorloch would make his wagers while Daffyd was out of sight, and then bring him in.

Daffyd looked to Jeff, who just said, "Go."

"Thanks again," Daffyd called back over his shoulder as he made his way over to the dartboard, already tasting the free cup of ale that was sure to follow.

Jeff finished his meal, thinking about what he would sing when he took up his guitar tonight. "The Wreck of The Edmund Fitzgerald" would be a fitting tribute, not that anyone would understand it. Perhaps, a few words of explanation would be in order. He still sang mostly in English, though he had learned a few current ballads and worked them in, to the delight of the audience. It was time to begin translating the songs where he could, or writing new words to go with the tunes if a translation didn't seem to fit.

He came out of his reverie when he realized that he had been joined by Father Ewan. "Hello Father," he said, shaking the priest's hand. "Sit. Please."

"Good evening, my son. And how are you doing?" Father Ewan took a stool and pulled it up to the table. "Sorry we haven't had much chance to talk in a while."

"Good to see you, Father." Jeff replied. "I've been wanting to speak to you."

"How can I help?"

"All that's been going on has me thinking," Jeff said. "I feel like I'm not doing nearly enough around here. These guys go out in the boats every day, put their lives on the line, while I feel like I'm freeloading."

"You're being a little hard on yourself there I think," the priest countered. "It's not like you sit and do nothing. You help Eldric, and I know he appreciates that. You definitely worked hard in the harvest, not to mention singing here several nights a week."

"Thank you for that Father, but harvest season is short, and as for Eldric, he already has an apprentice. I know Arthwyr's head isn't always in it, but that was his position long before I arrived. I certainly don't wish to provoke any animosity there. I owe Arthwyr that much at least. Then there is Burkellynn, The inn was fine with the occasional wandering minstrel or no music at all.

There is no reason for him to keep feeding me. I don't know why he still does."

Father Ewan laughed at the last point. "Well I can answer that riddle for you easily. He does it because Mairwen likes you."

Jeff blushed. That was a revelation. Jeff wondered *was it that obvious. Did others see what he didn't, or was the priest just more perceptive.* Then again it was possible that he knew things, he spoke to everyone. The notion that Mairwen might be interested in him was one that Jeff had been fighting for some time, despite his hopes. He didn't want to mess up an arrangement that he had grown to depend upon by trying to make something out of nothing if he was wrong about her.

"So you feel that you need to contribute more?" Summed up the priest. "I take it you've decided to stay here in Llewellynn? We've never really talked about the place you're from. Would you not be welcome there if you returned?"

"No. That's not the problem at all. I'm sure I'd be more than welcome. In fact they are probably quite worried about me. It's just not possible."

"Is it that far?" Father Ewan did his best to understand.

"Far? Yes. Across the sea, maybe a hundred times as far as Ireland. In today's fastest ships the voyage would take months. But that's not the half of it. Even if I got there, the place I left isn't there now. It's hard to explain. I don't know if you'd understand."

"Try me." The priest pressed Jeff to explain himself. If he was to be of any help at all, he needed to know what the problem was.

"What if the explanation goes against your entire understanding of the world? History is full of people who were burned at the stake for saying things that went against the established world view, even when they turned out to be right."

"Is what you tell me true?"

"Of course."

"And was evil at play? A pact with the devil, perhaps?"

"No. Not evil, just a machine." From the priest's blank expression, Jeff realized the man did not understand. At least that was better than branding him a witch. "It was an accident"

"Well then, if it goes against my understanding of the world, I'd say that I might need to understand the world a little better."

Jeff digested this for a minute. The old priest's response was far more open-minded and reasonable than he expected. "Thank you Father, I'll try. The thing is, until the day I came here, I would never have thought it possible myself. You see, I didn't just travel a distance when I came here, I traveled through time. I was twenty-one years old when I came here, but I won't be born for more than a thousand years. So you see, what I know as History, is still in the future. Anyway, I can't go back, it just can't be done."

The priest's brow was furrowed in confusion. "Well I'm not sure I understand how that can be, but I believe you. Your eyes say that you speak the truth, incredible as that may be." Father Ewan shook his head absently as he tried to absorb the revelation. "And I think maybe you're right about one thing. It might be better that this stays between you and me. Others might not be so understanding. It's easier to accept that you are a wizard, as some already do, and leave it at that."

"I agree. We might as well play it safe."

"So you'll stay here then," Father Ewan said. "What did you do in your country? Did you have a trade? A minstrel? You are obviously not new to entertaining."

"The music thing is just a sideline. I enjoy it, but I'm not cut out to make my living at it. Some day Burkellynn will wise up and send me packing. Then it's off on the road and I'm not the vagabond type. I like it here. I'd like to stay. Mainly I was a student. I was studying to be an engineer."

"An engineer? That is something." Father Ewan considered that for a minute. "I'm not sure how many bridges or roads we'll be building here anytime soon, but…"

"I'm not that kind of engineer, anyway."

"You don't have the look of a military man."

"No," said Jeff emphatically. "I was studying to design automobiles." Jeff's growing ability with the language still failed him. With no Celtic word at his disposal, he said the English one. "Of course you have no idea what that is. It's a kind of carriage, but one that doesn't need horses."

"Magic?" The priest's voice cracked.

"No magic. Another machine. We burn a fuel, it expands and we use the force of the expansion to turn the wheels. It's more complicated, but essentially that's it."

"I'm sure a wonderful machine like that would be very welcome, if you could build one."

"I wouldn't know where to start. There are a thousand things that I'd need that haven't been discovered or invented yet. We don't have the fuel, the rubber, electricity, lights, brakes. It's incredibly complex." The blank expression on the Priest's face told Jeff he still wasn't following.

Jeff pulled the cell phone from his pocket. He still couldn't go anywhere without it, despite its utter uselessness. He flipped it open and the display came on. Father Ewan's eyes grew wide at the sight of it lighting up. Jeff snapped it closed to save what little charge the battery still had. "With this, I could talk to people hundreds of miles away, but it's useless here. There's nobody to call."

"A carriage without horses and talking to people miles away…" The priest had a little trouble taking it all in, but thought it easiest to just accept whether he understood or not. "This place where you come from must be magical, indeed, if such things are possible.

"There are machines that do all sorts of things, things that you wouldn't believe. There are even machines that can fly. But there's no magic in any of them, just a thousand years of discoveries, one on top of another. Without all that background, I can't make any of them." Jeff had grown excited, talking about modern technology, but deflated when he reached the impasse. "Imagine being able to design a great cathedral, a monument to the glory of God, but if you don't know how to make the bricks or shape the stone, you can't even begin to build it."

"I see," Father Ewan said, his head bobbing slightly. "Can you make any of these 'bricks'?"

"Some," Jeff said.

"Do any of them have other uses?"

Jeff nodded.

"Start at the beginning. Those earliest discoveries must have been valuable in their own right at the time. Perhaps if you start with the simple things, concentrate on things you can do with the materials available, there might be a benefit."

"Good advice Father. I'll have to think about that."

"There is something else you can do, as long as you're looking for ways to be more helpful." The priest lowered his voice further and leaned in. "Something you are particularly in a position to help with."

"Sure, Father. What is it?"

"Keep an eye on young Arthwyr. " Father Ewan looked about conspiratorially, but no one seemed to be paying them any undue attention. "I'm sorry I can't tell you more, but help to see no harm comes to him."

"I'm not sure how much help I can be. I'm not exactly bodyguard material, but I'll do what I can." Jeff took up his guitar once again and Mairwen brought him a cup of ale to cool his throat as he sang. She let her hand brush across Jeff's shoulder as she turned to return to the kitchen. At the dartboard, the coolness had returned to Daffyd's expression. This time, Jeff felt as though he understood.

Maghnus was a minor king. He ruled a fiefdom in Eastern Ireland that included a town about the size of Llewellynn and several smaller villages. In addition to the farms and tradesmen populating his little realm, he owned three ships that traded as far South as Spain, East to Germany and Scandinavia, and even the Baltic, but that would be in summer. The brief periods when winter lost its grip, but it was too early yet to plant or plow, was the time for raiding. They would range in their ships across the Irish Sea, stealing anything of value.

Almost as important as the treasure they would steal, was the cargo that made their lifestyles possible, slaves. Men and boys would provide the labor needed to farm. Women and girls did the household jobs of cooking and cleaning and if they were pretty, all the better.

The chieftain stood on the deck of the lead ship. His brother Aongus at his side and his oldest son Phelan at the helm as the flotilla sailed along the Northern Welsh coast. Maghnus wore a battered Roman breastplate, a prize from his first such cruise when he was no older than Phelan was today. The Romans had been gone for a generation before he had taken it. It served as a reminder of the strength to be found in discipline and organization. He prided himself on his planning of each engagement, but once joined with the enemy, he was transformed. His freckled face reddened like a hot coal, fueled by his anger. More wiry and quick than he was powerful, when deliberation gave in to rage, he was a fearsome warrior. The combination was ideal for a leader.

Two other ships followed close behind, captained by his brothers Ruarc and Declan. Linen sails provided the primary source of power, but when the wind wasn't cooperative the boats could also be rowed by as few as four men or as many as twenty. They were making good headway with a southerly breeze as they rounded a point and entered a small bay.

"There!" Aongus pointed out a village as it came into view. Maghnus turned to the other ships and, using hand signals, gave the order to attack. Early morning was best for gaining the element of surprise, but today they were coming straight in from the west with the setting sun at their backs and that was almost as good.

The other two ships pulled alongside their leader for a simultaneous effort. Maghnus looked left. Ruarc stood in the prow of his vessel to get a better look at the target. His men readied for battle, weapons in hand. Looking to the right Maghnus saw Declan. He was a big man, standing six feet four and broad-shouldered. His height and long arms gave him a reach advantage over most men. In battle he carried an over sized spear with an iron blade at its tip, with a second smaller iron point at the butt adding balance. It was a formidable weapon and several of his men had adopted it as well. Satisfied all was ready, Maghnus turned his attention back to the town.

Once inside the bay and the boats were in the lee of the point, the wind died down. As one they quickly dropped their sails and the men leaned into their oars to row the last mile. Three ships, thirty men apiece, all desperate and violent men, intent on their prize, they raced for the shore.

A racket rose from the shoreline as the boats raced for their goal. Maghnus cursed as he heard someone banging a pair of cooking pots together, shouting for his neighbors to run. He could see people emerging from doorways, carrying children or belongings as they scurried off toward the woods. They had been seen.

A few minutes later the three ships grounded side by side on the shoreline. The moment keels touched sand the men were streaming over the rails and swarming through the village. No corner of the little town was untouched. Maghnus and Aongus strode down the street, weapons in hand while the men opened every door, emptied every cupboard and searched every loft.

It wasn't much of a town on its best day. It was too small even to have a name. But it hadn't seen its best in a long time. Several of the buildings showed damage from fire. There were empty foundations where more houses had once been. This part of the coastline had been ravaged by more than one band already.

At the center of the settlement was a large building, a meetinghouse or church, Maghnus wasn't sure, but it would make do for a headquarters. Not even bothering to try the latch, he kicked in the door. It was as empty as the rest of the town. He laid his sword down on a table, pulled up a chair and sat, his anger seething.

Aongus laid a rug in front of the king's chair as a collection point for the loot and started it off with a pair of silver candlesticks, all he could find in his search of the building. One by one the men came by and fed the pile as they scoured the town for valuables.

His brother Declan brought in a keg of ale he hoped would soothe his brother's foul mood. He was a mean drunk, but meaner still when sober. Once stoked, Maghnus' rage could only be quenched with blood. Unquenched, it was slow to ebb. Redness lingering on his ears told all to tread carefully.

When the keg was empty and the sun had long since set, the treasure trove was still a meager collection. Many of the men were afraid to face their king empty handed or with a trifle. Maghnus called off the search. Much as he would like to blame someone, it was nobody's fault.

"Is this everything?" He demanded. It was not uncommon for the men to hold back when the hoard was good. Today nobody dared.

"Yes, Sire," Ruarc said. "Phelan and I searched the men when they were through, nobody is holding back."

The older brother was pleased by the thoroughness, but pressed further, "Did anybody search you?" Ruarc held out his arms in invitation. Maghnus just smiled and questioned his brother further. "What about food?"

"Some." Ruarc listed the spoils. "A pig, some fowl, stores of wheat and vegetables, enough for a few days only."

Maghnus couldn't contain his anger in the chair. He sprung to his feet and walked to the door. "Surely, there are slaves at least?"

Beyond the door stood Declan with a group of men surrounding a captive. "Only one, Sire," Declan said, "An old woman. The rest escaped."

"Can she at least work?" The king bellowed.

"No, Sire." Declan barely uttered, "she is feeble."

"Kill her." Maghnus said curtly. It wasn't anger. He just didn't want to be bothered with her. He looked up at a sky that had gone to low clouds. The wind had changed and there were rumblings in the distance. "See to the boats. Foul weather is coming." He gauged the weather for a moment. "It will do the inhabitants of this pig sty good to spend a few wet nights in the woods. When the weather breaks, we burn the place and head south. We need some fresh hunting grounds.

Chapter 4 – Cub Scout Projects

Late at night, after his talk with the priest, Jeff lay in the straw of the loft and tried to sleep. There was no breeze rustling the trees. The cooler weather meant that the tree frogs and insects were silent. There was not a sound to distract him. It was a penetrating quiet. He never considered the noise of the freight trains that passed by his dormitory as a sleep aid, never mind that he would ever miss it, but he did. A wave of homesickness came over him and he fought it off. He had to accept that he was never going home and make the best of a life here.

The people of Llewellynn had shown him kindness and generosity since the day he arrived. They had taken him in and accepted him as one of their own without question. He felt he needed to find a way to repay them, to make a difference here, and he had an idea. He was going to have to start from scratch with the rawest of raw materials, but there were things he could do. He gave up trying to sleep and made a mental list of the things he would need.

Jeff was up at first light, despite his late night pondering and planning. By the time Eldric and Bryggyd arrived at the forge, he'd been busy for some time. He found some scraps of lead, copper and iron and worked them into the forms he'd need, then collected all the bits into a basket.

Jeff approached the blacksmith, "Eldric, Do we have a lot to do today?"

"Nothing special, why?"

"I stocked the charcoal, set up the fire, cleaned the tools and swept up. I was wondering if you'd mind if I took off for the day, actually, maybe a few days."

Eldric saw that those chores were indeed done. The forge looked like it was prepared for an inspection. "I suppose you could. Is there something wrong?"

"No, nothing wrong. I've just got some things I wanted to do," Jeff explained, "And I need a favor."

"What's that?"

"I need to borrow the cart, some tools, and to use the shed at the clearing, and these" He held up the basket with the bits of metal he had spent the early morning working on.

Eldric thought for a moment, "Sure, take what you need."

Bryggyd had brought breakfast for Jeff, and for Arthwyr who was just emerging from the loft, rubbing the sleep out of his eyes. She put the basket of food down and exclaimed, "You're going to need more food then," and abruptly turned around and scurried back to get more. Her pregnancy was now more pronounced, giving her more of a waddle than a walk.

Jeff piled his things into the cart. He pulled his cloak tight and started off to gather the things he didn't have handy. He had scarcely begun hauling the cart down the road when Bryggyd caught up with him, brandishing another basket, this one laden with enough food to keep him going for days. "I don't want you to go hungry, so I brought a little more." Bryggyd panted as she added the basket to Jeff's cart.

"Thank you Bryggyd, and I do appreciate it, but you really shouldn't be running around like this."

"I'll be fine," she responded defensively. "You take care as well."

Jeff's next stop was the glass maker, where he collected a stopped bottle and some glass tubes, one small one with a bend in it and one much longer, and a half dozen small jars with lids.

Jeff rolled the cart up to the inn just as the door opened. Mairwen came out shaking the crumbs from an armload of linen aprons when Jeff spoke up. "Mairwen! Just who I was looking for."

"Oh! Good morning, Jeff," Mairwen said. "What brings you by this early in the morning?"

"I need a gallon of your strongest vinegar," he explained, "and while you're at it, a jug of that cider you've been serving."

"Come," the girl answered, "I can get you the vinegar, but the cider I'm afraid, is just no good."

"Yeah, I noticed that. It's where I got the idea but, for what I have in mind it'll do just fine."

"Very well," Mairwen agreed, "You can pay me for the vinegar, but the cider well, in a few days, that'll just be vinegar too."

"Fair enough." Jeff loaded the two jugs into the cart and began the trek to the hills and the shed.

When Jeff arrived at the clearing he began unloading the cart. In a splash of sunlight at the center of the clearing he left the jugs of cider. He brought his equipment and tools into the shed, as well as the jug of vinegar. He unloaded his supplies, then looked around the shed and took stock of his surroundings.

The shed was a crude building, tall enough for a man to stand upright, but not much more, with a roof that sloped from front to back. Pallets of straw were set on either side and a small stone hearth was laid out on the dirt floor at the end opposite the doorway. It had no real windows, instead there were shutters front and back which could be propped open for light and ventilation.

The first thing he did was to set a small fire in the hearth and prop open the window in the front so that the little cabin didn't fill up with smoke. He used the glassware he brought to create a distilling apparatus. Before long, the vinegar had been transformed into a concentrated acid.

Jeff felt a sting in his nostrils as he divided the liquid between the smaller jars. By adding strips of copper and lead to each one they became crude batteries which he wired together to combine their strength. He connected them to a coil of wire wrapped around an iron bar and laid some iron pins alongside it. The pins instantly jumped over to the coil and hugged it magnetically.

For a few fleeting moments Jeff felt normal, like he was back in the chemistry lab at OU. It felt good to be on familiar ground, to forget for a minute about being marooned hundreds of years in the past.

When the last of the vinegar was done, he cleaned his gear and started it again, using the cider and then turned his attention to woodworking. He cut two sections from a cedar log, one, about the size of a hockey puck, and a second, cut as thin as he could make it. He hollowed out the center of the larger piece until he had made a bowl, leaving the walls as thin as he could make them without piercing them.

As he worked the wood, Jeff checked the progress of his distillery. The fermented cider came out the other end a concentrated liquor. It was harsh tasting but potent. He sipped a little more and felt a warmth in his chest. It calmed him.

He sanded the slice of wood even thinner and then glued it to the top of the bowl and sealed it with pitch. He etched a narrow groove across its diameter and inlaid one of the magnetized pins there. Jeff placed the disc in a bucket of water to see that it floated well. It did and it immediately rotated until one end of the pin pointed north. He painted a white arrow head on the north end and an eight pointed star at the center and then finished it all with a few coats of varnish to seal it.

Jeff admired his handiwork by the light of the fire, now the only light available, turning it over in his hands. "Perfect," he said out loud. "I just need to paint 'Pack 55' on the back and it'll be just like the one I made in Cub Scouts. After three years in Engineering School he would be changing lives with a project he'd done in 5th grade. Satisfied, he sipped some more of the liquor and took up his guitar.

Jeff returned to the village, shaking the cobwebs from his head left by the previous evening's "tasting". He spotted Daffyd on the way to the inn. "Daffyd," he called, "I've got something you're going to want to see. Come."

Mairwen was wiping tables when the young men entered. She finished what she was doing quickly and rushed over. Jeff greeted her, "I've got something for you." He raised the product of his labors.

Mairwen started to get excited until she realized he was holding one of the cider jugs. Somewhat disappointed, she took the jug. "You've brought back the cider? I told you it was no good."

"It's the stuff you gave me, but you'll find it much improved. " Jeff countered. "Bring two cups of this out for us. The rest you can try out on your patrons. Careful though, be stingy with it or there may be problems with your guests. It's quite a bit more potent than the ale. Taste it yourself, you'll see. Tell me what you think. But first, I need a bowl of water."

On the way to a table, Jeff caught a whiff from the kitchen and called back to Mairwen. "And two of whatever that is you're cooking. It smells delicious and I don't think I'll want that drink on an empty stomach."

Jeff and Daffyd had barely settled into their seats when Mairwen brought the drinks and a small bowl with water. "Thank you, Mairwen. Did you try the cider?"Jeff asked.

"Not yet."

"When you do, just sip it, but I think you'll like it. You too, Daffyd."

The fisherman did as he was told, tasting the concoction with a cautious sip. "Mmmm. Interesting," Daffyd said. "Feels warm going down." He took another sip of the liquor, savoring the flavor. "Is this what you wanted me for?" he asked. He took another sip. "Mmm. I like it."

"Remember the night you guys were stuck out in the fog?" Jeff began.

"I'm trying hard to forget."

"What you're drinking might help with that, but I have a better idea. This is what I wanted you to see." Jeff set the wooden disk on the table between them. "I've got something here that could keep the problem from happening again."

Daffyd examined Jeff's handiwork with some skepticism. "Thank you Jeff. It's nice." He looked over the stars painted on the top, then laid it back on the table. "Most of us are Christians. We pray to saints Peter and Andrew, as well as the Virgin, but others pray to the old gods as well. No sense leaving anyone out. So if you think this will help, we appreciate it."

Jeff chuckled, "Actually, this is a bit more direct than that. Let me explain. When you're out at sea, how do you find your way home?"

"Well, there are the landmarks, of course." Daffyd replied, "But when we are farther out, we steer by the sun and the stars."

"Exactly! And in bad weather, when you can't see the stars, like when that heavy fog rolled in?"

"That's when there's trouble. We wait. We pray."

"OK! Now, what if you had a way to know where the North Star was, no matter what the weather?"

"That would be great, but how?"

Jeff didn't answer at first. He just smiled and moved the bowl of water between them. "Which way is north?" he asked Daffyd, who pointed to the corner by the door. Jeff held up the wooden disk so that the little white star was at the top. "OK. Now watch this little star." With that, Jeff put the object into the water. The moment he let it go it began to rotate until the white star was lined up exactly with the corner Daffyd had indicated.

"Amazing!" Daffyd exclaimed, examining the disk for any strings. "I never knew you were a magician. Have you placed some sort of charm on it?"

"It's not magic at all." Jeff explained. "It's called a compass." He pointed out the iron pin set into the lid. "This is called a magnet. They actually exist naturally, but they are rare. However, they can be easily made from a piece of iron or steel."

"Take it with you, put it in your boat and watch it. Get used to how it works, and hopefully, next time the visibility gets bad, you can use it to find your way home."

"Here's to finding the way home," toasted Daffyd, as he drank deeply from his cup.

"I'll drink to that," Jeff added, raising his own.

Jeff smelled food coming behind him and looked around, hoping to see Mairwen again, but instead, it was Burkellyn with two bowls of soup. "Here you go boys, and they're on the house." He set the bowls down before them and went on. "That liquor you brought is tasty, and quite popular. What do you call it, and when can I get some more?"

"I'm glad you like it. It's called apple jack" Jeff beamed proudly. "If we can find some more hard cider I can have a little more in a couple of days. When that's gone, I'd like to try something else. It may take a few attempts to get it right, but with fermented barley malt we can make whiskey. That should be even more popular."

"If it goes over like this, I'd be happy to help with that," Burkellyn offered. "I can supply all the malted barley you need and we'll be partners. How soon can you start?"

"You've got a deal." Jeff agreed. "How's tomorrow afternoon?"

Mairwen came to the table with bread. Her father said, "Mairwen, I want you to meet Jeff here tomorrow afternoon. You're going to be making more of this new apple jack and another drink called whiskey."

"Yes, Father," Mairwen answered dutifully, but then turned to Jeff and gave him a little smile. "It's delicious."

"Speaking of delicious things, Mairwen, what was in that soup? I've never had any like it."

"Thank you, Jeff. It's tortoise stew." Mairwen blushed and hurried off.

Tortoise. Jeff never thought he'd enjoy eating a turtle.

Jeff and Daffyd spent the evening toasting Jeff's inventions. Jeff picked up his guitar to entertain the crowd. While he thought he was at his best, the crowd politely ignored him. Daffyd sat at the table, mesmerized by the floating disk. He played with it, turning it one way and then the other, only to watch it invariably find its way back to the north. Other patrons looked in to see what had him so occupied. Some were amused, some were amazed, others saw black magic in it and kept their distance.

Jeff decided to call it a night when he realized that only he and Daffyd remained and Daffyd was asleep in a corner. He got up and made for the door. He felt fine, but the room was messed up. The walls were moving and the floor didn't want to stay put. It was all he could do to walk out without knocking the tables over.

Outside the inn, the fresh air seemed to help as he staggered down the street until he tripped over a curbstone and ended up sprawled on the cobbles. He just sat there laughing for a bit before gathering himself together to make another attempt. He did his best to become vertical, but it was a losing battle until he felt a pair of hands on his arm.

"Here you go, sir," said a soft voice, "let's get you home."

Jeff looked over his shoulder. "Timothy?" He laughed. "You're up late."

"Yes, sir" Timothy replied. "Whenever I can't sleep, I like to walk. It's peaceful late at night."

"Well, thank you," Jeff chuckled. "This is great. I'm being led home by a blind man."

"I'm not entirely blind, sir" Timothy corrected. "I can see a little, especially up close."

"You seem to get around well enough," Jeff said. "How do you find your way?"

"Mostly from memory. The village isn't very big. I know every loose stone I ever tripped over, and I've tripped over most of 'em. Speaking of which, watch your step there." Timothy guided Jeff around a low spot but Jeff nearly stumbled again anyway. "At least it hasn't rained. That one puddles up pretty quickly when it does."

When they reached the forge, Timothy helped Jeff up into the loft and without another word, turned and walked away.

The next morning, Jeff's head was pounding his stomach queasy, and his mouth feeling like an old dirt road, but he pushed himself up and out of bed and got to work. He couldn't wait to get started. The focus on his projects was exciting but the chance to work alongside Mairwen, even more so. There was a bounce in his step that had been missing for some time. He hurriedly parked the cart and went looking for Mairwen. He met her at the door coming the other way, carrying two large earthenware containers of cider.

He shook his head. "Nice jugs!" He said in English, but didn't translate.

"What?" Mairwen asked.

"Sorry, old joke." Jeff muttered sheepishly. "Are you ready to get started?"

Mairwen was used to Jeff's occasional reverting to his native tongue so she let it slip without further comment. "Yes I am. Idwal had more cider at his orchard. I've got four more jugs and a sack of barley malt for the whiskey."

That'll be a great start," Jeff said as he loaded the cider into the cart alongside an assortment of parts made from copper and tin. "I spent the morning putting together some new equipment. This set up is a lot bigger than the one I used. We should be able to make a lot more and a lot quicker now that we know it works. One other thing though. Last night I got an idea for another project. Do you still have the shell from that tortoise?"

By now, Mairwen didn't question why he'd want an old tortoise shell. She dug it out of the trash. They loaded the cart with the cider and barley and found some empty barrels, a large one for the fermentation process and smaller ones for the finished product.

As they followed the winding path through the woods, Mairwen asked, "The thing you made for Daffyd, the…" She hesitated over the word.

"The compass."

"That's it," Mairwen said. "Do you think it will help?"

"It should. Can't do anything about the weather, but if they learn how to use it, they should at least know which way they're headed. We should probably develop accurate charts as well, but, at the minimum they'll be able to find land and beach rather than be blown out to sea."

"Well, that would be a great help," Mairwen said, cupping Jeff's cheek in her hand. "You should be proud."

"It's the least I could do. I feel like I need to give something back. Everyone here has been so good to me since I got here, especially you and your father. Eldric too. Besides, there are things I know how to do that are new here. Some that will make things better for everyone. I have to do what I can."

"I've never tasted anything like that apple jack. Was that your trade where you come from? Making liquor?"

"No. I've never made it before, but I knew the basic process, and as long as I needed the still, I figured, why not give it a try? If it's awful, and nobody drinks it, we'll pour it out. But, if it's potent, some people will drink just about anything. That could be a good thing too, considering I have no idea whether I'm doing it right."

In the clearing, they went to work right away. Mairwen showed Jeff how to ferment the barley malt. Jeff set up the new still and started it going with the cider, then made trips to the stream to fill the casks with water. Mairwen mixed in the barley malt while Jeff tended the still. As the first of the apple jack began to flow, Jeff filled a flask and stored it in the shed.

They worked steadily, side by side, Jeff doing all he could to come as close as possible to Mairwen. He felt a tightness in his chest and found himself holding his breath when they came particularly close. Mairwen, however, seemed oblivious. When they nearly bumped together, she side stepped to avoid the collision without a thought.

Jeff decided he needed a more direct approach. He looked up at a sky brushed with pink and gold as the red sun dipped into the west. "It's beautiful," he said, stepping closer, his heart racing. He smelled her hair. There were none of the perfumed scents that he would have expected in his previous world and yet he found her intoxicating.

"Yes it is," breathed Mairwen as Jeff put his arm about her waist. She looked up at the sunset, relaxed at his touch, then froze. "It's late! We've been concentrating on the work and I lost track of the time. I have to get back."

"I hadn't even thought about it." Shadows of trees stretched across the clearing and already the day's light was dwindling. "Where did the time go?"

"I'll have to hurry to get there before dark." Mairwen dropped what she was doing and rushed about, gathering up her things.

"I'll walk you home."

"No," Mairwen said. "Stay. Someone has to keep an eye on things." She looked back to the sun, winking out over the horizon. "I can make it back before dark if I hurry."

"OK," Jeff gave in and took her by the hand. "Just be careful." He said and kissed her. He held his breath, anticipating her response, hoping she didn't pull away, or worse, but she didn't. She returned his kiss and looked into his eyes. Jeff held her gaze silently clutching her hand for a moment, before releasing her.

"I'll be fine." was all she said before she turned and hurried down the road.

Jeff stood and watched her go. He didn't move until she was out of sight. He was sad to see her go and yet so full of hope for where things seemed headed. When she was gone, he scurried about collecting the tools and containers, putting things away in the shed until only the still itself remained. He placed a fresh empty container at the collection point and settled into the shed for the night.

With a small fire in the hearth to provide warmth and light, Jeff took out the Tortoise shell and etched out the framework he planned to carve from it. He worked at the project until late in the night, stopping from time to time to check on the still's progress.

In the morning Jeff packed the containers of apple jack into the cart and made sure the fermenting barley malt was secured in the shed and started back to town. It was a little early for the inn, so his first order of business was with the glass maker. Ferryll was readying his shop for the day's work when Jeff came in. The glass maker put down a piece he was polishing and greeted him. "Well, if it isn't Llewellynn's own wizard."

"I'm no wizard," Jeff said. "I wish you wouldn't call me that."

"Just repeating what I heard others say. I meant no offense."

The glass maker didn't sound entirely convinced but Jeff thought it best not to make an issue of it. "No, I'm sure you didn't."

Ferrill quickly changed the subject. "What can I do for you?"

"I'd like you to make something for me, actually a number of them. Using the clearest glass you can make, I want a number of disks of the same thickness at the edge, but progressively narrower at the centers." Using a piece of charcoal, he drew out a sketch of what he needed. "Can you do that for me?"

"I can make the disks for you, and with a good clarity, and I won't even ask for what use. But as for the thickness, they'll have to be ground using a polishing compound. It's painstaking work. I can show you how to do it, but I just can't spare the kind of time it would require."

"That would be just fine. Just get me started. Thanks."

"You can come back in a few days. I'll have everything you need ready for you."

Daffyd and Gorloch pushed off from the wharf and leaned into the oars. The river here flowed north before turning west toward what would, one day, be known as the Bristol Channel, and on to the Irish Sea. As light as the breeze was, it came out of the north so the little boat was headed right into its teeth, making the sail useless.

At the first bend, the pair shipped the oars of the little craft and hoisted the sail. Daffyd manned the tiller and Gorloch trimmed the sail to make the most of the light wind. As the sail filled with the zephyr, the boat heeled and picked up speed.

They were the last boat to leave the dock, but that was nothing new. As the youngest pair of fishermen in the village they were almost always the last to arrive in the morning. But they always managed to coax a bit more speed from their sails and arrive at the fishing grounds with the pack. As Daffyd guided the boat, Gorloch used the time to bait the hooks on their lines.

Nearing the point where they could make their next turn, Daffyd looked back over his shoulder at the lightening sky. Amid the pink and orange clouds rose the red ball of the sun. "I make it northwest. What says our friend?"

Gorloch leaned over to read the compass which had been mounted at the base of the mast. "Northwest it is."

Daffyd smiled at the news and gauged their progress to be sure he wasn't turning too soon. "Ready to come about," he called out before leaning into the tiller to bring the boat onto its new heading. Gorloch ducked as the boom crossed over, then readjusted the sail for the new course. Daffyd reoriented himself with the sun and calculated. "We should be due west now."

Gorloch again consulted the compass. "West," he said with a touch of irritation. "For two weeks now you've tested that compass every time we've changed course and every time it's been right. Are we going to keep checking it every time we alter our heading?"

"Okay. Point taken. I know it works, but I just want to be sure that it still works when we need it."

"It's really something." Gorloch mused. "Day or night, good weather or bad, it never fails. How do you think it knows which way is which?"

"Jeff explained it when he gave it to me, but that was also the night he introduced us to the strong drink so I'm a little fuzzy on the details." Daffyd did his best to recall. "He used a coil of copper wire to give it 'maggotism'. It's a kind of spell, I guess, that makes it always point to the North Star. My concern is merely that I want to know that the spell hasn't worn off when the weather turns bad."

They sailed on. Bit by bit making up the time lost in their late departure. The cod were running so they would be fishing in the deeper waters of the channel farther off shore. Light as the breeze was, the waters were choppy. Making headway required extra skill and so Daffyd and Gorloch easily caught up. They chose a spot and hove to by the time that the earliest arrivals were casting out their lines. No sooner did they get their lines into the water than the fish began to bite.

Jeff let down the cart as he crested the last rise of the road on its way into the village. It was downhill from here but it was a good spot for a breather. The casks of whiskey were heavy and he was glad for the cool weather. The hazy morning had evolved into a cloudy afternoon cooled by the northerly breeze. He looked down into the little town, veiled by the low clouds and to the river beyond. The wind was shifting. What had been a convenient cooling breeze would soon be a cold mist. The fire at the inn would be a welcome sight indeed.

He had a thought for the still and the rest of his stock back at the clearing. On one of his trips into town he had worked with Eldric to make a simple cylinder lock like the ones he had once used for his bicycle and a stronger hasp for the door of the shed. He hoped it would be enough but he had doubts.

Rested, Jeff took up his burden again. It didn't hurt knowing that Mairwen would be there. He hauled his load, letting gravity have its way, anxious to make his delivery and finally relax.

He hefted the first of the little barrels in the door of the inn. Mairwen spotted him and rushed over. "There you are! I thought you'd be back yesterday at least."

Jeff set his burden down on a table. "Once I fire up the still, it's best to just run continuously until finished and there was a lot of it. There are three more barrels in the cart and another back at the shed."

"You have been busy." Mairwen said. "Timothy is around here somewhere, helping my father. He can help you to unload." She moved into the kitchen and rearranged things to make room for the new supplies. "Timothy!" she called out. "Have you tasted it?" She laughed and added, "of course you have. How is it?"

"I'd have to say it's the worst whiskey I've ever tasted, but still, at this moment, the best that's ever been made," Jeff joked.

Mairwen was puzzled at his inconsistency but didn't question how both statements might be true. But then, not everything Jeff said made sense to her. "I'm sure that we'll improve over time as we gain experience." She stepped back, thinking about where to put the remaining barrels. "You said there was one more at the shed. Why did you leave it behind? Too heavy?"

"Well this was heavy enough, but no, the whiskey should improve with age in the oaken barrels, so I held some back." Jeff brought the first of the barrels into the kitchen and got it situated on a shelf by the remaining apple jack. "I think we should hold a little back each time until we can build up a supply of aged liquor, at least until we can see what it does for the quality."

"I think that's a good idea." Mairwen agreed. "At least as long as our supply can keep up with demand."

"Right. Which is why, even with all this, we need to plan on making more soon. The farther ahead we can get the better."

Burkellyn and Timothy came in bringing supplies from the root cellar. Mairwen ran to help. "Father, Jeff is back with the first barrels of whiskey."

"Excellent," Her father said, "and not a moment too soon. It's going to be a raw night out and the apple jack is almost gone. In weather like this it's the first thing anybody asks for. It makes them feel warm." He turned to Jeff and asked, "Is it good?"

"No," Jeff said, "but they'll love it."

"Good enough," Burkellyn roared and clapped Jeff on the back "I like you. You don't delude yourself." Then he called out to Timothy who was stocking the vegetables he had brought in. "Timothy! Mairwen can put those away. Help Jeff bring in the whiskey."

When the whiskey was in its place, Jeff led Timothy back out to the cart. "I have something here for you as well, Timothy!" A small box at the bottom of the cart held a carefully wrapped bundle. Jeff unwrapped the bundle revealing the frame he had carved out of the tortoise shell and four glass disks.

Timothy was puzzled as he stood waiting for whatever Jeff had in store. Jeff set the first of the disks into the frame. The clear polished glass resembled a small saucer. It was lightly tapered on one side, more so on the other, so that the center was narrower than the edges. "These are called glasses. Stand still," Jeff said as he placed the frames on Timothy's face. "Now cover one eye and look through that with the other." Timothy followed the directions and the puzzling turned to outright astonishment. "Tell me what you see."

Timothy was speechless for a moment, then blurted, "Oh my word!" He was stunned. "I haven't been able to see this well since I was a child!"

"Now try it with the other eye," Jeff suggested.

Timothy rearranged the frame to do this "Yes!" He exclaimed, "About the same!"

Jeff removed the frames, to Timothy's disappointment. He removed the lens and replaced it with the second. The second was concave like the first, but slightly more pronounced. "Now try this.' He then handed the frame back to Timothy, who set them in place.

Timothy was even more dumbfounded. "Amazing. This is even better. I never thought it possible. I can see!" He tried with his left eye as well. "Both eyes!"

Jeff took back the frame, this time Timothy was eager, and put in the third lens. Timothy tested the third lens, but his excitement was let down. "No, definitely better than the first, but, the second is still the best." He handed the frame back to Jeff.

Jeff installed the final lens. The last lens was different from the others, wider in the center than at the edges. "How about this one?" he asked, as he handed them over.

Timothy tried this one as he had the others, first one eye then the other. He shook his head as he handed the glasses back. "Not at all. I didn't think it was possible for my vision to be any worse, but that was."

Jeff put back the second lens in the right side then the third lens went in the left and made them secure. He handed the full set back to Timothy. "Take them, Timothy. They're yours. I'll regrind the first so that it is the same as the best, but even these will be a great improvement for you. Now let's get in out of the weather. It's getting damper by the minute."

At the door, they met Mairwen and Burkellyn coming out. "Was that everything, Jeff?" Burkellyn asked.

"Yes, that's it." Jeff answered. "But Timothy has a surprise for you." Jeff stepped aside so that Timothy could show them his new glasses. "Don't you Timothy? Show them how studious you look."

"I can see!" Timothy beamed. "Jeff made these glasses for me and now I can see."

Mairwen and Burkellyn were nearly as amazed as Timothy. "You're cured?" Mairwen asked. "How?"

"Not cured." Jeff offered. "More like corrected. His eyes are the same, but the lenses help him focus. The result is the same."

Mairwen stepped forward and examined the glasses. "I think it's wonderful" She stepped back as Timothy modeled the glasses. "It's an odd looking contraption, but if they help you see…" she said. "They make your eyes look bigger. I never noticed they were green." Timothy blushed.

As the group stood, admiring Timothy and his new found vision, Father Ewan came bustling out of the church. Timothy was the first to see him. "Hello, Father," He greeted, observing, "You look worried."

The old priest was perplexed by Timothy's new eye-wear. He hesitated for a moment looking at the glasses, not sure what to make of them, then remembered what he came to say. "It looks like we may be in for another long night." He said, looking up at the growing cloudiness and thickening mist. "I think we ought to make our way down to the waterfront."

The mist was definitely becoming thicker. Visibility was diminishing. Timothy saw the priest's concern. "Do you want me to ring the bell?" he asked.

"Not yet, Timothy," Father Ewan demurred. "While I would have expected them by now, if the fish are biting, they may have stayed to the last, or they might simply be delayed by the weather, going slowly but carefully. The bell can wait, but a few prayers are in order."

They all made their way quietly down the path to the wharf, pulling in their cloaks against the chill of the mist. Timothy stopped twice to wipe his glasses. Having discovered vision, he didn't want to miss a thing. At the wharf they found a small gathering already in progress.

Jeff looked out at the choppy surface river, straining to see the boats in the mist. The rough waters and the cold mist combined into an inhospitable environment. He didn't envy the fishermen at all. They awaited the return of the boats in the gathering gloom. The crowd grew along with the concern.

Daffyd and Gorloch were tired. All day long they'd bobbed relentlessly in the little boat. The waters were choppy when they arrived and as the day went on, the waves progressed into swells. Rolling with the motion for hours can take a toll, even if that was all you did, but the fishermen barely gave that notice.

What did have their attention was the fish. They were biting. As soon as they had arrived that morning they had begun to lay out their lines. Each boat used several, a hundred yards long and longer, a hook and bait was set at intervals every few yards.

The fleet spread out so as not to tangle the lines. Daffyd and Gorloch laid out each of their lines in turn, and when they were all out, went back to the first and hauled it in. All day long, the process continued. Lay out a string, haul one in, re-bait and lay it out again.

The baskets that held their catch were nearly full as they brought in the lines for the last time. While a few of these fish would be eaten tonight, most would be salted and put up for the coming cold weather. With the season coming to a close, every additional day they could go out, and each additional fish caught was a hedge against a long and difficult winter.

Still, when the holds were full, it was time to go home. Not a moment too soon for Daffyd. He was exhausted and miserable. The weather had gone from overcast in the morning to cold and damp. The clouds lowered until they practically met the waves. More a mist than a fog, but the effect was the same. Visibility was a couple of hundred yards at the most and the fleet was off shore more than a mile. Daffyd heard a bell ringing in the distance.

He looked in the direction of the sound and saw Dylan's boat was flying the pennant that meant come together. "Dylan's calling us in." He said to Gorloch, who was just finishing the last of the lines. They made their way through the swells toward Dylan's boat.

The fishing fleet, as they liked to think of themselves, consisted of six boats. They were small one man craft, except two, one shared by Gorloch and Daffyd and the other manned by Dylan and his son Morcant.

Dylan was the oldest of the seamen and took the mantle of leader. It was not an official title, but the men looked up to him for his experience. And he took on himself the responsibility for the safety of the group. When they fished offshore as they were today, he kept station closest to shore to maintain the bearing. So it was with some consternation that, when he called the far flung boats together, he saw them coming in from ALL directions. Even including the one he thought was east and shoreward.

As the boats gathered together, Dylan stood. Holding the mast of his little boat and balancing the best he could in the rolling sea, he addressed the fishermen, "I know many of you want to keep fishing as long as they bite, but this weather isn't going to cooperate much longer. I think we ought to head in while there's light."

With some reluctance the men muttered assent as Dylan turned his boat to sail for home. No sooner had he raised his sail and set course a cry rang out. "Where are you going?" yelled Rhys, waving his arms to get Dylan's attention. "Land is that way!" Rhys pointed off in another direction entirely.

Dylan dropped his sail again and hove to. It seemed there were as many opinions on the true direction of land as there were sailors. "The wind's been from the north so we should be going that way," said one voice.

"But the wind's changeable today. I don't know that we can rely on it." came another.

Dylan looked up at his telltales, the little ribbons attached to the sails and mast that caught the slightest breeze. They would show the true direction of the wind even as the boat sailed on. The telltales on his own boat disagreed as the wind seemed to be blowing in circles.

"I have no intention of sailing off, halfway to Ireland while we figure out which way to go," bemoaned Siorus, who had a reputation for obstinance. "We should probably lash together and wait out a break in the clouds."

Dylan shook his head. "No, that won't do at all." He looked across at the boats bobbing and rolling in the brewing seas. "I don't fancy spending a night in this chop. Never mind should it get any worse." He stood again and surveyed the distance, or what he could see of it, looking for any sign of land. "We need to do the best we can to find our bearings and get in."

Finally Daffyd decided to weigh in. He stood in his boat pointing assuredly after consulting the compass. "The closest land is there." He said, trying his best to project his voice. He pointed again at a slightly different angle. "The mouth of the river should be there."

"Who says?" barked Drest, "a mermaid?" The men laughed nervously as Drest went on. "What makes you so sure?"

Daffyd laughed along with the rest of them, then responded, "No mermaids, I'm sorry to say, but a gift." Daffyd moved to the compass that was mounted alongside the mast. "It's called a compass. It was a present from my friend Jeff and it always points to the North Star."

"So now we trust our lives to a minstrel?" Siorus chided defiantly.

The others either laughed or muttered derisively until Gorloch chimed in. "It's true!" Gorloch checked the compass himself, and pointed north. "North is there!" he asserted. "For weeks I've checked it every time we changed course. It's never been wrong. Day or night, good weather or bad, whether you could see the North Star or not, it points in the right direction." Daffyd could sense that the others were coming around. Nobody wanted to spend a night out on the water in this weather. "The first time I saw it at the inn, it even worked inside."

Daffyd surveyed the faces of his brother fishermen. What they were looking for, he thought, was decisiveness and action. He raised his sail and dove for the tiller as the sail filled in the light breeze. He drew in the sheet, the line controlling how far the sail boom can swing out, and adjusted it to best advantage. He didn't hesitate. He didn't look back. With an overhand wave, he called out over a shoulder "follow me!" and sailed for home.

Rhys quickly followed. Then one by one the others did as well. Siorus sat defiantly until he was the last, but when he found himself being left alone, he went after the others as quickly as his boat could go.

Daffyd could easily have outpaced the others. His boat was faster and his skill as a sailor was superior. So he subtly let air off his sail as he crested a wave or let the boat heel over just a bit more than necessary here and there. He never looked back but he knew they were there and he took care not to get too far ahead lest the others lose sight of him as he made straight for the river's mouth.

The wind freshened enough to blow off the mist, revealing the point of land at the mouth of the river. Right where it ought to be and not a moment too soon. The next gust came in stronger still, whipping the tops of the waves into a froth as Daffyd brought the little boat around on a heading upstream into somewhat calmer water.

As Daffyd made his turn, he finally looked back at the other boats. The mist had cleared enough that he could see them all. Now visibility was the least of their concerns. They were spread out in a line astern like a necklace on the water, fighting their way through the foaming swells. One boat in a trough so deep all Daffyd could see were the mast and sail, the next crested a wave exposing the hull right down to the keel.

With the weather turning foul, the townspeople gravitated to the waterfront just as they had done before. Standing at the dock, Jeff was first to see Daffyd's boat emerge from the mist. "That's Daffyd!" He called out. "They're coming!"

"Yes! There they are!" Shouted Timothy, the glee in his voice was unmistakable. Whether out of concern for the fisherman or at the joy of sight itself was debatable.

Each boat rounded the point while the wind continued to build. The sailors sensing a change in the weather for the worse took full advantage. Sailing close hauled, the booms held in tight they raced for the wharf. The men were leaning as far over the rail as they could, bringing their weight to bear, and still the opposite gunwales skimmed the surface, even going under as the boat crested the chop.

Confident the others would find their own way in from here, Daffyd sailed on as swiftly as he could go. Increasing the gap over the others as he tacked his way upstream, he noticed a small crowd gathering at the wharf.

Daffyd came racing in after the last bend so fast Jeff thought they would wreck against the dock. But, at the last possible moment, he executed a neat little turnabout into the wind, dropped his sail, then drifted easily the last few feet into the dock. He and Gorloch began tossing the baskets holding the fish onto the wharf.

The wind kicked up even higher and a gust nearly swamped the close-hauled boats, and then the rains came. One by one the boats came in with all haste, anxious to get out of the weather, the fishermen rushed in. As they arrived, the crowd gathered at the wharf began to help with the unloading, glad to see that another candlelight vigil would not be needed.

Siorus was last to arrive, heeling over so far with the wind and already riding low with her heavy load. His boat was taking on water with every whitecap she broached. He came in much the same way Daffyd had but with all the others tied up there wasn't room for the maneuver at the wharf so he headed directly for the careening beach and grounded. He jumped out and, with the help of Timothy, hauled the boat up onto the beach, and rolled it to one side to spill the water out. Timothy wiped the wetness from his glasses then cheerfully took up a share of the load and carried it in.

That night the inn was one big celebration. The elation of the returning fishermen, fueled by the introduction of whiskey, made for a raucous evening. Daffyd soon found that he couldn't put his cup down empty without finding it refilled almost immediately. Never one to turn down a free drink, he basked in the attention. Neither was he one to hog the spotlight. He reminded everyone that it was Jeff who made the compass that had been responsible for their return. And so, the village's newest resident found his tankard bottomless as well.

Since Jeff was drinking ale, the effects were not so immediate. Still, not wanting to be rude, he figured the only way to avoid a drunken stupor was to give his mouth something else to do. He took up his guitar from its peg.

Winding through the crowd, he found himself face to face with Father Ewan. "It seems you've made yourself quite productive. I never did have any doubt, but you've exceeded my expectations."

"Thank you, Father. I'm glad to help, but really, it was nothing. The compass is common where I am from."

"Call it what you like." The priest stepped aside to let Jeff take up his usual spot in the corner. While, from there, Jeff could see and be seen throughout the room when he sang, it was farther from the tables and allowed them a touch more privacy for their conversation. "The results speak for themselves."

"I'm just glad I could help and that everyone is safe."

Father Ewan stepped closer and spoke quietly. "In light of your newly demonstrated resourcefulness, there is another matter I'd like to discuss."

"Go ahead, Father." Jeff was surprised at the conspiratorial tone.

"You've been watching out for young Arthwyr as I asked?"

"Yes, Father."

"Is there something you know about that might offer the boy some additional protection. In case someone…"

"Might try to harm him?" Jeff finished the priest's sentence for him, his brow rising in surprise. "I was thinking more on the lines of protecting him from himself." Jeff couldn't imagine anyone wanting to hurt the boy. He seemed harmless, wouldn't hurt a fly, and was liked by all who knew him. "Who could possibly?" He gasped.

Father Ewan waved off the question. "Another time, perhaps. I can only say that it would not be good if certain people knew of his existence. Perhaps there is something else that is *common where you are from,* that might offer some protection. He's in good hands with Eldric, but it could be that brawn is not always enough."

Jeff weighed what the priest was saying. He never was the type who got into fights so he wasn't sure how much help he could provide. "I'll do what I can. Sure." He replied, but without much conviction.

"I have faith in you and I know I can count on you to keep this to yourself." The priest took a step back. He went on in a full voice so any nearby might hear, "I'm not sure I approve of the liquor you've brought us, but today was a good day and we thank you." With that he nodded and left Jeff to his music.

Jeff played his guitar and sang his songs late into the night while fighting a losing battle to remain sober or something like it. Human spirits were high and liquid spirits flowed freely. Revelers came up to request their favorite songs and, one by one, the seamen came by to request a compass of their own. Without hesitation, he agreed.

When the celebration wound down, Jeff helped Mairwen, Burkellynn and Timothy with the cleanup, a larger task than usual.

Timothy manned his broom, actually finding debris with it for a change.

"Well, Jeff. You were right about two things." Mairwen observed as she swabbed down a particularly filthy table. "I tasted the whiskey and it is harsh, but it's rather popular just the same."

"It will get better with practice." Jeff assured her.

"I hope you were able to secure things at the clearing. I'd hate to see all that work go down the drain."

Jeff chuckled at the choice of words. "The drain is the least of our worries, but the throats of some of these guys could definitely be a problem. I did take a few precautions, but I'm not sure it's enough. That shed is so rickety that a lock on the door is only a minor impediment to a thief when all you need to do is pull a few boards apart to get in."

"It looks as though it could fall over all by itself."

"I don't think it's quite as bad as that, but until we can build something more solid, I'll have to come up with something."

"You certainly helped the fishermen today. It could have been a bad day out there when the storm blew in, if not for you." Mairwen stepped closer and she looked into his eyes. The lamplight sparkled in her eyes as she squeezed his hand. "You made me proud." As she kissed him, Burkellynn pretended not to see.

Chapter 5 – The Apprentice

Cynwrig had inherited a little farm on the edge of town. A vegetable patch, a field of grain, and enough pasture land to support a few cows, some pigs, and a small flock of sheep, it wasn't much, but it was home for him, his wife Fhinna and their five children. It was a meager existence, but they made do.

He had never been one for outward showing of emotions, except for anger. He kept his emotions bottled up pretty well but, when his temper flared, the anger found its way to the surface. When it did, other men learned quickly to give him a wide berth. He was a big man, almost a head taller than any other man in the village. And, while he didn't have the brawn of the smith, he was broad shouldered and powerful. His size, coupled with the adrenaline of anger, made him a man not to be trifled with.

From sun up to sundown he worked hard, but found no joy in it. He paid little mind to his wife and of his children, even less as long as their chores were done. On those few days he had any energy left when the farm work was done, he could usually be found at the inn. Now that the older boys, Deinol, Berwyn and Mercher were taking up some of the load, that was becoming more frequent. If only the younger one, could be counted on as well.

One fine fall day, Mercher was off with Cynwrig taking a hog to market. The task of minding the sheep fell to the youngest brother, Rhydderch He led them to a corner of the pasture where the grass was abundant and sat in the shade of a tall spruce tree. Before long he grew bored with watching the animals mill about chewing the grass.

Rhydderch pushed his way between the branches and disappeared into the spruce. He leaned the staff he used to prod the wandering sheep against the trunk and began to climb. The spruce was a perfect climbing tree, perfect at least if you ignored the sap clinging to your hands as you climbed.

High in the tree he could see the entire pasture. In fact from this vantage point, he could see all the way home and, in the other direction he could even see the bell tower of the church. When he pressed down on a branch he could look out over the wetlands to the river and even the sea. He mused about what it might be like to travel to distant lands.

He wasn't sure how long he had been daydreaming when he snapped out of it, so he hurriedly counted the sheep to confirm that none had wandered off. When all were accounted for, he relaxed and soon was again lost in tales he had heard of magic and kings, of wizards and dragons, anything but the hum drum of normal life.

The sun was nearly touching the distant sea when he was roused by the bleating of his charges. He looked around frantically for any sign of danger and found, instead, his brother Berwyn. No danger to the sheep at least.

Berwyn was in a foul mood as he thrashed around the pasture looking for Rhydderch. "Rhyderch!" He called out. "Where are you, you little runt?" He pushed apart the branches of the spruce, but never thought to look up. "Asleep somewhere no doubt. I'll spot that red mop of yours from a mile away, and when I do, you'll be in for a thrashing.

Rhyderch held his breath, afraid that the slightest sound would give him away. He was in for a rough time whenever he got home, but nothing like that he'd receive if his brother got his hands on him in this mood. Silently he watched Berwyn round up the sheep and usher them off. Only when it was dark did he climb out of the tree and venture home to take his medicine. He would miss his dinner, but at least his mother could prevent a severe beating.'

The more Jeff thought about what Mairwen had said about security at the still, the more he knew she was right. The new hinges were fine, the hasp and padlock would discourage the well meaning, but a determined thief would barely be slowed. The shed itself was so flimsy that all one needed to do, if they really wanted to break in, was to dismantle the door. If he wanted to be sure the stock would be safe. He was going to have to come up with something else. He was pretty sure that he could devise a simple alarm system, but the clearing was so remote that if he wasn't in the area, he would never hear it. The noise might scare an intruder off into the woods initially, but, when nothing else happened they would return. He needed to find a way to discourage thieves enough that they would give up.

    He dwelt on the alarm idea for some time, thinking how it might be wired into the shed before dismissing it altogether and focused on the wiring itself and came up with an idea. Make the wiring the deterrent!

    Taking another page from his basic electronics classes, he went to the forge and built some components, resistors, capacitors etc.. He designed, and after a little trial and error, constructed a circuit that would build and store an electrical charge. It was strong enough to deliver a jolt that would make anyone think twice about trying a second time, but wouldn't kill anything larger than a moth.

    Jeff took his device to the clearing and, using a fine bare copper wire, he installed it. He wove the wire into the door and windows. He connected it to the latch, the hasp and the hinges so that anyone trying to remove either the door or shutters would make contact. A simple gate switch behind a crack in the wall he could poke a thin strip of wood through and push up the arm of the gate, breaking the circuit to disarm it. Finally, he refilled the cells of his battery with acid and connected it to the system.

    He stepped back and admired his work. The wire was fairly unobtrusive, not really hidden. It needed to be visible to work. He gathered himself up, then reached out and took hold of the latch. A stab of pain ran right up his arm to the shoulder, his armpit throbbed, and his muscles contracted involuntarily, pulling his hand away from the offending hardware. Though it was no surprise, a yelp escaped him as he shook his arm to ease the pain. "No!" he thought, he certainly didn't want to do that again. With a fair degree of satisfaction, he inserted his wooden key, then shook out his arm again.

With his immediate security concern taken care of, he pondered the priest's cryptic request to keep an eye on Arthwyr. Simply watching him posed no problems, but if anyone ever did try to cause him harm, what then?

He had always been fairly fit. In fact, his work at the forge had made him stronger than ever, but he had never been one to solve his problems with his fists. In all the time spent in places like the inn, he was usually capable of using humor to defuse a situation before it got out of hand. A person with a grudge was different. He was going to need an ace in the hole.

Jeff busied himself with the still as a diversion. He had found in the past that he was more likely to come up with a solution if he didn't try to concentrate too hard, especially when the solution needed to be out of the ordinary.

He worked into the evening, occasionally testing his product for quality, then sat picking out a tune on his guitar as the fire burned down, lost in the music.

A quiet night at the inn drew to a close early. At least the rain had let up as the sun set but it was cold, a wet raw cold that crept into your bones. The wind wasn't terribly strong, but strong enough to make chill penetrate deeply. It was the kind of night that only those with nowhere else to go, who found their own homes to be inhospitable, found their way to the inn.

The guitar hung on its peg as the lone patron of the inn needed no entertaining. The man sat, slumped in a chair by the fire, a half empty cup of whiskey at his side. Occasionally he would shift in the chair or mutter a few words under his breath and Jeff thought he might rouse and decide to call it a night, but then a moment later he would be snoring.

Jeff could usually count on a few moments alone with Mairwen at the end of the night. On a slow night like this he hoped to have more than a few minutes. As the patrons left, most right after dinner, his hopes rose. All but the last guest. He was considering how to politely rouse the man and convince him that it was time to go. He bent down to tend the fire, soaking in the warmth as he turned a log, bringing up the flame, when he felt a blast of cold air as the door opened and closed. He looked to the door, but saw no one. *A gust of wind? Probably. A voice? No... Just the man muttering again* he thought, as he added another log and stood.

Jeff went about the room to be sure that once the final patron left, they would be done for the night. Burkellynn had already turned in and Mairwen was in the kitchen, shutting down for the night. *Just a few more details,* he thought as he wiped a table, when he felt a tugging at the tail of the flannel shirt. "Sir?" said a little voice. "Could you help?"

Jeff turned to see a young boy with a face full of freckles and hair the color of a new copper penny. His head barely rose above the level of the table tops. "Sure," he began, "What is it?"

The boy froze. He stood for a moment staring at the T-shirt emblazoned with the fish and the lettering "MARLIN". His jaw dropped and he stepped back. "You're the wizard!" he whispered.

Jeff was amused at the thought that he might inspire such awe. "Not a wizard," he said, "just a musician, a man like any other."

"People say you're a wizard." The boy countered with just a touch more confidence in his voice.

"Do they? What do they say?"

"They say you came on a bolt of lightning when there wasn't a cloud in the sky." The boy explained, his voice gaining in strength as his apprehension faded. "They say you cured a blind man and taught a box to point North. You make a potion that makes men drunk. Then there's the cabin in the clearing...."

Jeff digested what the boy was saying. He had no idea he was having such an effect. "What about the cabin?"

"It's enchanted," the boy said. "The door stings like a bee if someone tries to get in." He lowered his voice again. "I've seen it myself."

"You tried the door?" Jeff asked, a hint of annoyance in his voice.

"Oh, no!" The boy, shook his head and backed up a step. "I'm smarter than that, but I've seen others."

"Good for you," Jeff leaned in close and whispered, "Between you and me though," he looked both ways as if he thought someone might be listening in. "I'm not really a wizard." Bending down so that their foreheads nearly touched he went on, "there isn't anything I've done since I got here that you couldn't do if you knew how." Jeff stepped back and straightened before continuing in a full voice. "What's your name son?"

"Rhydderch." the boy answered, "on account of my hair. It means, *The Red.*"

"Well, it certainly suits you," Jeff chuckled. "You can call me Jeff." He shook the boy's hand and went on, "You were asking for help. What can I do?"

The boy led Jeff to the man snoring in the chair. "It's my Dad. My mum sent me to fetch him, but I can't wake him." He shook the man again by the arm, evoking a snort and a murmur, but little else. "Da! Wake up!" The boy shook the sleeper while shouting in his ear to no avail then said, resignedly, "It's no use."

Jeff considered the situation. "Looks like it's the hard way or nothing." He pulled his cloak in tight against the weather outside. By this time, Mairwen had heard the voices and came in, hoping to see another paying customer. He addressed her as he hoisted the man onto his feet, pulling his arm and shoving a shoulder into the man's armpit. "Our friend here is going to need a bit of help getting home. I'll see you later." The boy ran ahead to get the door and Jeff followed him out. "OK, Red, show me the way."

They walked in silence as the boy led the way to the farm outside the town, Jeff occasionally resetting the man's weight to keep him from slipping to the ground. The cold damp air at least had the effect of rousing the man from his stupor. He was a long way from conscious but his legs contributed somewhat to the process of walking, leaving Jeff mainly responsible for balance and navigation.

Rhydderch timidly broke the silence. "You said back there that even I could do what you did, if I knew how. Is that true?"

"Absolutely!"

"Could you teach me?" Rhydderch ran ahead a few steps and turned to face Jeff, then skipped along backwards as he pled his case. "I'd work to repay you, like an apprentice, clean up, fetch things. I'm good at that."

"Doesn't your family need you at the farm?" Jeff didn't need to get in the middle of any family trouble.

"Sometimes, like at harvest time, but mostly my brothers do the work." When they had reached the farm, the boy ran ahead to open the gate. "I don't like farm work all that much. Mostly I run errands and the like. Sometimes I watch the sheep. My brothers say I just get in the way, so they wouldn't even miss me."

"I'll tell you what," Jeff thought that it might be nice to have some help here and there, so he was inclined to bargain. "I'll make you a deal." The boy froze in place while Jeff laid out the terms. "First of all, IF your parents say it's OK, and IF you do all your chores around the farm, and I want you to do more than you're doing now, especially at harvest time. Then OK, I'll teach you and you can help me out. Deal?"

"Deal!" agreed the lad.

"Excellent." Jeff confirmed as they reached the door to the little farmhouse. "Now, let's get your father inside, and you can work it out with them tomorrow."

In a church on the southern coast of Wales, Maghnus held council with his top lieutenants. The wind howled outside, blowing out the last gasp of winter but the men took no notice. A crackling fire fed by timbers from the house next door kept the chill at bay. A dozen men helped themselves to a feast laid out on the altar, slabs of mutton, breads, dried fruit and a cask of ale. The rest slept, curled up in darkened corners. Those who weren't off beating the cold in another way, with the unwilling aid of captured women.

Phelan sat beside his father but didn't participate in the conversation, obeying his father's oft repeated admonition to listen and learn. "When the weather breaks, we'll cross the bay and continue south." Maghnus said.

Ruarc's head wavered from side to side. "I think we should explore these waters a bit more first." "This has been the richest prize we've seen this year," Declan said. "No sense leaving while there's more here for the taking."

"As we move upstream, the bay will narrow and we'll be bottled up. Another storm like this one could trap us," Maghnus said.

"But this is probably the last storm of the season," Ruarc said.

"I think you said the same thing a fortnight ago."

"Others have done so and come back with riches. I've heard the stories," said Declan.

"And if a band didn't come back, would we hear those stories?"

"The men are happy for once. They want to keep going while the looting is good." Aonghus finally weighed in. "Spring will be here soon. We'll want to be getting back for the planting. Heading South takes us farther from home." His brothers muttered their agreement. "I say we work our way up one coast of this inlet and down the other and then straight back to Ireland."

"Aye." Declan and Ruarc said, almost in unison.

"Then that is what we will do." Maghnus deferred to his men.

Later that night, the wind died down and the storm moved on. Maghnus and Phelan left the church and stood near the boats. In the crisp air, lights twinkled in the distance across the inky black of the water.

"Why did you back down?" Phelan asked. "You're the king."

"Their arguments were sound." Maghnus put an arm over the boy's shoulder. "If they had said to move on, I might have argued to stay, as long as both sides are heard. Sometimes a leader gains more power by giving a little bit away."

 Chemistry had never been Jeff's forte. He passed the required courses easily enough and then moved on, forgetting much of what he'd learned. Besides, it was one thing to measure out samples of a pure substance from well labeled jars and combine them in a textbook experiment. It was another thing entirely, to find those samples in their natural states.
 There were three ingredients that Jeff was going to need. The first was easy. Charcoal. He took what he needed from the forge and ground it into a fine powder to fill a large jar.
 The second ingredient was sulfur. The hot spring that fed the town's baths provided the source. For ages, trace amounts of the element had collected on the rocks where the spring bubbled to the surface, coating them in a yellow rime. Since the water had been diverted for the baths, only a trickle made the surface anymore leaving behind the dried stones. Jeff had only to scrape the foul smelling yellow powder and collect it.
 He carried his samples, to the clearing and locked them away in the shed, then continued out the road in search of his third ingredient. Where the stream crossed the road he followed it to the rent in the cliff and the uninhabited cave. He crept into the cave and stared intently into the blackness, giving his eyes a chance to adjust. When his sight allowed him to make out some detail, he opened his cell phone for the first time in weeks and turned it on. He held his breath while it came to life. It still had a charge.
 In the dim light of the phone's display, crystal deposits on the walls glistened. Jeff hoped he was right about what they were. He scraped the crystals to fill the last of his containers and returned to the clearing.
 He set up a work area well away from the still or the shed, where no stray spark could find its way. He used his cloak as a windbreak against light breezes when it was warm enough, but worked only when no wind or rain threatened and only in full daylight so that he wouldn't require any lamp, candle or firelight.

Eventually he would need to find a way to chemically refine his raw materials if he was to produce any kind of quantity. In the meantime the best he could do was to visually sort by color, picking out the purest white crystals by hand.

For safety's sake, Jeff worked with only the smallest quantities, never more than a thimble-full, as he tried using each ingredient in different proportions. It was a lot like trying to open a combination lock by trying all the possible permutations except that each one gave a slightly different result.

He set out tiny samples of each combination on a board. He took a stick from the fire and blew out its flame. Carrying it over to the board, Jeff looked around the clearing and then up and down the road to be sure he was not being watched. All clear.

He blew on the ember until it glowed red and lowered it to the first sample. The powder burst immediately into flame and consumed itself in seconds. He lit the second and it burned too, but with less enthusiasm as did the third. The fourth burned even more slowly before guttering out. When he touched the coal to his fifth sample, the flames leapt up with a hiss, startling him. "Ooh! That's more like it."

Each round of samples was prepared using what he had learned in the last. Each time he got better and more consistent results. Each time, he looked about him for prying eyes. Secrecy was always a concern but this time it was critical. As he cultivated the notion that he was a wizard, the townspeople grew to respect and accept him more but he didn't want to overstep. If respect turned to fear, it could evolve further into suspicion and distrust.

Jeff prepared six very promising samples. He touched off the first one. *Pssssssst* it went as it burned furiously. Jeff smiled. The second and third spluttered a little less excitedly. When the fourth was touched off, it went all at once with a *FOOM*. "Yes!" he said. He knew he was close, and for the first time, sure that he was on the right track. He blew on the ember to revive it as a portion had been blown off, then lowered it to the fifth sample. *WHUMP*!

That was it. He was sure of it, but how would it react when it was confined. To find out, he had hollowed out an acorn. His hands shook in excitement as he filled the acorn shell with more of his compound, packing it tightly. He inserted a few strands of hemp twine that had been rolled in the powder as a fuse. He sealed it all with wax and set it down on a stump.

He lit the fuse, then quickly stepped well away and waited. It spluttered and Jeff was deflated, thinking he had been wrong. His shoulders sagged as he let out a sigh. He took a step toward the acorn to see what happened when the smoldering fuse caught the charge. *BANG*! Jeff recoiled, shook off the stun, then let out a whoop. "Yeah!' he said dancing in a circle in celebration.

It didn't have the power or the snap of the firecrackers he knew, but it was unmistakable, He had just invented gunpowder. That notion was still sinking in when a small voice behind him brought him out of his reverie.

"I knew you were a wizard." Jeff turned to see Rhydderch coming up the path, his red mane flowing in the breeze. The boy had come to see if Jeff would make good his promises of apprenticeship. "But don't worry, I won't tell."

Jeff's mouth hung open for a moment. In all the excitement, he hadn't even thought to look around again before he set the thing off. "You made it!" he said, trying to hide his shock. He put an arm over the boy's shoulder and led him around the clearing. Let me show you around a bit, then we'll get started." Jeff's mouth hung open for a moment. In all the excitement, he hadn't even thought to look around again before he set the thing off. "You made it!" he said, trying to hide his shock. He put an arm over the boy's shoulder and led him around the clearing. Let me show you around a bit, then we'll get started."

He and gave him a brief summary of the use of the still. He showed him how to disable the security system in case he needed to get in when Jeff wasn't here. They topped up the acid in the batteries and then Jeff explained magnetism. "I thought this would be a good place to start." He handed the boy the rough-cut parts of a compass float. "I promised the other fishermen they could each have their own compass. How would you like to be the one to make them?"

Rhydderch grinned, taking up the pieces. Speechless, it was all he could do to nod his appreciation. The subject of gunpowder never came up

Jeff turned the compass float over in his hands, admiring the craftsmanship, running his fingers over the smooth surface. It was beautiful. The last of six, each more perfect than the one before it. The compass rose on the top was painted with painstaking detail and lettered with care. The wood glistened with several coats of highly polished varnish that would protect it from the effects of water for years to come. "Nice work," he said. A smile came to Rhydderch's face. "Better than I could do," Jeff continued, and the smile became a grin. The boy had spent a week working on his assignment and brought it here to the inn for Jeff's approval.

Jeff dropped the disk into a bucket to be sure it floated properly. It bobbed high in the water as it whirled around to unerringly point North. He ran a hand through the boy's hair, tousling it further, "You definitely have a good eye for detail." He put the floats aside in the corner by his stool for the fishermen when they came in that evening.

"This gives me an idea," he said, reaching into his pocket. He undid a leather wrapping and gave the boy the remaining lens he had been carrying since giving Timothy his glasses. "I'm going to put you in charge of re-grinding this. I'll show you how and get you started. When you're done we may even want to fine tune the ones he's using. I think you might be capable of improving it."

Rhydderch was visibly excited at the prospect of surpassing the teacher. Jeff went on, "We can start on that tomorrow. In the meantime, you can help me with something else. Come on." He strode out of the inn and down the street, the boy trotting along behind. At the forge, they got the cart as well as a hammer and an assortment of chisels then turned back up the road and out of town.

With the town still visible behind them, Jeff left the road stepping through the tall grass of a meadow. Rhydderch did his best to keep up. "Aren't we going to the clearing?" he asked.

"Not this time," said Jeff, climbing to the summit of a hill topped by a polished granite monument.

Jeff stood for a moment looking at the stone. As appropriate as it had been when it had dominated the plaza behind the office building, here it looked incongruous. Jutting up from the meadow grass it was a blatant urban anachronism in this ancient pastoral setting. A reminder of how far away he was from the world he knew.

The brass plaque still commemorated the stone to a man who wouldn't be born for centuries. Jeff's unevenly bearded face looked back at him in the mirror-like finish. He selected a chisel for Rhydderch. The boy held it in place while Jeff pounded it with the hammer, first from one side of the plaque, then from the other, until the metal separated slightly from the stone.

Rhydderch traded the fine pointed chisel for a heavier one, allowing Jeff to bring a fuller swing to bear. Jeff hefted the hammer in a two handed grip while Rhydderch held the chisel low on the side of the plate. It made a dull "chink" when he struck. Rhydderch repositioned the chisel higher and Jeff brought the hammer around again.

"It's coming." Rhyddech said as he wedged the chisel in deeper. Jeff brought the hammer down in an overhand arc and the plaque let loose with a clang. "There it goes!" he said triumphantly.

Their act of vandalism left a gaping hole in the granite stele. Jeff didn't like defacing the monument, but he had his priorities, and right now the brass plaque was more valuable for what it could become. The brass was a fine alloy of a purity that was unmatched in current technology. He had enough reservations about the casting process and whether his design for the project would be adequate. He couldn't take a chance on the material. He gathered up the tools and Rhydderch followed with the plaque for the walk back to the forge.

Eldric and Arthwyr were ready for them when they arrived. They had built up the fire higher than they usually did when working iron, the coals piled high around a crucible, and were eating a lunch that Bryggyd had brought. Over the last weeks her belly had changed its focus, away from getting larger and toward moving lower as the baby dropped in preparation to making its debut. It was making it harder to get around now, but after protesting for so long that it didn't, Bryggyd wasn't about to admit it now. "Are you boys hungry?" she asked.

"No, thank you, Bryggyd.," Jeff said. "The fire looks about ready. We don't want to waste it." Eldrich and Arthwyr went back to the forge, chewing their last bits as they went. But Rhydderch was visibly dismayed.

Bryggyd had to turn sideways to pick up the basket. She tossed the boy a crust of bread and some cheese. "Thank you, Ma'am," he said, taking them to a corner where he could watch the work while he ate.

Jeff and Eldric used heavy hammers to smash the plaque to bits while Arthwyr and Rhydderch gathered up the pieces and fed them into the melting pot. As they waited for the temperature to build and the brass to melt, Eldrich asked Jeff, "Do you want to tell me what all this is for?"

"Not really. We'll see if it works, then I'll explain it for you."

"Very well," Eldric said. He was a man of few words and so, if Jeff wanted to leave the subject alone that was exactly where he would leave it. Arthwyr, who had been quietly listening in with curiosity, was disappointed.

Eldric supervised the fire itself while the other three took turns at the bellows, pumping it feverishly without letup. The coals burned furiously, white hot as the brass began to liquefy. Between turns at the bellows, Jeff placed a mold of fired clay at the edge of the coals. Though he hadn't worn them for weeks, he donned his sunglasses against the brightness of the fire and the hot golden metal.

When Eldric was satisfied with the bubbling liquid metal, he and Jeff used a pair of tongs with long handles at each end to lift the pot out of the fire. They painstakingly tipped the crucible to pour the molten brass into the form of the mold and set it aside to cool.

After a short respite Eldric announced, "OK gentlemen that's enough" as he paced a few plugs of iron on the fire to be worked. "There's a lot of fuel on that fire and I don't aim to see it go to waste, so let's get back to work."

Jeff took a long draught from the dipper of cool water Bryggyd had offered. Sweat rolling off him despite a cool breeze he handed the dipper back with a nod of thanks. Bryggyd's face was contorted, her eyes widened, her brow furrowed and her mouth agape. "Are you OK?" he asked.

Bryggyd gathered herself together after a moment. "The baby moved," she said. "I'm fine." She took up the basket she had brought the lunch with and turned to walk back to the house. Instead, she froze and doubled over, grimacing with a pain. Eldric was at her side before she could fall. He swept her up as if she weighed nothing and carried her off.

"Rhydderch, go fetch the midwife," Jeff said. "Don't worry about the forge, Eldric. I'll take care of things here. You just see to Bryggyd. We'll be fine."

Eldric called back as he bustled his wife home, "Be patient with that casting. Let it cool. I don't intend to redo it." He carried her off kicking and complaining, seemingly deaf to her protestations. Not until she threatened violence did he put her down with a forlorn look on his face.

Bryggyd looked at him and had to laugh. "That's very sweet," she said, and she kissed him "but I'm going to be a mother, not an invalid. I'm still quite able to walk." She pulled his arm around her and together they walked to the house.

Eldric felt ill at ease. At the forge he knew what to do. At the forge he was in charge. At the moment he had neither of those comforts. The midwife was in the other room with Bryggyd. He would wait as long as he could bear it, but when his patience ran out and he felt he had to do something to help, he went in and the midwife would shoo him away. If a simple scolding wasn't enough to send him off, she would give him an errand to run. This had the benefit of making him feel needed and usually kept him away longer. Sometimes the errand was actually helpful, like collecting and bringing in the linen towels and bandages hanging from a line behind the house.

Jeff had insisted, as the baby's arrival came near, that every towel and bandage to be used in the birth be washed in boiling water and air dried, every metal utensil washed in boiling water and kept in alcohol, which he provided. It seemed an odd request, but he had been adamant and it was easier to comply than to argue and so they had gone along. He seemed obsessed with killing germs, little tiny beings so small they couldn't be seen, that he said caused disease and infection. Well, the art of medicine had so many superstitions, who knew which to follow.

The midwife complained of Jeff's meddling, but Eldric had put his foot down. "People are calling him a wizard because of the things he does. If he says it's a good idea, I think we should do it," he'd said. "Besides, what could be the harm in it?" The midwife had no answer to that.

The sun had gone down, Rhydderch had gone home, and Jeff and Arthwyr had shut down the forge when they went across the street and found Eldric sitting outside his house. "Still no baby," greeted the blacksmith.

"What are you doing out here?" asked Arthwyr.

"Once I'm inside, it's only a matter of time before I find my way to the bedroom. The midwife got tired of kicking me out, so now I'm banned from my own house." Eldric got up and paced nervously. "I can't stand the waiting."

"Waiting is always stressful." Jeff consoled, "But then you've been waiting for months now, a little while longer won't hurt."

An infant's cry from inside the house overwhelmed Eldric's self control. He threw the door open and came face to face with the midwife coming the other way. "It's a boy!" She announced. "Congratulations, now you can go to your wife."

Eldric rushed in to be with his wife and new child, Arthwyr and Jeff on his heels. He found Bryggyd in bed looking like she had just finished a marathon, then wrestled a bear. To him she'd never been more beautiful. "Eldric, "she said. "Come and meet your son."

Jeff was amazed that such a powerful man could be so gentle as he took the baby into his arms. "He's beautiful, Eldric," Jeff said as the older man's pride filled the room. "Lucky he takes after his mother."

Eldric was too happy to take offense at the remark. Besides, he was thinking the same thing. He leaned his face over, nuzzling the baby. "Ow!" Came a startled cry as he tried to raise his head and found the baby had his beard firmly gripped in his fist. "He's a strong one, like his father. Cormac! A strong name for a strong young man."

News always travels fast in a small town, but never so fast as when it has been anticipated. A contingent of the town's women led by Thyllwy'n, the mayor's wife made their way into the house. Some brought blankets and swaddling clothes for the baby, others brought food. Very soon Jeff determined that he and Arthwyr were lost in the crowd. They backed out of the room and went to the inn. No one in the house noticed they had left

With the arrival of the baby, Eldric spent little time at the forge. He would show up in the morning only to find Arthwyr and Jeff at work, everything in its place, and work being done. It did his heart good to see the younger men picking up his slack, making his presence unnecessary. Seeing no reason to stay, he took advantage of the opportunity to spend time with Bryggyd and the Cormac.

For Jeff the timing could not have been better. Covering for Eldric meant hanging around the forge, and he needed to be there anyway. He freed the brass casting from its mold and inspected it. There were no flaws that he could identify and so he mated it to a wooden stock he'd had the wood carver make. That was the easy part. The real challenge was the mechanism.

There is an old adage in engineering that you design what you know. So, rather than design the pistol with the hammer lock associated with flintlock weapons, in Jeff's design, the trigger used gears and a spring to rotate a barrel-shaped grinder against a small piece of flint, like in a cigarette lighter. For the master gear he used an American quarter. The ribbed edge provided a handy guide for cutting the gear-teeth. He used a dime for the drive gear, though smaller, it still needed to be cut down in size.

He had considered driving the gears directly with the trigger, but decided it would be too hard to control the jerking and maintain his aim, so instead, he used a spring with a bolt to cock it and engage the gears. He made the flash pan with a lid that closed tightly so that it could be primed in advance and fire quickly when needed.

All the time he worked on the pistol, Arthwyr looked on with interest, but managed to keep his curiosity in check. He was dying to know what Jeff was working on, but, since Jeff clearly didn't want to talk about it, he was afraid to bring it up. Jeff dry tested the mechanism. He pulled the bolt back, cocking the spring, then pointed the pistol to the floor, and pulled the trigger. When the spring was released the grinding wheel spun against the flint, sending a shower of sparks over the pan.

Arthwyr could restrain himself no longer. "What is it?" he asked. "What did you make?"

"It's a device for starting fires," Jeff lied. "I still need to make the fuel it needs, but I think it'll work."

"I thought it might be some kind of weapon," said Arthwyr, deflated, "You being so secretive about it and all."

"Nothing so exciting," Jeff continued his misdirection, "Sorry to disappoint you."

"No problem. But you know we could..." Arthwyr decided that as long as the subject had been broached, he might as well press the issue. "You know... as long as Eldric isn't here. We could make a sword."

"Sure we could," Jeff played along. "And I'm sure it would look just fine..."

"It would be beautiful." Arthwyr was encouraged. "I knew you'd agree."

"As long as all you want it for is to look good." Jeff continued.

What do you mean?" Arthwyr was taken off guard.

"Well, neither one of us has ever made one before." Jeff explained. "And sword smithing is a very specialized skill. So we might get it right, but if not, it could break the first time you tried to use it. Sounds like a good way to get yourself killed.""Not to mention, a waste of my iron." bellowed Eldric, as he stepped inside the forge. "Enough talk of swords. Let's get back to work."

Chapter 6 – Trymme

"I'm heading up to the clearing. How is our liquor stock looking?" Jeff asked Mairwen, coming up behind her to give her a little squeeze.

"We'll be alright for a while yet." she replied, then noticed the pumpkin he was carrying. "What do you want with that?" It was a sad excuse for a vegetable with several soft spots and discolorations.

"I found this in the root cellar," Jeff explained, "Mind if I take it?"

Mairwen laughed musically. "If you can use that poor thing, then welcome to it."

"Thanks," he kissed her lightly on the cheek. "I've got to run, I'll see you later tonight." Jeff carried the pumpkin out the door with him and hustled up the road. He was due to meet with his apprentice and didn't want to have him waiting. When he walked up the last hundred yards to the clearing, Ryhdderch's bright red hair broadcast the fact that the boy had beaten him there again.

"Wizard!" The boy called out when he saw Jeff's approach. He had taken to referring to Jeff that way when they were alone. Jeff protested to no avail, but secretly the idea of it appealed to him.

Taking Ryhdderch on as his apprentice was working out well for Jeff. The boy did odd jobs, allowing Jeff to get more done. As a result he had built up a stock of gunpowder which he kept in a keg painted white to distinguish it from the liquor stocks.

Jeff had a feeling that the boy's attention to detail and artistic eye would translate into a talent for lens making. In actual practice the boy exceeded expectations and Timothy now sported a pair of glasses that all but eliminated his disability. Jeff was so impressed with those results he gave the boy a new assignment for another pair of lenses.

"You're early!" Jeff called out as he put the pumpkin down on a stump. "Are you sure all your chores are done?"

"They're done." Ryhdderch replied defiantly.

"You know I'll check." And he had checked. Several times over the past weeks he had gone by Ryhdderch's house to talk with his mother. Not only was the boy keeping up with his chores, but he was doing more than ever. For the first time he seemed anything but indifferent. The change was more than welcome. "Let's see what you've got."

Ryhdderch pulled out a linen cloth and unwrapped it, revealing two lenses, one nearly as large as his palm, and a second that was no larger than his thumbnail. Jeff inspected each one. It was excellent work. Certainly, they were better than he could have done himself. They were well polished, and more importantly, evenly shaped. He looked through the lenses at a straight edge, turning them and rotating them, seeing no waves in the lines.

"You are amazing!" He praised. The boy beamed at the approval. "Are you ready to see what we're doing here?"

"I can't wait," was the reply.

"The first lenses were to fix a problem," Jeff explained, "Timothy's eyes couldn't focus properly so the lenses corrected that. Now we'll see what a lens can do for eyes that work fine." Jeff took a coin from his pocket and held the large lens over it. His apprentice leaned in for a better look. The coin looked as large as a melon, the tiniest details became distinct and clear.

"Yes!" Rhydderch was intrigued. "I guess I saw that when I was working on them, but I just thought my eyes were playing tricks."

Jeff gave the lad a lesson in the basics of optics and lenses. He drew a diagram in the dirt to show how different focal lengths affected the rays, then he drew in a second lens to show how they might work together. He reached into the folds of his oversized robe and pulled out his contribution to the project. "While you've been busy with those," he announced as he produced a tube made from stiff hardened leather as long as his forearm. "I've been busy as well." He held the tube by its ends and pulled, revealing a second tube inside the first, nearly doubling its length.

The larger lens was fitted into one end of the telescope and the smaller one into the eyepiece at the other end. Jeff adjusted the focus then showed Rhydderch how to sight it across the clearing. "Do you see the bird there?" He asked .

"Wow," Ryhdderch was awestruck, "I feel like I ought to be able to reach out and touch it." Fascinated he looked about in different directions, testing the telescope's capabilities.

"I thought our sailor friends might appreciate that when they go far from shore." Jeff suggested, "but, no rush. The moon is almost full. Why don't you take it for now, look at the moon with it, the stars, whatever, anything but the sun, it'll hurt your eyes. Then we'll talk." The boy's face lit up at the offer. Jeff waved him off. "Go on, check it out. I have some work to do."

Rhydderch trotted off with his prize throwing a 'thank you' over his shoulder. Jeff waited until the mop of red hair had completely disappeared before he reached into his robe again, this time brandishing the pistol. It was unloaded, but he had been carrying it around for some time with a charge in the pan to test whether it could be relied on.

Jeff checked the primer charge and was assured it would be ok, then he cocked the spring and leveled the weapon. When he pulled the trigger there was a hesitation for a moment but the powder caught and belched flame and smoke. A satisfying grin spread across his face as he re-primed the pistol and loaded it for the very first time. He tamped down a measure of powder and added a larger one of shot, bits of iron he collected after sweeping up at the forge, and tamped that down as well.

He took a position ten paces from the stump and cocked the spring. He took aim at the pumpkin and held his breath as he squeezed the trigger. It was not the almost instantaneous report of a modern gun, more a quick succession of steps. Spark! Flash! Bang! The pistol bucked in his hand as it discharged. The shot quickly spread out from the short barrel, obliterating the pumpkin and taking pieces off the stump as well.

Jeff walked up to the stump to inspect the damage to his target. It was total. The stump didn't fare much better, splinters were blown off both sides and it was peppered with holes. He had a weapon now that he could be confident with, but if any bystanders might be involved, he would need to replace the shot with a solid bullet.

This could change everything, he thought. And then the thought continued, *this could even change history as he knew it.* He hadn't given a single thought as to how his "inventions" might affect a past that didn't otherwise contain them, or to what the ramifications of their addition might be. But, the pistol was too big to ignore. *Well, people have been calling me Wizard for weeks. Maybe it's time I stop denying and embrace it. If everything I do is credited to magic, it'll all just become a part of legend I can live with that.*

A few miles up the coast from Llewellynn lay the village of Trymme. It was a larger town, sitting in a cove with a protected harbor and so they saw more trading ships. A street ran along the waterfront with houses and shops on one side and moorings for boats on the other. At the center was a wharf where the larger trading ships unloaded and a second road began, heading directly inland.

A grand stone house, built in the Roman style, sat on the corner where the two streets met. It had a commanding view of the harbor, making it the center point of the waterfront and, with its adjacent warehouse, the perfect headquarters for Trymme's leading citizen. Devlin, the home's master, was a merchant and trader with a fleet of ships and wagons that ranged over much of the known world.

Devlin looked over his wagon's load, then went to the warehouse to check his inventory to be sure he wasn't leaving behind anything he might later need. "Mercher!" he called out.

A head poked out of the doorway of the house. "Yes, father," answered his youngest son.

"Get the grey mare harnessed up to this wagon," the merchant ordered as he grabbed a couple of blankets from a pile and added them to the load. "I want to be well on our way before noon."

Devlin's three older daughters were off raising families of their own. Their weddings cemented various business ties for their father. His two older sons captained his ships. They traveled to far off ports, bringing back Russian furs, Spanish silver and oranges, Egyptian cotton and all manner of exotic goods, and were gone eight to ten months a year. This left Devlin, when he was home, alone with his wife Bronwyn, their youngest child Gwenhwyver and Mercher, who traveled with his father now.

Devlin entered the house as the boy ran to see to the horse. When he went through the parlor he found his daughter sewing a fine green material. He stood over her, his arms outstretched. The girl put down her sewing and stood to put her arms around her father. "How long will you be gone this time?" She held her grip around his neck, immobilizing him.

Gwenhwyver was a beauty and her parents doted on her. She had golden hair and green eyes that sparkled like emeralds in the fairest of faces. She was of that awkward age where she was no longer a child, but not yet a woman. She would soon have any number of suitors. Devlin would have liked to cement another business arrangement through her betrothal, but Bronwyn hoped at least one of her daughters might stay in Trymme. Devlin raised no objections as she paraded every promising unmarried man and boy in the village by her daughter. So far, the girl showed no interest in any of them.

Devlin leaned over to let his little girl hug him until his back began to complain. When he could no longer stand the pain, he merely straightened up until her feet were off the ground. "A few weeks, as you are well aware," he good naturedly upbraided her.

Gwenwhyver relaxed her grip and let herself slide down until her toes hit the floor. "I just don't want you to forget about my party. Mother is planning it for May. I hope you'll be back."

"I'll be back in plenty of time," he reassured her, "I certainly don't plan to miss out on a chance to meet your future husband." he added, only half in jest. "Where's your mother?"

"Behind you." The girl giggled. Devlin hadn't noticed Bronwen standing there.

Bronwyn had been bustling about ever since early morning, making sure her husband was prepared to take his journey. She draped a scarf over his neck. "Summer isn't here yet." she teased, "I don't want you coming back with the shivers." She used the scarf to pull his head toward her and kissed him warmly.

"Hold that thought." The merchant said. "I'll be back as soon as possible." He pulled the scarf tight around his neck and went to the wagon.

Satisfying himself that the horse was properly hitched, he climbed aboard. When Mercher clambered in alongside him, he handed over the reins. "You're driving son." he said, "I'm just along for the ride. Next time you'll be on your own, so show me you're ready."

Mercher smiled as he took the reins and gave the horse his command, "Giddap." As they plodded up the road, they were startled by a shout, followed by a pair of youths who ran across the road right in front of the wagon, one chasing the other, then disappeared behind a house.

Before they were out of town, they came across the pair again. The red haired youth had caught up with the other and was astride him, clearly getting the better of him. Devlin just shook his head.

Habren had no sooner sat down to take up her mending than she heard a commotion outside. "What's all that about?" She called out to her son Cefin.

"Bryn and Rhys are at it again" said the boy. "Fighting in the yard."

Habren rose from her perch, dropping her work. She took a deep breath to compose herself and went out to break up the fight. Rhys was a twelve year old boy that lived down the street who had been teasing her ten year old daughter Bryn mercilessly for some time. She went around to the side of the house to find the pair rolling around the yard. She grabbed the redhead by the arm and yanked the two apart before more damage could be done.

"He started it." her daughter protested as her mother dragged her back inside. The brown haired boy got up and wiped a little blood from his nose. Bryn was a tomboy. She could outrun any boy her age in the town, and apparently the same went for fighting.

"I don't care who started it." Habren snapped, directing her daughter to the waiting laundry. "Maybe you should put all that energy to work." Bryn sullenly picked up the wet clothing as her mother added, "He probably just likes you."

Bryn puffed out her lower lip, "Well I don't like him!"

With all his new projects, Jeff spent less and less time at the forge. When he was in the village he made it a point to help Eldric if he was needed. He did, after all, still sleep in the loft when he was in town and had taken over the shed completely. On the other hand, a village the size of Llewellynn provided only so much work for a blacksmith.

Jeff helped out through the morning and, as happened often, they finished their work before noon. With only a few light jobs for the afternoon, Eldric banked the coals of the fire. "Why don't you boys go get yourselves something to eat." He suggested. "We'll pick this back up in the afternoon."

Arthwyr had his apron off and hanging on its peg, cheering, "Sounds good to me," and was out the door in seconds. Jeff just smiled as he wiped down his tools.

Eldric hung the tongs he'd been using and turned to the younger man. "I'm sure that pretty girl at the inn wouldn't mind seeing you." He said. "Why don't you go too?"

"Thank you, Eldric." Jeff said, as he hung his own apron and started for the door, only to be blocked by the mayor coming in.

"Thank goodness you're here," spluttered Caradog, catching his breath. "I need you. Come quickly, both of you."

Afraid to waste his breath explaining further, the mayor turned abruptly and waddled up the street, Jeff and Eldric at his heels.

Caradog huffed and puffed as they made their way up the road. The smiths kept pace easily, held back only by good manners and the fact that the mayor had not revealed their destination. He led them to the public baths, but then turned off the road and stopped at a puddle midway between the bath house and the old hot spring.

"There! You see!" The mayor gasped. "You've got to do something!"

Jeff was bewildered by the mayor's exasperation. The puddle hardly rated such urgency.

Eldric bent to examine the water. He dipped in his hand and brought it to his nose, his face contorting at the smell. "Sulfur!" Standing he continued. "We're going to have to dig it up to repair." The ancient ducts channeling the water from the hot spring to the baths had sprung a leak. Turning to Jeff, he directed, "I'll get the tools. You go find Arthwyr."

Jeff thought he had an idea where to look for the boy. Rather than walk up the hill toward the inn, he went down. He crossed the little wooden bridge at the mill stream and went into the ruin of the old Roman Barracks. As he made his way through the rubble he thought he heard an argument in progress. He proceeded cautiously, being as quiet as possible to avoid detection. He peered around a corner and saw Arthwyr but he was alone.

The young apprentice faced a wall with his back to Jeff. In his right hand he brandished a stick as though it were a sword. "Winded, are you?" He goaded the wall. "Take a deep breath. It'll be your last."

Jeff watched quietly as Arthwyr thrust and parried with his imaginary opponent. These were not the delicate, precise motions of a fencing duel. Each slash and thrust of the imaginary sword was a potential killing blow. They spoke of the desperation of a life and death battle. Unaware of his audience, Arthwyr went on with his struggle. With sweat beading on his brow, Arthwyr wind-milled his "blade". He swept his sword high, then low, he back peddled, then attacked. He parried an imaginary blow, then pushed off.

With a powerful overhand slash the tip of Arthwyr's stick clanged when it struck a stone and sparked. Only then did Jeff realize that the "sword" was not a wooden stick at all. It was a heavy iron bar. He'd never had any doubt that the work in the forge strengthened the boy. Still, he was impressed with the ease with which Arthwyr handled his weapon.

Arthwyr kept up his attack at a feverish pace, working himself into a lather. He blocked, stabbed, slashed, parried and thrust in every possible direction. He took a step back and hesitated a moment, then lunged forward, but he stumbled. He went down onto one knee, catching his balance on the butt of his "sword" without losing control of it. Without looking up, he drove the still upturned point of the poker hard into the wall. The tip of the poker gouged the stone with a shower of sparks as he came back to his feet, then stepped back and took a breath.

"I don't know what it did to you, but I think you've murdered the wall." Jeff chuckled as he stepped forward. Looking at the wall, he saw that it was scored over and over. Arthwyr's misstep had been a feint he'd practiced many times. "I hope it deserved it."

Arthwyr was flustered. He had no idea anyone was watching. "I... Practice," he said as he fought to catch his breath.

"Don't worry about it," Jeff deflected. "Take your time and pull yourself together, but I hope you didn't wear yourself out. Eldric needs us and I think it's going to be hard work."

Jeff led Arthwyr to the site of the leak and found the puddle growing larger, forming a rivulet that soon would cross the road on its way to the wetlands and the river. They had no sooner arrived than Eldric was there as well, handing out mattocks and spades.

They worked feverishly in the sun, the spring day becoming warmer. Stripped to their waists, the sweat poured off their bodies as they piled the dirt high. As if the digging were not hard enough, the trench soon filled with water turning the dirt to mud that was both heavier and slippery. The mayor brought them a bucket so they could bail it as they went. They rotated positions as one man would break up the dirt with a mattock, a second shoveled it away and the third bailed the water as fast as it collected in the hole. Eventually, they were able to uncover the problem.

The Romans had run the water from the spring to the baths via a pipeline made by hollowing out tree trunks. The system worked very well until this particular section, an oak tree trunk twice as thick as a strong man's thigh, developed a crack. The crack had grown and eventually split the side of the pipe.

Eldric stanched the flow by caulking the crack with oakum, a sticky patch made from hemp rope and tar. He pounded the oakum deep into the crevasse, then slathered more tar over the surface. It would work well for a while, but inevitably, the crack would spread if the pipe were not replaced.

With the leak stopped, they were at last able to bail out the trench enough for Eldric to take measurements. The log was as long as a man is tall and cut so that it interlocked with the next one and sealed with tar. Eldric measured it from end to end, around its girth. Satisfied he had the dimensions he needed, he climbed out of the hole and reassured the mayor. "It'll take a few days, but we can fix this."

A log of oak with a fine grain lay between a pair of crossed timber braces so that it was level. It had been cut to a length, just longer than needed, to allow for last minute adjustment.

Eldric bustled about lining things up. He marked off the exact center of the log then used a hand drill to start a hole. He laid an iron bar across a pair of andirons and adjusted them until they lined up with the hole perfectly. On one end of the bar he attached a hand crank and on the other, a drill bit. Using progressively larger bits, he re-drilled the hole over and over until it was as large as a man's fist and an inch or two deep. He blew the hole clear of sawdust and wood shavings, made sure everything was still aligned properly, then went back to the smallest bit again. When he had attached the bit, he backed out and waved Arthwyr in to take his place. Though he fought to hide it, he was clearly winded.

"Go ahead Arthwyr," he said, gulping a breath. "You do the same." Arthwyr stepped up and took his turn at the drill. Determined to show his worth, he turned the crank over, hard and fast. "Save your strength, son. It gets harder as the hole gets wider," Eldric told him. Arthwyr kept on without a word as if he hadn't heard him. He became sweaty and his breathing labored as he uncomplainingly went through drill bit after drill bit. His face registering relief as the final bit reached the bottom of the hole.

Eldric again reset the apparatus, and when he was satisfied, nodded at Jeff to take his place. The smaller bits weren't so bad, but as the gauge increased, so did the difficulty. Jeff strained to make his way through to the last bit, then caught his breath and looked on as Eldric made his inspection. Progress was agonizingly slow, the bore, depressingly shallow.

Jeff compared the now three inch hole with the eight foot log, mentally calculating the effort it would take to bore through to the end. It would take days. A tap on his shoulder broke his reverie. Deciding Arthwyr must be ready for another turn, he stepped out of the way, only it wasn't Arthwyr, it was Trefor, the weaver. He noticed others standing at the door. Cynwrig and his son Berwyn were there and of course Timothy. Even the overweight mayor stood in line to do his best. Before this repair was finished, every man in the village would step forward to pitch in and do his part.

Maghnus and his men plied the coast of the narrowing waterway. No pirate ever likes the idea of being bottled up and blocked from the sea, but so far there seemed no one of consequence on the water, and the rewards had been well worth the risk. They kept the land to port as they worked their way up the channel, hitting targets of opportunity along the way. They sacked village after village, filling the holds with treasure and slaves. A few more strikes and it would be time to return home.

The channel narrowed to a point where the risk seemed too

great, with no advantage to pressing further. The three ships crossed over and headed west along the south bank. Nearing sundown they came upon a cove that was home to a good sized town. They sailed on by, so as not to raise any alarm, hove to out of sight and waited out the night.

Early in the morning, as the very first light began to bleed into the eastern sky, the three ships made their way into the cove. They rowed slowly but silently. The predawn air was still, so the sails would have been useless. Using the oars alone offered the additional advantage that the boats had a lower profile, making them all but invisible coming out of the blackness.

As they drew nearer, Maghnus signaled his brothers to fan out. His own ship continued directly on to the wharf at the center while the other two went to head off any escape to the flanks. The rowers shipped their oars and let the boat glide the last few yards into the pier and men leapt over the side to bring the boat in to a berth without a sound. Leaving a handful of men behind on each boat to guard the treasure and slaves, the band flowed over the rail in silence, like so many cats.

Since childhood, Maghnus had been enamored of the stories, songs and legends, told of the Roman legions. He was enthralled by tales of their heroism of course. But even more so, he was intrigued by the formations, tactics and strategies with which they defeated their foes. They could be as important as strength or bravery. He saw himself as an Irish Julius Caesar, carrying a Roman short sword instead of the battleaxe favored by most of the raiders. Still, what he had here was no army. They were a band of cutthroats and nothing more. They would follow his orders when it suited, but they won their battles primarily through fear, savagery, superior numbers and the element of surprise.

Maghnus sent his two quickest men up the cross street to prevent escape via that route while the rest began going house to house, then he headed for the big house on the corner.

Bryn was up at first light as usual. It was her job around

the house to see to the chickens. She hated getting up so early, but if the birds were not fed at dawn, they would raise such a racket that everybody in town would be up before long. She was carrying a bucket of feed to the coop out back, her feet leaving tracks in the early morning frost, when she saw two armed men running up the street in front of the house. She froze until she began hearing noises, crashing sounds, yelling, screaming all throughout the town.

She took a step toward the noise, but then she saw two more men coming in her direction, one with an ax, the other with a bow. Before she could turn back, they had seen her and started to run. Bryn dropped the bucket of feed and took off with the men in pursuit, but they were no match for her speed.

Cut firewood lay in a neat pile along a low fence that ran back to the chicken coop. Bryn cleared it without breaking stride. On the way over it she heard the *thunk* of an arrow striking wood. She ran on until she reached the barn belonging to the farm at the edge of town before she dared a look back. The men were well behind as she ducked inside the barn.

Bryn knew she couldn't hide in the barn for long but she was glad to have the shelter of the walls while she caught her breath. She had moved into a stall occupied by a chestnut mare when she heard the door at the other end of the barn slide open. One of the first two men she had seen run up the street had come after her as well and now he started to search the stalls.

She whispered into the horse's ear to relax her as she slid up onto the mare's back, then gathered up as much mane as she could to hang onto and kicked the horse into action. The mare bolted out of the stall and turned toward the open door, nearly riding down the man as he tried to grab the girl. They broke out into the morning light, crossed the pasture then lept the fence onto the road out of town. Bryn held on for dear life, her knuckles white.

Bronwen awoke to the sound of the front door being smashed in. Heavy footsteps pounded up the stairs. Her heart racing, she went looking for a weapon. By the fireplace, she spotted an iron poker. *Better than nothing.* She heard things crash in the kitchen and doors being splintered throughout the house. She wasn't sure which way to go until a scream from her daughter's room decided for her.

A young raider named Adamnan was first to reach the big house. Anxious to show his worth to his king, he bounded up the stairs in search of the inhabitants and burst into the first bedroom he found. The young girl inside shrieked at his entrance.

When Bronwen got there, an armored man was trying to carry Gwenwhyver off. Her daughter was kicking and screaming, writhing about, and stabbing repeatedly with a knitting needle trying desperately to find a vulnerable spot. Bronwen swung hard with the poker, hitting the man over the head with an audible clang stunning the man and putting a big dent in his helmet. It should have been a killing blow, but the helmet did its job. Adamnan let go of the girl, but instead of collapsing in a heap, he roared in a mix of rage and pain and turned to face his attacker.

The young raider swung his battle axe to fend off the fierce attack of a mother protecting her young. Bronwen stepped back and deflected the weapon with her poker, nearly losing her grip against the powerful blow. The blade whipped past her ear and bit into the bedpost. The boy pressed his attack, the young girl momentarily forgotten, and raised his axe again when an intense pain shot through his arm. Gwenwhyver had found the gap in his armor at the neckline and plunged the knitting needle deep. With his right arm hanging limply, barely able to hold onto the axe, never mind swing it, Adamnan raised his empty left hand in a feeble effort to ward off the next blow from Bronwen, but the blow never came.

Maghnus, trailed by his son Phelan had followed Adamnan into the house and up the stairs, arriving just in time to witness the girl's attack on their shipmate. Bronwen, unaware of their presence, was focused on her daughter's assailant. She made no attempt to block the chieftain's sword as he thrust it deep into her side. The blade cut through organs and arteries, blood flowing equally from the wound and her mouth as she collapsed on the floor.

"Mother," screamed Gwenhwyver. Her knees buckled. She dropped to the bed, frozen by the trauma of her mother's death and sat, sobbing, the fight gone out of her.

"Pity," Maghnus muttered to no one in particular, assessing Bronwen's lifeless form. "She would have made a welcome addition to my household." He turned his attention to the maiden, now lying prostrate on the bed, bawling loudly. "The kitten's not ripe yet, but she'll be a beauty soon enough." He addressed his son. "Bind her," he commanded "and take her to my ship." He reached down and took her by the chin, turning her face, appraising her. "And spread the word. HANDS OFF! She's to be mine when we return to Ireland,"

Bryn rode on, surreptitiously looking over her shoulder for pursuers, though none seemed on her trail. Outside of town she crested a hill at a fork in the road where she needed to choose her destination. From her vantage point atop the horse, she could see up and down the coast.

Directly behind her was Trymme, still in an uproar. To the left was a little village, so small Bryn didn't even know its name. She could see a few wisps of smoke rising from the houses there testifying to an earlier visit from the raiders. Those people would have enough troubles of their own. To her right, beyond her sight, lay Llewellynn and her best hope for refuge. She turned her mount in that direction.

Maghnus held court on the pier in front of the warehouse as the raiders assembled the loot from the village. The other two ships had been brought alongside for the loading of the goods and the slaves. Those inhabitants of the town not lucky enough to have escaped but not among the dead, were already bound and below-decks. A steady stream of raiders bustled between Devlin's warehouse and the ships. Today's raid was easily the most rewarding thus far.

"A nice haul," the chieftain apprised. Men were still coming in with goods and valuables found throughout the town. "This will be the best raiding season we've had in years."

"There's a good bit of food as well," Aongus said. "This would be a good place to stay a while. Shall I organize a feast for this evening?"

Maghnus looked out at the channel and across it to the far shore. "I'd like to." He pondered for a moment before going on. "But I'm a little uneasy. We're a bit too vulnerable. We're all too visible here in the harbor, and the channel is so narrow, there'd be no place to go if we were attacked."

Maghnus weighed the options. It would be good to give the men a rest in comfortable surroundings. A feast would go a long way to lift the men's spirits, but then so would a triumphant return home. The risk was too great. "I think not," he decided. "Let's get packed up. I want to get out to where this channel opens before someone decides to come after us."

"Very well," His brother said. Caution would rule the day. He went off to pass the orders to his subordinates. Word went out to round up the men still foraging through the town in preparation for an early departure.

Bryn pressed on periodically walking or jogging alongside her mount. She stopped twice when the road crossed streams, but just long enough for both horse and rider to drink and gain a second wind, then onward again. With each hill or rise or bend in the road she hoped to see a village or settlement, only to be disappointed when the view revealed another stretch of empty road,

She crested a ridge, where the view extended out to sea and up and down the coast better than any since she left Trymme. Ahead, she could finally see the village of Llewellynn, not far away, but across a shallow river ford. Behind her, smoke made it clear that much of her home village was burning.

One other sight gave her a greater chill even than the sight of the town in flames. The three ships that were in the harbor when she made her escape had left and now they were rounding the point where the channel narrowed and headed this way. Bryn urged the mare onward. Finding refuge was no longer her only concern. She had to get to the town ahead of the raiders and warn the people there.

The hardwood tree would certainly be durable. That was the point, but the quality that made it so desirable also meant that the work drilling through it was slow going. As the bore deepened, progress slowed even further due to the need to clear the shavings. Jeff put in another turn in the morning, taking over after the last of the fishermen left to catch the morning tide. He pushed himself hard, trying to make headway, determined to get it finished as quickly as possible.

Out of breath and running with perspiration, he stepped out. He turned to the door and met a welcome sight. Ferris the glass-maker was there to do his part, but more importantly, so was Mairwen. She carrying a basket and a blanket, dressed in a white linen blouse, a blue woolen skirt and sweater that brought out the color of her eyes. Her blond hair draped over her shoulders. "I thought you might need to take a break, so I brought lunch." she offered.

"You thought right," Jeff said. He kissed her lightly, but couldn't keep his attention from the basket. "What did you bring me?" he asked as he lifted the blanket from the food. He couldn't help himself from quipping. "Are you expecting a chill?"

"No silly!" Mairwen blushed, "I thought you might like to have a picnic."

"Excellent idea!" Jeff agreed. He took the basket from her as they went out into the street, holding hands as they strolled up the road and out of town.

"How is it coming?" Mairwen asked.

"Slowly," Jeff said, "there is still a good way to go before we turn it all around and start from the other end. Hopefully the holes will meet up in the middle."

"The really amazing thing though, is how the whole village has pitched in. I don't think there's a man in the village or a boy over the age of twelve that hasn't taken a turn at least once. Even the mayor tried his hand and it's no secret he's not used to hard labor. He was sweating like. Well, he was sweating profusely."

"When something affects everyone, it's only right that everyone helps out," Mairwen observed.

"That it is. But still, it's nice to see it actually work that way, no one shirking their duty."

They left the road and walked through the tall grass up the hill where, months ago, Jeff had made his first appearance. Something seemed odd, but Jeff couldn't place it until they reached the top. Then it was obvious. The monument was gone.

"Someone took the stone!" Jeff felt a loss. The gray base was still there. The hole that once held the brass plaque, a glaring wound. But the pink obelisk was missing. A furrow gouged from the soft earth pointed out the way it had been dragged off.

"What was it anyway?" Mairwen asked. "Was it important to you?"

"No. Not really." Jeff's shock subsided. "A memorial to a man who discovered some things, then started a company to discover more."

"Did you know him?"

"No. I never met him." Jeff opened the blanket, spreading it out and set the basket on one corner. "It was a comfort for me though, a reminder of home whenever I passed by here. It's my own fault, in a way."

"How is that?" Mairwen wondered.

"People were afraid of it at first, I think." Jeff explained as they flattened the blanket into the grass, "Once I took the hammer to it and removed the plaque, people knew that it could be defaced without consequences. Now that stone is probably adorning someone's fireplace."

"Why did you do it?" Mairwen did her best to smooth out some of the lumps under the blanket.

Mairwen set out the food, bread, cheese, some roasted goose, and a pot of ale. They ate their lunch quietly. Jeff's hunger took over, so he barely stopped for a breath. Mairwen didn't want to distract him until he slowed down. When he did, she brought the conversation back to a subject that had been on her mind for some time. "You miss your home, don't you?"

"Yeah, I do." Jeff sighed, a hint of a quiver below his lower lip. It was still a bit painful to him, so he generally stayed away from the subject. "I miss my family, my friends."

"Spring will be here soon. There will be traders." Mairwen went on, not quite sure she wanted to hear his response. "You could probably get passage on a ship to take you home, or if not directly, surely by way of a port in France or Spain…"

"I'm not going anywhere," he reassured her. "There are no ships that could take me home, and even if they could, the place I left isn't there now."

"That's sad." Mairwen took his hand. "It must be hard to know you can never go home."

"I've learned to accept it." Jeff looked into her eyes, so blue in the sunlight. "But even if I could go back now, I wouldn't. Not if I couldn't take you with me."

It was what she was hoping he would say, but was afraid he wouldn't. He kissed her, and she leaned back onto the blanket, the tall grass rising around them. In their own little world, they explored each other, sharing the joy at being loved. There were bells ringing.

Mairwen stiffened and sat up, a quizzical look on her face. Jeff was taken aback. "What is it?" he asked.

"The church bell!" She answered. "Something's happened." They tossed everything back into the basket and grabbed up the blanket. "We've got to get back!"

Chapter 7 – Alarm

By the time Jeff and Mairwen reached the church, a large crowd had gathered. Most of the villagers were already there. The people gathered around the mayor and a red haired girl holding the lead of a gray mare, frothed with sweat. Throughout the crowd people speculated about the emergency, their voices growing more agitated. Thyllwy'n, the mayor's wife, came out of the butcher shop with a large goblet of water for the girl. She gulped it down.

Mayor Caradog stepped up onto the church steps to address the crowd. "Young Bryn here has ridden from Trymme to warn us. Raiders struck there this morning and may be coming here next. Tell us all what you saw, lass."

The girl, not quite Arthwyr's age, was sweating almost as much as the horse, her freckled face reddened by exertion. She handed back the goblet and spoke haltingly as she fought to regain her breath. "I left the house at first light to feed the chickens and gather the eggs like I always do, but before I even got to the chicken coop, I saw armed men running through town." Bryn's voice climbed in pitch and began to crack as she related her story. "I ran off, and I'm a pretty fast runner so I got away at first and hid in a barn, but they came after me. I had to get away so I took the horse. I didn't want to steal it." Her voice trailed off, trembling and her chin began to quiver. "But, they would have killed me, I'm sure."

"You did well," the mayor said reassuringly. "And don't worry about the horse." Caradog needed to know more about the attackers so he interrogated further, "How many were there? You saw their boats?"

"Three boats that I saw. A lot of men... Seventy-five? Maybe a hundred, dressed like soldiers with armor and weapons."

Despite the warming spring day, Jeff felt a chill pass through him. They faced a reality he had only known in his previous life through movies and television or as a lesson in far off history. The faces of those around him showed a fear no different from his own. He thought back to his first cold night here, spent huddled in the woods, and shivered again. The one saving grace was that, as the scene played out this time, he could understand the words of the town folk as the decided what to do.

Well, you've given us some time and we thank you for that." Caradog then addressed the crowd. "More than likely, they'll be here tomorrow. We must assume the worst and make ready. There are several hours of daylight left. We must use them wisely. Go. Check every house to make sure no one is left behind. Bring food, enough at least for a few days. We'll need to share. We can be well inland by nightfall and on to Aquae Sulis tomorrow. We'll be safe there until we're sure they've left and we can return. As to valuables, bring only those you prize most if they won't slow you down. Hide the rest if you can do it quickly. But if they find nothing it will only infuriate them and they'll burn the village to the ground."

"What about my mother? She can't walk all the way to Aquae Sulis," said Orson the tanner. His mother was almost seventy and barely able to walk.

"There are a few wagons. I'm sure we can find her a ride." He turned to the blacksmith. "Eldric! That goes for Bryggyd and the baby as well."

The crowd muttered approval for the most part. Then, one defiant voice spoke out. "I'm not leaving!" It was Arthwyr. "Go if you want, I can't blame you, but when the raiders arrive I'll be right here waiting for them. They killed my parents and I vowed years ago to kill them if ever I get the chance or die trying."

"And die you will," came an anonymous response in the crowd.

"Then I die proud and good for my word, "Arthwyr challenged. "Who's with me?"

"I am" said Daffyd, stepping over to Arthwyr's side, followed by Corwain and three others. "I'd rather die fighting than live in fear." Emboldened, villagers began to step over to Arthwyr's side until the groups were nearly equal. "Come on, the rest of you." Daffyd went on, "There may be a hundred of them, but there are at least that many of us."

"Only if you count every soul in the village," Gilliam the weaver said, "including Orson's mother." The last comment lightened the air somewhat and the crowd laughed. "Even if we do match their numbers, those are fighting men. How many among us has ever killed a man?"

"I've felt helpless all my life, until now." Timothy said as he stepped forward, wearing his new spectacles. He stood straighter and taller than Jeff had ever seen him before. "For the first time I feel as though I can defend myself and those that have looked out for me when I couldn't. I never want to feel helpless again."

"What is it with men?" A tall, plain woman spoke up from the back of the crowd. Her husband, a much smaller man stood by her side. "Why does it always have to come to war? You go off to fight and leave it to the women to clean up your mess." The heads of several more women bobbed in agreement.

"This is not a fight of our choosing. It comes to us," said Cynwrig. The big farmer stepped across to join those in favor of standing, followed by his older sons. "And it will keep coming to us until we put a stop to it."

The village population was divided almost equally. Both sides murmured and grumbled. Faces began turning toward Caradog, looking to him to break the impasse. The mayor avoided their glances in hope that the decision could be arrived at without him taking sides.

An unlikely voice spoke next. Henwyneb was one of Llewellynn's oldest citizens. A candle maker and shop owner, he was the last person anyone expected to speak out for a fight. "Most of you are too young to remember the last time they came. I'm not. We made it to the woods easily enough, and watched as they looted the town. They burned my house to the ground just for sport. I rebuilt then, but at my age, I won't do it again. I'll fight."

Eldric stepped forward then, joining those aligned with his apprentice. "The raiders rely on two weapons more than any. Surprise and fear. We know they are coming, thanks to our young friend here, and I for one, am not afraid of them. We can stand up to them. They don't expect a fight. We can hurt them enough that they never come back, but we need every man. Who's to say that they won't just burn the village out of spite if we leave."

Again, there was a shift. More men came over to the side favoring a fight until only a few hold outs remained. Gilliam led them across the divide shaking his head as he went. "I still think it's foolhardy, but I'll not turn my back on my neighbors," he said.

Jeff stood back and listened as the crowd slowly came around. He was thinking about the promise he had made to Father Ewan. He wasn't sure this was the sort of thing the priest had in mind, but it seemed to apply and he took his promises seriously. He still felt enough the outsider that he didn't feel right pushing them into a decision but, once they seemed committed, he stepped forward as well. "What we need to do is turn the tables on them. I think we can prepare a few surprises for them that shift the balance into our favor."

"Very good." Mayor Caradog started barking out orders. "First, we need all the help we can get. So if there is anyone that isn't already here, get them and bring them."

"Next, we need to know what we're working with. Everyone go, get anything you have that can be used as a weapon, bring it. Extras too, if you have 'em. Somebody will use it. Collect them here for Eldric. He'll organize the ranks of defenders. When you get back, we'll go from there.

Jeff looked out through the crowd for a mop of red hair and found it. "Rhydderch, lately there have been woodsmen working near the clearing, see if you can find them. While you're at it, there is a white keg in the shed, bring it back with you but be careful with it. Eldric." He caught the blacksmith's eye, "I'm going to need that water pipe we're drilling."

Rhydderch worked his way over to the newcomer. Bryn had finally caught her breath and relaxed somewhat. They stood for a moment, nervously looking at one another, not sure what to say. Finally Rhydderch croaked, "Hello."

"Hi," Bryn said shyly, embarrassed by the attention, but

intrigued by the boy with hair as red as her own. The two stood eye to eye for a moment.

"I like your hair." Rhydderch ventured. It was as far as he got before the mayor shooed him off to complete his mission.

Jeff made his way through the crowd to Timothy. "I could use your help, Timothy. I have something special in mind." He said as the meeting broke up and he started off toward the forge.

"Yes," Timothy nodded, "you usually do." He followed Jeff anxiously to see what the young man had in store.

At the forge, Jeff looked over the log for a moment, then pointed to a spot near the bottom of the bore. "We need to drill a hole here, down into the center." He indicated point a bit farther along. "Then cut the log here. We'll also need to reconfigure the hand cart. I'll help you with all of this, but I also need to go back and forth to check on the defenses."

"You do what you have to." Timothy took up a drill to start on the hole. "I'll be fine here"

The raiders loaded their plunder aboard the ships and made sure the prisoners were secure. Over the objections of those who wanted to stay and rest a few days, they sailed south and west, hugging the southern shore. Late in the afternoon they rounded a point where the channel opened up. Maghnus breathed a little easier when the far shore fell away, allowing for more sailing room.

They sailed on after sunset, looking for a good spot to disappear for the night. Aongus pointed out a light twinkling in the twilight. On a bluff overlooking a small river flowing out toward them through the salt marshes was a village. It was smaller than Trymme, but no less inviting.

"I see it," Maghnus acknowledged his brother, "What do you say to one more before we go home?"

"Good idea." Aongus considered the approaches to the village, "Our ships would be under cover up that stream as well. It might be a good place to stay a few days once we're secure. The men could use a rest before we make the crossing home."

"We could all use a rest and this looks a good spot." Maghnus directed his helmsman to steer toward the mouth of a creek just to the southwest where they might heave to for the night. "It's agreed then. Have the men get some rest. We'll attack at first light.

Eldric presided over the weapons as they were brought in. There were few legitimate weapons, some knives which Eldric suggested they lash onto rake handles to make spears and a couple of hand axes. Cynwrig brought a scythe with the blade turned so that it extended straight from the handle instead of at an angle. The rest were farm implements, pitchforks, hoes, shovels and such.

When Jeff returned, he inventoried the growing arsenal. "It's not much," he said, shaking his head. The sense that they'd bitten off more than they could chew was mounting and the consequences of failure could be devastating.

"We'll have a fair number of spears as well," Eldric said. "Arvel has several of the women working with him, putting together some shields as well. They'll be heavy, probably too heavy to carry into battle, but we won't be moving. And Orson will have some leather armor, really rough stuff, just double thickness rawhide, but it will help."

There was some good news at least. Jeff hoped there would be more. "Wizard!" a voice called out from the edge of town. Jeff looked up the road for Rhydderch's copper locks, and found them at the head of a procession. He was flanked by a woodsman named Owyn on one side, which was welcome enough news, but on the other side, carrying the white keg, was Wahlgren, the hunter. Behind them were several more men, woodsmen with their axes and hunters with their bows.

"Welcome, one and all!" Jeff said, shaking hands and clapping the backs of the men as they passed. "I hope our little friend here didn't misrepresent our situation."

"He said there was a party!"

They all enjoyed a good laugh, but then Owyn spoke up. "He made it clear to all of us that you are expecting trouble with the Irish raiders. If you're planning on putting up a fight, we would love to be a part of it. They've been a scourge on this coast for far too long."

"Well, I've got to say, I'm glad to see you." The Mayor stepped forward, offering his hand in welcome, "I was beginning to feel that we may have been rash in our decision to stand."

"And you may yet regret that decision," Owyn said, "but we can hope that by tomorrow night those scoundrels will regret it even more."

"Well spoken, friend." Jeff waved the men in. "It's time we organized our defenses." He sought out the eye of a fisherman and found Gorloch first. "I've been assuming they will land at the wharf. Is there any chance I'm wrong?"

"None," Gorloch said. "It's the only spot near the village where the water is deep enough for any sizable boat and the shoreline is not all marsh. Anywhere else up the coast would just take too much time. It's the wharf and the careening beach."

Jeff's head bobbed in understanding as he pointed to a spot on the road to the wharf, just before it started up the hill into the town. "We'll make our stand there."

"Wouldn't it be better to be at the top of the hill?" asked a voice in the crowd.

"Good point," said Jeff. "And usually I would agree it is easier to defend when the invader has to attack uphill, but there are two reasons that this time is different. First, is visibility. From here we can see them coming, it's true, but they will see us before they even leave the ships. If they know we are waiting for them, they will be much harder to beat." Jeff gestured toward the spot where the trail to the wharf started to rise. "Down there, they won't know we expect them until they make that last turn. Second, the ground here opens as it climbs the hill."

The crowd fanned out along the top of the hill behind the in to see what Jeff was talking about. "At the crest, we would have a wide front to defend and they might be able to flank us. Down there, the dry trail is at its narrowest, and we will make it even more so. If they try to flank us there... Well, a man trying to climb out of that swamp is easy prey."

The crowd murmured approval so Jeff continued, thankful for all his hours spent watching History Channel. "We need to build an abatis, a kind of barricade, there. Actually we need two," Jeff gestured with his hands to illustrate, "in a V shape, so that the ends are out in the marsh, and the center is open. That is where we will meet them, at the center of the V." He saw the woodsmen nodding in understanding as they saw what he had in mind. "If anyone has another idea, please, bring it up. The only stupid question is the one not asked."

"What if they don't come?" demanded Siorus.

"Then we'll have done a lot of work for nothing won't we?" Mayor Caradog was quick to respond. "But tell me Siorus, if they don't come after all this, which will you be more, disappointed... Or relieved?"

"Relieved," Siorus said.

"Then let's get ready in case they do." With that, the mayor closed the meeting.

Owyn gathered his men together to start the work, several of the townspeople joining them. Jeff approached Wahlgren, putting an arm around his shoulder as they conspired. "You know that boat you were hunting from the day I met you?"

The hunter grunted assent. "I've seen a few like it in the creeks around here. I think we might put them to good use."

Jeff took his arm from Wahlgren's shoulder and cupped his hands to his mouth. "Rhydderch!" He was rewarded promptly with the appearance of not one but two mops of red hair. "You and your new friend there, grab as many kids as you can and give Wahlgren a hand gathering reeds and marsh grasses. The hunters will show you what to do from there. And somewhere along the way, go get the telescope. We'll need that as well."

The woodsmen felled a spruce tree and dragged it into position. The branches that would face the invaders were cut at the point where they were about the thickness of a man's thumb, stripped bare, then sharpened to a wicked point. On the villager's side, the limbs were sawn close to the trunk. The cut limbs were trimmed and sharpened as well and anchored in the ground as stakes with their points adding to those of the tree. A second tree was laid on top of the first, head to toe, and prepared the same way as the first, and then the whole process was repeated on the other side of the road.

Eldric admired the barricade. The spikes facing the marauders were vicious. Only a fool would even attempt to pass through those barriers. Pleased with that progress, he called the men together to discuss his plans for the men themselves.

"We'll be organized in three ranks," he explained. "The first rank, the ablest men with the best weapons will span the gap between the barriers. That'll be me in the center, the woodsmen to my left, Cynwrig, Deinol, Gorloch, and Orson to my right. Behind us will be the second rank, made up of all the men with spears, to support us and plug any gaps that open up. The rest will be spread along the two barriers to make sure none penetrate there or manage to get around through the marsh."

Arthwyr retrieved the iron bar he'd used for his sword practice from the old ruin and took it to the forge. When its tip glowed red, he pounded it flat and worked it into a point, repeating the process over and over, extending the flattened end and giving it an edge on both sides. When the sun was hanging low in the west he had managed to flatten less than half its length. He put what he had to the grinding wheel and mounted it at the end of a staff. It was half sword and half spear.

He carried his handiwork to the staging area. Eager to take his place with the defenders, Arthwyr had no doubt Eldric would put him in the forefront, but when it came to the key positions he wanted to be the first person that came to Eldric's mind.

Arthwyr approached the blacksmith with his makeshift weapon. "You forgot about me," he said.

"I didn't forget you," Eldric said, "you'll be in the second rank."

"But I should be in the front," Arthwyr objected, "I was the first to step forward. If not for me we would be half way to Aquae Sulis by now."

"That was a brave of you. You made me proud" Eldric turned the sword/spear over in his hand. "But I have a responsibility to look after you. This is an awkward beast at best. I just can't put you in the first rank to go head to head against their best with it."

"There's time," Arthwyr pleaded. "I can keep working on it, make the blade longer…"

"And it will still be soft iron, no match for the weapons we'll be facing."

"You treat me like I'm a child." Arthwyr pouted.

"No," Eldric put his hands on the young man's shoulders and looked him in the eye. "If I did you'd be going into the woods with Father Ewan and the women. You can fight. You've earned that, but without a proper weapon, you can't be in the first rank."

Arthwyr knew there was nothing more he could say. He dropped the weapon in the community pile and walked off.

Arthwyr was angry. He was insulted. He was utterly depressed. He left Eldric behind and wandered the streets of town. His eyes welled up but stopped short of tears. "Wouldn't even *be* a fight if not for me," he muttered. "I'm the one that didn't want to run." He dragged a forearm across his nose. "It should be me there, in the center of the front row." He'd shown the courage to stand up to the invaders when no one else had, only to be shunted aside. He wasn't a boy any longer. While Eldric's argument had made sense, his logic and reason faded compared to Arthwyr's emotional need to be at the forefront.

Arthwyr found himself in the old ruin. The place always made him feel good and so, without thinking, he sought it out. The warrior spirit of those who dwelt here in ages past had a calming influence, but not today. Today, it just infuriated him more.

He picked up a stone the size of a hen's egg and threw it against the wall. It made him feel better to get out some of the anger, so he did it again. It did feel good, but wasn't enough, so he hefted a larger stone, one the size of a small melon. When he threw that one he felt much better. He picked up a stone the size of a cabbage and heaved it with all his might. With great satisfaction it smashed into the wall, breaking in two and leaving a large mark on the wall. Two more boulders flew with similar results but when he hefted a third, it fell from his hands. Underneath the spot where the last boulder had lain, was the hilt of a sword.

The crosspiece of the sword hilt was corroded, the pommel was loose, and the leather wrapping was in tatters, but there was no doubting what it was. Arthwyr stooped to pick it up, but it wouldn't move. He removed more stones to see how it was wedged in place only to find that the sword was lodged in a large slab of limestone. The stone was too large to be moved and, try as he might, he couldn't pull the sword blade out of it. So he ran back to the forge.

Arthwyr returned with the heaviest hammer he could find, a long handled sledge meant to be wielded with two hands. He brought the hammer down relentlessly, sending chips of stone in every direction. As pieces crumbled away, Arthwyr realized it was not limestone at all, but cement the Romans had poured as a foundation. Thud, thud, thud the hammer went with each strike and then a hollow sound as the slab split in two, revealing a fine blade. After generations locked in the stone the blade was unblemished.

Arthwyr took up the sword and it came free of the stone. He tested its balance with a swing to each side and broke into a grin. The weapon felt natural in his hand, almost as if it had been made for him. He hurried back to the forge where he cut a strip from a leather apron to re-wrap the hand-grip. He buffed away the corrosion on the parts that were exposed then sharpened the edge. When he was finished there was no doubt in his mind that it was the finest weapon of any kind in the village.

Jeff paid a visit to Orson the tanner. He normally gave the place a wide berth, the acrid odor of the chemicals kept most people away. Today however, that unpleasantness faded to insignificance when weighed against the need for protective gear. Orson had already been joined by half a dozen women huddled about the little cabin hunched over sheets of rawhide, feverishly stitching them together.

"How are we doing, Orson?" Jeff said cheerily as he entered the workshop.

"Given the time available," Orson said, "It won't be pretty, but we can have some protection for those in the most danger. We have enough material for a dozen of these, so those most exposed will be a little better off." He showed Jeff one of the garments they were making. It was a leather chest protector with straps over the shoulders and around the back, to give it a snug fit. The leather was roughly tanned and crudely cut. Two layers had been hastily stitched together with a few studs sewn into them.

"The studs will add a little extra protection, but not much." Orson pointed out the metal buttons sewn into the front of the piece. "We could do better with metal plates but there isn't time to fabricate them. I had to make do with what I had."

"I have an idea." Jeff ran out the door to find the potter. A few minutes later he returned, carrying a stack of earthenware saucers. "Can you find a way to hold these in place between the layers?" He asked.

"Sure. We can do that, but the first time one of these is struck, it'll shatter." Orson commented, "What's the use?"

"In a long fight, where you can expect to be hit again and again, it would be of very little use, that's true," Jeff said, "but a single strike will be stopped cold. In any case, it'll be better than without."

"Good point. There's nothing to lose since they are certainly no better without." The tanner held a few of the little plates against the garment and thought about it for a moment. "We'll get on this right away. I'm sure we can make use of these." Jeff left him to work it out.

The night was still with a chill in the air. At well past midnight the barricades were finished and the waiting begun. A number of whetstones were being circulated for anyone wishing to put a finer edge on his weapon or just to busy themselves. The mayor looked over the defenses, hoping they would prove adequate, fretting that they wouldn't.

The men began to take up their positions for the coming fight, speaking in hushed tones lest their voices carry to the invaders through the stillness. Burkellyn joined the men guarding the abatis, carrying a large kitchen knife. Gilliam looked at it and sneered. "We're facing an invasion, not preparing dinner. You call that a proper weapon?"

The innkeeper responded, "Perhaps not, but it is a proper knife for slicing a pig," The others nearby laughed uneasily, glad for the distraction.

Orson arrived wearing one of his vest and carrying a couple of others. The women who had been helping him brought the rest. A linen vest had been sewn with pockets to hold the ceramic plates, and then the whole thing was stitched in between the layers of leather. Metal studs protected the spaces between the plates and held them in place as well. It was crude but functional.

Men paired up to don the armor, pulling each other's straps tight. A voice complained "I can't breathe." only to be answered by another, "Good! Then it's finally tight enough."

Eldric pulled on his own breastplate and struggled to adjust it until he felt a hand haul the strap across his back tight. "Much obliged." he said, as the unseen hand tightened the remaining straps.

"You're welcome," came the reply from his apprentice.

Pulling the leather this way and that to satisfy himself that it was secure and wouldn't loosen in the struggle, Eldric turned to face the young man. "I see you decided to join us."

"Was there ever any doubt?" said Arthwyr.

"No, none," Eldric said, "but I haven't seen you for a while. Where have you been?"

"Busy," Arthwyr said, presenting his sword for the blacksmith's approval, "working on this." The sword was beautiful. The hilt was re-wrapped in new leather, its parts tightened, the blade polished so that it gleamed, its edge honed to a razor sharpness.

Eldric admired the weapon with wonder. The entire village had been searched for anything that might be helpful in a fight and nothing remotely like it had been found. "Where did you get that?" He asked.

"I found it in the stones of the old Roman building," Arthur said. "You said the reason I couldn't be in the front rank was that I didn't have a proper weapon." Arthwyr cut to the chase, "I think this should qualify."

Eldric had been snared by his own words. He had hoped to keep Arthwyr out of the worst of the danger, but there really was no argument left, short of simply saying 'NO' and 'Because I said so'. Arthwyr was no longer a child. He was taller than some of the men in the village and his years in the forge made him stronger than most. He picked up the last chest protector in the pile and presented it to Arthwyr. "You're going to need one of these if you're to stand in the front rank," was all he said.

The rattle of wheels on paving stone sent several men up the hill to help Jeff and Timothy roll their burden down to the barricade keeping it as quiet as was possible. What had been the hand cart was now a carriage for the maple tree turned water pipe, now converted again into a makeshift cannon. Three iron rings reinforced the gun, one on either side of the touch hole and a third a few inches short of the muzzle, leather straps and coils of rope secured it to the cart. The handles of the cart had been rearranged lower, to become skids when the gun lurched back in recoil. It was crude and Jeff had some very serious doubts about it holding together, but if it did, it could be the difference between life and death for many. It could mean the survival of the village all together.

For ammunition, Jeff had three cannonballs made by chipping an iron ore node until it was round and of the proper diameter. The first round, however, would be scatter shot. Chunks of iron, scraps of metal, nails, all packed in together made for a nasty surprise.

The cart was wheeled to the bottom of the hill and positioned at the center of the gap between the barricades. The last piece of the defense was in place. All they were missing was an enemy and that would only be a matter of time.

While the men finished the last of the defensive preparations, the women of the village put together a breakfast of bacon and sausages with bread. When it was ready they brought it down the hill in a procession led by Father Ewan in the cool pre-dawn. Mairwen and Thyllwy'n, the mayor's wife, with the help of Rhydderch and Bryn, passed out the food as the women sought out their men - husbands, fathers and sons - for words of encouragement and a last minute embrace. Father Ewan brought them together for a prayer.

"Dear Lord," Father Ewan prayed in a low voice, his head bowed and his arms outstretched, calling in his flock. The villagers gathered round, bowing as well and holding hands, taking comfort from the blessing. "Protect the men of this village. We did not seek this fight, but it has found us. We stand here today as the army of David stood before the Philistines. Lord stand by us and protect us as we are your servants. Amen." A muted chorus of amens ran through crowd before the priest addressed them again. "Now spend some time with your families, after that I'll lead the women and children to safety in the hills to the east."

Mairwen and Jeff stood face to face, holding their four hands together, their foreheads touching, in wordless quiet. Mairwen looked up at Jeff and broke the silence. "Do you think they'll come?" She asked, holding back her tears.

"I'd like to have hope that they won't," Jeff kissed her finger tips, "but Bryn seemed fairly sure they were headed this way. She's a sharp kid."

Mairwen stiffened at the thought, her fingers tightening around his. "I couldn't bear to lose you."

Jeff put his arms around her reassuringly before continuing. "We've arranged a pretty rude reception for them though. There's still a good deal of danger, but I think we'll be alright." He ran his finger tips through the hair over her ear, pulling a few errant strands away from her face. "Now go give your father a hug. I don't think he's quite used to having to share you."

Mairwen went to have a moment with her father and Jeff found his apprentice. "Red!" the boy stepped up, "We need a lookout. Take the telescope and climb up in the bell tower. Keep an eye out for the first sign of them. I'll have Timothy stand below you so you don't have to shout, and take your friend so you don't fall asleep."

"Don't worry." The boy promised, "They won't sneak up on us." He pulled out the spyglass from his cloak and led Bryn to the church. They climbed up to a perch in the bell tower from where they could see well out into the channel. Rhydderch scanned the horizon with the glass for any signs of trouble. In the East the steel grey pallet of the sky was mixing hues of lavender and blue with just a touch of deep harvest orange as the sun prepared to make its debut, while in the west, the last vestiges of the moon extinguished themselves far out to sea, leaving just enough light to silhouette a ship as it approached.

Bryn looked on as well, watching as those defending the approach to the little village took their positions. Older men and boys who were not yet men lined the barricades with clubs and pitchforks or whatever was at hand. In the gap between the roadblocks were Eldric, Arthwyr, Deinol and Cywrig and the woodsmen with their axes. Behind them stood a second line of men, mostly carrying spears. Each man gathering strength from those nearby. Fear of letting down friends, family and community outweighed the fear of the attackers.

Behind the ranks on the left flak was Idwal, the farmer who owned the orchard at the north end of town on his horse. The only other horse in town, the one Bryn had come in on, topped by

Rhydderch's brother Berwyn mirrored Idwal to the right. Together they made up the town's cavalry, each man armed with a spear, standing off to the sides of the barricade.

Bryn turned her attention back to Rhydderch who was still looking intently through the telescope, wondering what use there was in looking through the tube. "Was that your father?" Bryn asked Rhydderch, pointing to Jeff as he readied the cannon for battle.

"No." He said, "That's my father down there." He pointed to the men straddling the gap between the barricades. "The one with the scythe."

Bryn looked down at the men until she spotted Cynwrig. The scythe was distinctive, extending over the heads of most of the men. "He's tall." She said, "Then who was the other man, and why is he always telling you what to do?"

"His name is Jeff and he's a powerful wizard," Rhydderch boasted. "And I'm his apprentice."

Bryn was not so easily impressed by the young man in the flannel shirt and jeans. "Just because he wears funny clothes doesn't make him a wizard." She declared flatly.

"Oh, but he is." Rhydderch objected, "He uses a magic called science, and he's teaching me. I helped him make this." He handed her the telescope and helped her to look out toward the channel with it. "See for yourself."

Bryn looked out through the glass. People fifty yards away looked like they were at arm's length. She stifled a gasp and raised the glass to the horizon, anxious to see what it did at a greater distance. She was working up to admitting the power of the invention when a sight made her stiffen. Hurriedly, she gave the glass back to Rhydderch and pointed. Rhydderch raised the glass to his own eyes and found them immediately. Three ships in single file, rowing silently into the mouth of the river. It was beginning.

Chapter 8 – Attack

The raider fleet entered the river as soon as the early morning light allowed. They rowed silently up the stream in single file, Maghnus in the lead as usual, followed by his brothers. The chieftain brought his ship around to a berth at the wharf. He always took the prize location, while the other two slid onto the careening beach.

The fighting men poured over the rails quickly with ease. The town was set well back from the landing. So, rather than stream immediately into the town as they had in Trymme, they collected together on the wharf to avoid having a leading invader being spotted and the alarm being raised before the rest arrived. The three leaders brought their men together for a final check then led them toward the village.

Walking up the causeway road, Maghnus could smell bacon on the morning breeze. It smelled inviting. He relished the idea of people going about their morning unaware of his presence and the danger he represented. In a few minutes he would be turning their lives upside down.

The road followed the course of the creek fed by the mill stream and the hot spring. The opposite bank of the brook was a wall of tall reeds over which the men could see the rooftops of the taller buildings, the inn, the mayor's house and, of course, the church and bell tower. The stream reversed itself as it neared the town then doubled back along the bottom of the hill where it splitting between the mill stream and the hot spring runoff.

Maghnus led the band of marauders around the last bend. He came to a halt, sword arm outstretched as a signal to the others. The entire village manned a barricade blocking the path. Turning around was the last thing on his mind. It was natural that some people would fight when they were cornered, or to defend their families in their homes. They were generally dispatched quickly and without emotion. This was different. People standing like this in, open defiance, made his blood boil.

"Insolence!" Maghnus steamed at the affront. He quickly

assessed the defensive position. The barricades were impossible and there was no use trying to go around. A direct assault on the gap between the barricade was the only choice. "Declan!" He shouted for his brother, no need any longer for stealth. "Bring up your best spear men and shields! Form the box!"

Gwenhwyver cried until she could cry no more. She cried at the loss of her mother, then she cried at her capture. She cried in the uncertainty of what the future and these barbarians had in store for her. She was taken into the dark hold of a ship and secured to the timbers along with a handful of others. It was cramped and the hold had a terrible stench and she cried at the conditions. Once the ship set sail, she cried again at the thought of never seeing her home again. When her tears were all gone, she considered her situation. It was bleak to be sure, but the one thing she knew for certain was that the tears wouldn't make it better. She began to take stock of her surroundings.

All the rest of the captives in the hold were women save one, a boy about her age with a nasty looking black eye and bruised face, she thought he might be useful if an opportunity to escape arose. One of the women looked familiar, from her village but Gwenhwyver couldn't recall her name, the others ranging in ages from children to adult, but none old, must have been captured on earlier raids.

Her captors didn't come below-decks often once they were secured, but she could see glimpses of them through the hatch from time to time. In the first rays of sunlight in the early morning, the men on deck made ready for another foray. Helmets and armor were secured. Weapons were sharpened. Shields were taken up. The ship bumped to a halt against a pier and they went over the side leaving just a few guards behind.

"None of the men left on deck are wearing armor." She whispered to the boy tied up alongside her.

"No talking down there!" A voice called down from the deck, the tone was hushed, but an edge of venom managed to come through. Gwenhwyver recognized the man that broke into her room yesterday standing guard. He was unarmored and shirtless, revealing a bandage on the shoulder where she had stabbed him. "The others will be back soon with food, "he added, "and if you don't shut up you'll get none."

Gwehwyver was famished. When the boats stopped for the evening the prisoners had been untied, one by one, and allowed on deck to eat a little bread. Other than that she'd had nothing since before she was captured.

The phalanx was an intimidating sight, bristling with weapons, shields and armor. It seemed invulnerable. As the formation moved inexorably forward, approaching the gap, the townspeople facing them backed slowly away. After a few steps, they backed into a cart that had left behind them and had to split their line. Maghnus smiled when he saw this. It was the sort of mistake he expected from peasants like these. He had drawn abreast of the barricade. When he was clear of it he would give the order to rush headlong into the defenders.

The defenders lined up on either side of the cart stopped backing up and readied their weapons, some of them looking nervously to the man who stood behind the cart. *A leader perhaps*, thought Maghnus. The man was wearing an ill fitting cloak and held a lighted taper, but didn't otherwise appear to be armed. He lowered the flame until it touched the hollow log atop the cart.

"A little fire will do you no good now," muttered Maghnus as he raised his sword over his head then shouted, "ATTACK!"

Nobody heard him. The only thing anybody heard was the thunderous roar of the cannon as it erupted flames that leapt out singeing the first of the attackers, they were so close. A cloud of acrid smoke enveloped them all, stinging their nostrils with a sulfurous bite. Chunks of iron tore through wooden shields like paper, through bronze armor like tin foil, and finally through bodies.

So tightly were the men packed together that what missed one man went on to hit the next, or the next with the heavier pieces often piercing a second man or even a third before coming to rest. A dozen men were dead before they hit the ground, a dozen more, frightfully injured.

Maghnus surged through the opening, followed by Phelan. Others followed suit in a sporadic rush to meet the defenders.

Some of those at the rear of the pack, not the bravest of the bunch on a good day, headed for the boats at the cannon's first roar, as did many wounded. The rest, still a considerable force, rushed headlong at the defenders. They streamed past the abatis, over the bodies and through the smoke to avenge their brothers.

Cynwrig was first to meet the onslaught. Two great strides took him to the edge of the gap where a specter was emerging from the smoke. With a roundhouse sweep of the scythe, he cut the man down only to be faced by Aongus right on that man's heels.

Aongus stepped inside the arc of the weapon that took down the man in front of him and attacked. He struck quickly with his battle axe. Cynwrig was able to parry the blow with the shaft of his weapon, but only just and was now on the defensive. Aongus swung again and again, forcing the big man to backpedal.

Aongus was a seasoned fighter. He was wary of the reach of the long-handled blade, particularly in the hands of a big man and worked hard to keep him off balance. His attack came from every angle possible to keep his foe from setting up for a clean shot at him, but in so doing, his attention was focused too narrowly. For all the fury of his attack on the big man, he never saw Burkellyn's knife before it slid under his breastplate. The stabbing pain brought down the raider's guard and Cynwrig brought the scythe around again, ending Aongus's life. With Aongus out of the way, Cynwrig waded into the throng of invaders, mindlessly cutting down one after another.

At the center of the line, Eldric had passed up the shield in favor of an iron poker that just felt more natural in his hand. In the other was his ever-present hammer. A raider shot out of the smoke with his battle axe held high and fell on Eldric in a fury. Eldric parried the attack with the poker and brought his own weapon up. The man raised his wooden shield to meet the blow as Eldric smashed down with all his considerable might. The blacksmith's hammer caught the shield dead on, splintering it and continuing on to shatter the man's arm. The raider bellowed in agony and dropped his axe to take hold of his useless shield arm, but before he could turn away, Eldric brought the poker around to his helmet then caved in his chest with another massive hammer blow.

Wahlgren had lain on the floor of the little boat for hours and his joints were beginning to stiffen. He and the other hunters had taken the boats up the stream as soon as the camouflaging was ready and worked them into the scenery where the stream doubled back. From there, they could command the road from the barricade nearly all the way back to the wharf with no danger of overshooting into the townspeople. The need to be in place ahead of time meant he'd already been here long before the women brought out the breakfast. His stomach protested when the smell of bacon reached him, but it wouldn't be long now.

Sounds of footsteps and the light rattle of armor passed the hunter's position. He was tempted to try to sneak a look as they went by, but Jeff had been adamant that they should wait for the signal. Wahlgren wasn't quite sure what that would be but Jeff assured them, "You'll know it when you hear it." So, he waited, his grip tightening reflexively on his bow.

Muted voices told him their defenses had been discovered. Someone shouted orders and the commotion grew only to be shattered by a deafening thunderclap. Now Wahlgren understood, that was the signal, he threw off the reeds covering him and stood in the boat drawing back the bowstring, as did the three others.

In the dim early morning light it was hard enough to see, made even worse by a dense cloud of acrid smoke. Walhgren could make out a crowd of men clamoring to push through the barrier. One man, obviously a leader, was exhorting those not wounded back towards the fight. Wahlgren drew back his bow and took aim, then let fly an arrow that spitted the man's neck. Other arrows sang through the air as the rest of the hunters joined the fray.

An Irish bowman took aim over a low spot in the barricade. Wahlgren put an arrow in his back before he could finish his task. "Cedric, Brian, shoot their archers!" Wahlgren directed his men. A number of the raiders in the rear of the pack had had enough. They ran headlong toward the boats. Wahlgren yelled to the hunter farthest downstream. "Haydin, don't let them escape." Haydin concentrated his fire on the uninjured.

With the archers' threat eliminated, Wahlgren concentrated again on putting his arrows into the backs of those still trying to break through the barricade.

Jeff and Timothy rushed to get the cannon reloaded, first swabbing the barrel with damp rags to be sure no hot embers remained behind, a particularly dangerous possibility considering the cannon itself was flammable, then added the gunpowder which he had pre-measured into a linen bag. Finally one of the cannonballs was pressed into place and the touch hole was primed. When Jeff was able to look up from the process he was encouraged to see the villagers holding their own in the fight, particularly on the right where Cynwrig, methodically mowed the invaders down. He was more concerned with the left flank. Maghnus burst out of the smoke and faced off with Owyn and another woodsman named Pedr. Behind the chieftain, his son followed through the gap then turned right and met Arthwyr.

Arthwyr entered the fray with his sword singing as it swept through the air. His young foe countered his sword strokes with powerful thrusts of his war ax. The young men were evenly matched and it was a frantic brawl, each man desperately doing everything he could to bring pain and injury to his opponent. Several times Arthwyr brought his sword to bear in ways that should have produced wounds that degraded the young man, if not outright incapacitated him, only to be thwarted by the lad's heavy armor. The young raider wore a copper helmet, bronze breastplate and wristlets, as well as shin guards. Phelan was a skilled fighter in his own right and so they fought on in a stalemate.

Maghnus took on the two woodsmen at once. Despite the odds, the chieftain's relentless attack kept both men off balance and he forced them back. Jeff grew concerned that this might be the beginning of a breakout and reached into his cloak for the pistol. He checked its prime once again and cocked the spring.

Maghnus pressed his attack, his sword much quicker than the woodsmen's axes. Owyn's ax lunge went wide and Maghnus sidestepped it easily responding with a sweeping roundhouse slash of his blade which Owyn quickly ducked, only to find that it's true target had been Pedr. The sword opened a gash in Pedr's leg, sending him sprawling.

Two of the spear-men in the second line moved up to help Owyn while Pedr scrambled out of the way, but to Maghnus, they were a minor obstacle. The raider parried the spear-points away then delivered a murderous slash to Owyn that struck his chest with a crack, sending him to the ground.

Expecting the pirate king to deliver a killing blow to the woodsman, Jeff raised his pistol. His concern turned to shock when the man surprised him. Rather than move in to dispatch Owyn, he turned and raised his sword for a killing blow directed instead at Arthwyr's back. Arthwyr was still locked in combat with Phelan, the pair exchanging blow for block and slash for parry, neither able to gain an advantage over the other. He was unaware of any danger from the rear.

As Maghnus wind-milled the sword blade, Jeff squeezed the trigger and watched in the agonizing slowness of the adrenaline rush as the blade arced higher and waited as the pistol's spring released, turning the gears. The wheel ground the flint showering sparks onto the pan igniting the powder in a flash. At last, the pistol bucked in his grip as the ball was expelled. It

struck the chieftain in the back of the head, piercing his copper helmet and ending his life. The sword continued its arc beyond the two younger men and came to rest, impaled on a tree trunk in the barricade.

Phelan heard the shot and saw blood spray from his father's head. He screamed, "NO!" His momentary distraction was enough for Arthwyr to finally find a vulnerable spot with a slash to Phelan's sword arm. The wound was barely significant, but it brought the young man's attention back to the immediate. He looked around and found himself alone. When Arthwyr lunged again, he sidestepped then backpedaled past the barricade and out of range. "Back to the ships!" He ordered to the few men still attempting to break through the enemy's line and rushed headlong toward safety. He had difficulty keeping his footing as he made his way off the battlefield, there were so many bodies in such a tight space. Picking his way through the dead, he recognized his uncle Ruarc among them, an arrow through his neck.

The raiders broke ranks and began running for their ships with Arthwyr and Deniol close on their heels and a mob of Celts not far behind. The horsemen soon overtook them, running down the fleeing raiders with their spears. Some raiders stopped to help the wounded, others stayed back to fight and delay the pursuers. The rest ran headlong for the boats.

When Phelan came within sight of the boats he commanded the crews left to guard them, "Shove off!" he shouted, "Pickup who you can, but get going quickly."

Brocc, guarding Ruarc's' boat called back, "We must wait for your father."

Phelan never broke stride as he came up the path, "He won't be coming."

"Then Ruarc, Aongus, Declan?" Brocc had trouble taking in what Phelan was saying, but his men began shoving the boat off the beach.

Phelan reached his father's boat and clambered aboard. "None of them," he said matter-of-factly, as he pushed the boat away from the pier and slipped his war axe into his belt. Mullen was already in place at the steering oar, so Phelan sat at an oar and put his back into it. The last survivors of the attacking force scrambled aboard their ships and made for open water.

Jeff raised the muzzle of the wooden cannon for the greater distance and sighted on the leading vessel. He touched off his second shot and watched a great plume of water explode well beyond the boats. Timothy swabbed the barrel again and they reloaded. Jeff readjusted the aim to compensate for the miss, he had little hope of doing any damage but wanted to harass the invaders all he could.

The cannon roared again, but this time, instead of a jet of water, the ball struck home. It smashed through the steering oar of the last boat and took Mullen with it, leaving behind only a bloody smear. With the steering oar gone, and pushed by the cannonball, the boat lurched to port and grounded near the beach.

"Good shot!" Said Timothy exuberantly.

"Pure luck!" replied Jeff, extremely happy with himself, "especially since I was aiming at the first one."

The men who had been guarding the ship during the battle went over the side quickly and swam to the second boat, which stopped nervously to pick them up, over Phelan's objections. The young prince was determined to bring all the boats out with him until Arthwyr and Berwyn reached it with more on the way. He gave up the notion of defending and dove after the others.

The moment Phelan hit the water he knew he was in trouble. He was a reasonably strong swimmer, but his heavy armor took him straight to the bottom. He struggled to free himself, but the battle and his escape had already left him winded, and there wasn't much time. He never surfaced.

Gwenhwyver heard the thunder. She hoped that when the marauders finished with this village that they would at least wait for the storm to pass before sailing on. She didn't relish the idea of riding out a storm in the little boat, besides the more time spent here, close to home, the better the chance for a rescue. Sounds of commotion began to reach her as the band of raiders ransacked the town. She hoped the townspeople had the chance to flee. That sentiment wasn't entirely altruistic.

She genuinely hoped no one else had to face what she was going through, but she also didn't look forward to adding more captives to the already crowded hold, and fleeing was the only chance since, after the way these men went through her little town, it was obvious resistance was futile.

Sounds of the battle reached her, making it clear that many in the town had been unable to escape. She despaired for them. It felt good to be concerned for someone's welfare other than her own.

Excited voices and clashes of weapons grew nearer. She heard horses as well and that surprised her. She wondered where they were kept. She doubted that the other boats' holds were any deeper than this one.

The boat was suddenly underway again and the thunder boomed again. Gwenhwyver thought, perhaps the raiders didn't want to be caught ashore in the rain, but that really didn't makes sense. Then, when the thunder boomed once more, the whole ship shook violently and veered, leaning to one side and scraped to a halt.

She saw the sword-point before she saw the man. He was armed like the others had been, but his armor had a crude unfinished look to it. He was young and had a kind face, smiling, not frowning like every other man aboard. For the first time in more than a day, Gwenhwyver felt unafraid.

Rhydderch watched from the bell tower as the battle unfolded below. He knew Jeff would want to know how many there were, but he lost count long before he ran out of men. As the horde worked its way up the causeway road, Rhydderch found he didn't need the telescope anymore and snapped it shut.

Tension mounted as the invaders neared the barriers and Rhydderch reached over to take Bryn's hand. She looked back at him and they shared a brief smile. That moment was shattered by the roar of the cannon. Rhydderch was the one person with any idea what Jeff might have in store and yet it far exceeded his expectations.

When the smoke cleared, he was appalled by the number of bodies left in its wake and yet cheered somewhat by the devastation for the change in the balance it produced. When the two sides met he was riveted on his father and brother. Cynwrig wielded the scythe with abandon, cutting down an after man. Rhydderch watched in both fear and awe until the noise, a much smaller noise than the cannon, but still unmistakably made by the wizard, after that the attackers broke and ran for the ships.

When the first of the Irishmen were nearing the boats, Bryn took up the telescope to see better once more. Arthwyr, without the help of the telescope could just make out the two ships retreating and the villagers storming the one remaining, when Bryn cried out, "oh my god!", then thrust the telescope back in his hands and rushed down the ladder. Rhydderch went after her as best he could.

Burkellynn and Arvel started walking up the hill as the women and children returned. What had been an orderly procession when it entered the village, splintered as it passed the inn as, first the older children then the younger wives broke into a run down the hill to find their loved ones.

Near the front of the pack, Burkellynn spotted his daughter Mairwen. Arvel waited for his friend as his daughter ran to him and threw her arms around his neck. "Father!" she exclaimed, "I'm glad you're alright." The innkeeper hugged his daughter feeling the relief flow through them, but before he could even respond to her, she had shrugged out of his grip and sped on down the hill.

Watching his daughter run down the hill into Jeff's arms, the pair embraced, then kissed then embraced again, Burkellynn said to Arvel, "I always knew this day would come, but that doesn't mean I'm ready for it."

Arthwyr reached the ship right behind Berwyn, too late to prevent the escape of the young raider he had fought at the barricade, by the time he leapt aboard, his adversary had disappeared beneath the waves. The deck was deserted, so he turned his attention to a hatchway that led to the hold.

With his sword tip leading the way, he crept down into the hold. In the dimness of the early morning the hold was pitch dark, a perfect opportunity for an ambush and he sensed the presence of others. As his eyes grew accustomed to the light, shapes in the hold grew more distinct. People to be sure, but not fighting men. They were captives, tied to the timbers.

The first person he could see clearly was a young girl, perhaps his own age. Her blonde hair was disheveled, she wore a soiled nightdress and there were bruises, yet he thought she was beautiful. He smiled. "It's going to be OK," he announced, "It's over. You're all safe now." His final action with his sword this day would be the cutting away of their bonds.

When the villagers chasing the fleeing raiders reached the captured vessel some clambered aboard in case Arthwyr needed help, others stood at the pier or on the beach hurling insults and curses at the fleeing ships in a celebration led by Mayor Caradog. When Arthwyr emerged from below-decks with the newly released captives a cheer rose from the crowd. The defense of the town had been an exceptional victory, but undoing the damage already done was a bonus no one expected.

The captives coming out on deck joined the villagers in their celebration, cheering, giving hugs and kisses, some throwing japes of their own at the raiders, all save one. A woman in her thirties had come out joyously as any, but when she saw the two ships making their way out to sea, she moved to the stern and stood alone watching them retreat with tears in her eyes.

The mayor approached the woman, quietly. "You're safe now," he spoke softly, putting an arm around her shoulders. "They can't hurt you anymore."

"I know." The woman sniffed. "The tears are not for me. When the men came, my children were doing their chores. My son ran for the woods and I believe he escaped, but if he did, it was only because the men were intent on capturing my daughter. She runs quickly for one her age, so there is hope, but the last I saw they were right on her heals. I have to assume that, if she lives, she is on one of those boats."

"I see," the mayor began to lead her ashore where the crowd worked its way back toward the town. "Tell me about her, won't you." It always helped he found, when people could talk about their trouble.

"Well," the woman held back her tears the best she could. "She is eleven and so she is a handful at times, but she means well. The boys are always teasing her about her hair, its bright red like mine. I tell her to just ignore them, but sometimes she can't. Sometimes I can't blame her, so sometimes I have to break up fights. And now she's gone." At that she could hold back the tears no more

Caradog did his best to console her as they made their way up the causeway. "It's still possible though, that she was never captured. She may not have been on the boats after all."

"But I must have hope that she is, the alternative would be too much to bear," the woman sobbed.

The mayor saw first one, then a second, copper colored mop of hair threading its way upstream against the flow of the crowd and the crowd parting to make way. He turned to the woman and said, "Maybe not."

"Mother!" Bryn's voice called out as she flew into the woman's arms.

The surviving Irishmen sailed all day and well into the night, only stopping when they could go no further. When the wind cooperated they sailed, and when it didn't, they brought the captives on deck and forced them to row. They found a protected cove where they could heave to in calm water, but remain out of bowshot from the shore and stopped for the night, the two boats lashed together. After a meal the men met to discuss their next move.

"What happens now?" Cavan said what everyone was thinking. "We go back to Ireland and act like nothing changed. It was just another voyage?"

Hoyt had always been a thorn in the side of the leaders, so it was not unexpected that he had a different point of view. "In these two ships, there is a treasure that would have made sixty men very happy, and that's after Maghnus and his brothers took the lion's share and now there are but twenty of us to share it." Mutters of agreement rumbled through the boats. "I say we go back home and split this evenly between us and live out our lives with a certain amount of comfort."

Nods of agreement escalated to cheers. "I'm for that." called out one voice. "Yes, me too," added another, and finally, "We should put it to a vote." The volume built until it was cut off.

"NO!" Protested Bearchan. Throughout the day the men, one by one, had shed their armor in favor of comfort as the distance between them and the danger increased, all except Bearchan. He had remained fully armed in anticipation of this moment. This discussion had been inevitable and he had considered his response, weighing the potential gain against the risk and found the risk worthwhile. He stood on the deck with his right hand on his battle ax in a subtle gesture of intimidation. "I am Maghnus' cousin, the last of that line apparently, and as such I should be his heir."

Bearchan looked out at the men for support as he went on. "We go back to Ireland, each man with a double share, and with me as your leader." He found Dooley in the crowd and made eye contact. Dooley was the biggest man among them, at least now that Declan was gone, and he was well respected by the men, if Bearchan could enlist his support, he could quell the little rebellion at the onset.

Dooley stood and approached Bearchan with his right hand outstretched. "We certainly cannot ignore the claims of the last of Maghnus' line" he said as Bearchan clasped his hand. Bearchan shook Dooley's hand enthusiastically, looking out at the others for their reaction. He never saw Dooley's other hand as it took hold of his belt right behind the axe and boosted him over the ship's rail and into the water. The water was calm, but deep and Bearchan fought desperately against the weight of his armor and clambered at the boat to pull himself back in. Dooley calmly picked up an oar and pushed Bearchan under the waves with it.

When the bubbles stopped rising to the surface, Dooley took his seat once again. "I believe we were about to have a vote on Hoyt's proposal. All in favor?" A loud chorus of ayes made it unanimous. "Then I'd say, to anyone who hasn't done so, finish your dinner and let's get some rest. Ireland is still a long way off."

After the last cannon blast, Jeff stood watching the villagers chasing off the last of the raiders, cheering in triumph. "Thomas," he addressed his helper, "I think we can ring the bell now. Let Father Ewan know it's safe for the women and children to return."

"Right away." said Thomas, as he trotted up the rise to the church, nearly being knocked over first by one then another red-headed child. Watching him go Jeff spotted the aid station that had been set up in the rear, tending to the wounded. Pedr was there, his leg being wrapped in bandages, but there was no sign of Owyn. Fearing the worst, he went in search of the woodsman. Jeff looked to the spot where Owyn had gone down. The woodsman was struggling to his feet. Jeff rushed to his side, amazed that he might still be alive, much less able to rise. "I thought you were dead." he blurted, putting an arm around him as he slowly came upright.

"Sorry to disappoint you," Owyn responded with his wry sense of humor, "but it's your fault if I'm not." He brought his hand up to his chest and pulled at a gash in the rawhide vest. A puff of dust wafted from the opening as the pulverized remains of a shattered plate sifted to the ground. "Your idea worked like a charm. That man would have killed me for certain if not for this." At the aid station he stripped to the waste. He was bruised, and that would look even worse tomorrow, a rib might be cracked and there was a cut, but it was all superficial and should heal fully in no time.

Timothy rang the church bell triumphantly until he was sure even those deepest into the woods were aware that it was safe to come back. When the returning crowd reached the barricades some of the men removed bodies of the invaders to make the passage easier for the rest others began searching out friends or family members they'd lost track of in the confusion.

The mayor stepped up on the cannon and waited for the bell to stop ringing before addressing the crowd. "Friends, this is a good day. We've defeated a powerful enemy, and defeated them soundly. It was not without its cost, but those we've rescued today are testimony to the wisdom of the decision to fight, and for that we owe a debt to young Arthwyr, who refused to run away."

The crowd cheered. A chant started low then grew as it spread "Arthwyr, Arthwyr, Arthwyr." The young apprentice, standing beside Gwenhwyver was at once, proud and embarrassed. The mayor waited for the chant so subside before he continued.

"This was our fight, and we fought it well, every one of us." Again the crowd expressed its appreciation for the mayor's words. "But we did not fight alone. There are those among us whose fight this was not, and yet they stood with us, shoulder to shoulder, and to them we are indebted as well." More mutters of approval spread, focused where the woodsmen and hunters had gathered.

Caradog turned and looked at Jeff, speaking to him directly, but for all to hear. "And then there is our adopted citizen. I knew you'd have a few surprises for them, but you far exceeded my expectations."

This time the crowd roared and another chant grew. "Wizard, wizard, wizard..." Jeff knew there was no point in protesting, the title was going to stick.

"Now we have people in need of medical attention and others who've lost family members." The mayor brought them back to the work still ahead. "And we have guests in need of food and clothing. I ask you all to help where you can once again and then when we've seen to the living we'll attend to the dead."

The crowd began to break up. The former captives were lead to the inn for a meal and a chance to clean up. Caradog offered his hand to Jeff, who was looking over the makeshift cannon, a split rand down the length of it from the touch hole to the iron ring that girdled the muzzle. "I never would have thought a hollowed tree could speak so loudly," he said as he shook the young man's hand.

Jeff couldn't take his eyes off the crack, running his fingers up and down its length, feeling its depth, "It's a wonder it didn't kill us all," he replied.

"Perhaps," consoled the mayor, "but if it had, we'd be no more dead now than we'd have been if you hadn't had it."

Chapter 9 – The Minstrel

The captives were brought to the inn to be fed. All of them were hungry, but those who had been held the longest were especially so. The boy with the bruised face was Gareth, a carpenter's apprentice from the Welsh side of the channel who had been among the first to be caught. Boys his age are basically bottomless pits anyway, but after several days in the hold of the ship with meager rations, he was insatiable. Thyll'wynn and Bridgid brought plate after plate, and the boy was always the first and last stop. Biscuits and jam, bacon, cheeses, fruits and bread, whatever they brought he ate. As conversations went on around him, several times he looked like he wanted to chime in, but couldn't bear to stop eating to do so

When the wounded had been attended to and the captives fed, they all turned to the grim task of the Irish dead. The limbs were cut from the trees of one barricade and then stacked upon the other and set ablaze as a pyre for the bodies of the invaders after they had been stripped of anything of value.

Warm clothing was brought for those in need, as they had only what they were wearing at the time of the raid, then those who wished it were taken to the baths. Many of the townspeople were there already, despite the weather, answering some unconscious need to cleanse themselves.

As evening fell the village came together at the inn in a gathering that quickly overflowed into the street. Tables were brought out and lamps and candles were lit. Whiskey and ale flowed like water. The women of the town all did their part, each household bringing a dish to be added to the buffet.

Caradog donated a large tray of smoked meats and added it to the fare. When he stepped up on a stool, the crowd grew hushed. "I'm not going to give a speech," he said and the whole town roared in appreciation. "Just have a good night. We've earned it." He finished abashedly and stepped down.

With the party getting going, the mayor pulled together the former captives along with the fishermen and Jeff. "I just had one piece of business to attend while we are all together and before our heads have become fogged." Looking to each of the guests in turn he prefaced, "first I have to say you are all welcome to stay, but tomorrow, for those who want, the fishermen have offered to take you home. The young ones will surely go home as long as one exists, but for the rest of you there is the choice."

Gareth was first to respond, "There's no place there for me to go. I've no family to return to. I was a carpenter's apprentice, nearly finished and ready to move on anyway, in a little village in Wales. The pirates burned the village to the ground. If I'm to start from scratch, I'd just as soon do it here."

"And I'm sure old Arvel could use a hand." said Caradog, accepting the young man. "He's a good carpenter, though not one for conversation. Never mind asking questions, but if you watch him you just might learn a thing or two."

Nesta, a young woman from the welsh coast, considered the offer. "The little village I come from isn't much, but it's home and I'll never be able to repay you all for your kindness as it is. So if you could be so kind as to take me home, I'll not impose on you anymore."

"I can take you," Newlin volunteered.

That left only Habren and Bryn to decide. The two redheads sat close to one another, neither quite ready to let the other out of sight. "I have to find my son." Habren asserted. "There's not much else in Trymme for us, but Cefin needs me still."

"Daffyd's boat can take you both, if he leaves Gorloch behind." The mayor responded, more to the fishermen who nodded agreement. "There is also the matter of the horse. Find its owner and let him know it's here. We can work out the return later."

"As for the youngsters, Dylan's boat is biggest, so I hope you can accommodate them." When Dylan nodded his agreement, the mayor stood up from the table and eyed all the food that was laid out. "Let's eat!" he declared.

The whole town was in a festive mood as they did their best to forget the horrors of the day and dwell instead on the triumph.

Jeff and Mairwen worked their way up and down the tables, sampling the dishes, drinking ale, singing and dancing to traditional music. They were inseparable. As they moved about the celebration, occasionally they found themselves apart. When they did they quickly came back together. Neither could bear to be away from the other very long.

After a dance left him a little winded, Jeff steered them toward the shadows. In an alley between shops, they found a little quiet. With his arms about her waist and her hands clasped behind his neck, he was content just to look into her eyes, bright blue, even in the dimly reflecting light.

Mairwen broke the silence, "I was so worried something would happen to you, "she said, gripping him tighter.

"All I knew was that they had to be stopped in order to protect you and the village." Jeff recounted, "The thought that if we weren't successful I might not see you again was just too much to bear. I knew then that I had to get through it in order to be here with you now."

Jeff held her closer still, searching for the courage to say what was on his mind. "I'm not sure what the custom for this is, so I'm just going to say it. Mairwen, would you marry me?"

"I think that's the ale talking," Mairwen deflected, "and a bit of nerves."

"I admit the ale has made it possible for me to say it," Jeff insisted, "but, I was going to ask you at the picnic. I know I love you, and this morning I decided that it couldn't wait any longer, so I ask you again, will you?"

"In that case, then yes," Mairwen kissed him passionately, "I love you, too. Now let's go find my father."

The fishermen fanned out across the channel, returning those captured to their homes. Daffyd's boat hugged the coast making the final turn into the cove and brought Trymme into view, even from a distance the devastation was apparent. Habren became visibly upset as they grew nearer the town and the extent of the ransacking came clear. All of the buildings showed some signs of fire, many of them were gone altogether. Two days since returning to their homes and the cleanup had barely begun.

Daffyd brought the craft up to the pier, the only thing in town that seemed to have escaped the marauders' wrath, and tied it fast. He helped Habren and Bryn over the rail and they walked up the wharf. Before them, on the corner of the two streets, the large house that was Gwenhwyver's home stood, unburned but heavily damaged.

The mayor of Trymme, a man named Ithel, lived up the street, about half way to the little house that was Habren's. It seemed a good place to start. The fires had all, long since been extinguished but throughout the town the smell of smoke pervaded everything at a time normally reserved for wildflowers. When the trio arrived they found the mayor on the roof, replacing thatch that had been burned away. When he saw Habren and Bryn he nearly fell off the roof.

Scrambling down the ladder, Ithel embraced Habren warmly and greeted Daddyd. "We thought we had lost you!" he said, still in shock. "Both of you actually. How did you get away? What happened?"

Habren single-mindedly changed the subject, "In good time, but first, my son. Have you seen Cefin?"

"Yes, he's here" the man assured her, "And he's fine. Can't say the same for your house though, I'm afraid. Meical and Delwen took him in. I think Rhys was disappointed it wasn't you though, Bryn." Ithel led the trio to Meical's house. "Come, you can tell me all about your adventures on the way."

"The raiders went to hit Llewellynn next, but Bryn got there first and they were waiting." Habren did her best to explain, "I can't tell you much about that, as I was still tied up in the hold, but the town fought them off and even managed to rescue us. Daffyd here was kind enough to bring us home."

"Looks like we all owe you and your village a debt of gratitude," Ithel said, with a tip of the hat to Daffyd.

Daffyd accepted the praise, "I don't think we need to worry about that band anymore."

Before they reached Meical's house, the door burst open and banged shut behind an excited Cefin. The boy ran to his mother's arms followed by Delwen and Rhys. There were hugs and kisses, and profuse thanks for taking care of the boy, but before long Rhys and Bryn were back to old habits and the little reunion broke up.

Habren wandered to the spot that had been her house, followed by Daffyd and the kids. The house had been reduced to a pile of cinders, and not a very big one at that. They never did have a lot of possessions, so there was no sense sifting through the rubble.

Bryn went through the yard to the chicken coop. It was smashed and the birds were gone. "Ooh the birds!" she cried. She hated the chore of taking care of them, especially the cleaning, but she had grown fond of them just the same.

Habren looked around and came to a conclusion, "There's nothing left here for us," She sighed, "Daffyd? Can you take us all back to Llewellynn?"

"If that's what you want," He knew it was not an easy choice. "It'll be cramped, but we can fit."

"I got by taking in wash and sewing." Habren said, "It will be a long time before this village has much need for services like that."

"Then back to Llewellynn it is," the seaman agreed, "But first, we have to see a man about a horse."

Taking the shortest route, they retraced Bryn's steps, but going wide of the woodpile, to the farm at the edge of town. They found the barn was gone, but the house still stood. Daffyd knocked at the door, it was opened by an older man. "Yes?" he asked.

"I stole your horse." Bryn's voice trembled. "I didn't mean to, but the men were coming and…"

Her voice fell off to a squeak, but Daffyd quickly stepped in. "The horse is in Llewellynn and its unhurt," he asserted. "We can make arrangements to get it here soon, but we wanted to let you know where it is."

"Well then you've saved it." The old man leaned over to look Bryn in the eye. "That horse is the only animal I have left. I'm sure if you hadn't taken her, she'd be gone as well. So, thank you."

Bryn was clinging to her mother's skirts in fear of his reaction. When the old man spoke, a weight lifted off her and she sniffed back a tear, "you're welcome."

In the other boats, the rest of the captives who wished all returned to their homes. Enit, the youngest of the children didn't know the name of her village, but Nesta knew she had been in the hold when she arrived, so it was a simple process of backtracking from there. Teary scenes of reunion erupted in each of the villages on their return.

When the captives returned home, the story of their rescue and of the battle went with them. While many might question the accounts of people who were tied in the hold during the battle, especially the children's, their very presence and safe return built instant credibility.

In the days following the attack, the village returned to normal. People went back to their daily lives, wildflowers took root in the ash that had been the barricade, the water pipe to the baths was eventually fixed, and the town became, once again, a quiet little seaside village.

Habren found space for herself and her children, taking in laundry and sewing to support them. Gareth settled in with Arvel and did his best to expand the carpenter's business. Cynwrig found new appreciation for farm work.

Tales of the attack spread around the countryside, some accurate, some exaggerated. As the legend grew, so did the number of travelers and curiosity seekers, going out of the way to see the town of fame and the town prospered. Nowhere was this more apparent than at the inn. Gwenhwyver had taken up residence there while she waited for her father's return and found herself put to work on busy days, not that she contributed much to the operation. When they really needed help, they found it from Habren.

If there had been whispers calling Jeff a sorcerer before the attack, they were quite in the open now and he made no effort to stifle them anymore. In the warmer weather he put aside the ill-fitting cloak and wore again the flannel shirt and tshirt. The Marlins shirt was beginning to show signs of wear from the constant use, but he wore it often as a reminder of home. The flannel shirt was enough to ward off the evening chill without being overly warm, and had the additional benefit of concealing the pistol still stuck in the wide leather belt next to the big bronze buckle.

Jeff worked with Rhydderch, teaching him the basics of astronomy. Any real study of the subject would need a more powerful telescope and so they continued in refining the lens making process. To do so, Rhydderch made a series of lenses, each one slightly higher in magnification, and in both concave and convex shapes.

With Rhydderch's attention on the painstaking process of grinding lenses, Jeff had a project of his own. He was developing the process of making paper using wood pulp and cloth fibers, mostly linen, and succeeded in producing a reasonable quality, somewhat heavy, but durable. He wanted still to make it finer, but mostly he wanted to be able to produce it in greater quantity. That would come in time, for now, it was enough to move on to the next phase.

A derelict olive press provided the mechanism, now he needed skilled hands. In the carpentry shop he showed Arvel and Gareth a small wooden block, on one face of which he had carved the letter I as an example. He unrolled a sheet of paper to reveal a carefully lettered alphabet in both upper and lower case, and described what he needed. "I want to use these as forms for a bronze casting, Arvel. They need to be very uniform in both size and spacing. Do you think you can carve me a complete set?"

Arvel turned the little block over in his hands then passed it over to his new apprentice. "The hands are willing," he explained, "but the eyes betray me. Gareth can do it though." He stepped closer and lowered his voice, " Don't tell him I said so but he does pretty good work." Gareth pretended not to hear. The old man led Jeff to the corner and went on in barely a whisper, "Those glasses you made for Timothy. Do you think they could help me, or are they only for the blind?"

Jeff put a hand on the carpenter's shoulder reassuringly, "No," he said, "I think we can do something for you. Come by later, when Rhydderch is there and we'll see what we can do."

Jeff lugged in a barrel of whiskey, still warm from the distillery. "Burkellynn!" he called out. "I've got more rot gut for you." He gave a quick nod to Arthwyr and Gwenhwyver in passing as he carried the barrel in.

"Oh, good!" Eldric said. "The party wiped out our supply. You know where it goes, the spot's empty."

Jeff hefted the barrel into position on the shelf. "I know. I rushed this one through. I'm sure it's dreadful, but nobody seems to care." He stepped back to let Burkellynn tap the keg and felt a hand on his shoulder.

"Could I have a word with you?" asked Father Ewan, who had come in on his heels. They steeped away and gave Burkellynn some room to work. "I'm concerned about Arthwyr." he whispered, "Fighting off the invaders will bring notice to us, that is unavoidable, but he's been parading around with that sword ever since. It's been three days now, it focus's the attention on him."

"I think he sleeps with it," Jeff joked, "He has a right to be proud of it, and of himself, but I see your concern." He looked around the inn for a moment, then had a thought. "Don't worry about a thing, Father," he said then huddled with Burkellynn who had finished with the keg.

The innkeeper approached Arthwyr and Gwenhwyver at their table and cleared his throat. "Ahem." When the couple looked up, he spoke, "I've been thinking, Arthwyr, of using the weapons and so on, taken from the Irish to decorate the walls of the inn." He pointed to spots around the room as he went on, "a shield there maybe, an axe on the rafter, perhaps a breastplate on that wall. What do you think?"

Arthwyr snapped up the idea, "I think it's an excellent idea," he said, "the whole village can join be a part of it."

"It couldn't hurt," Gwenhwyver added, "the place could use a few little touches."

"I'm glad you agree," Burkellynn surveyed the walls thoughtfully, stopping at the fireplace, "We need something special there, don't you think?"

"Yes," Arthwyr agreed, "but what?"

"A symbol, perhaps, of the town's defense." Burkellynn said, "Can't use the cannon, the wood's all been put to use, besides, it wouldn't have fit." Then as if by chance, his gaze fell on Arthwyr's sword. "That's it! Unless you think you'll still be needing it. I mean, it'll be here if you do."

Gwenhwyver took the young man's hand in hers and prodded him. "What better symbol of the town's strength than your sword?" She asked excitedly.

Arthwyr was cornered. With the reluctance of a child giving up his security blanket, he removed the sword from his belt. He did his best to smile as he turned the sword over to the innkeeper. "I would be glad to have my sword in such a place of honor," he said.

Three weeks later, Jeff found himself at the altar of the little Roman church with Mairwen at his side. Burkellynn walked her down the aisle with his hair brushed back until the waves rippled across his head. In a spotless linen shirt he looked uncharacteristically neat and unruffled to those used to seeing him bustle about the inn, belying his nervousness as he kissed his daughter and gave her away.

Father Ewan was reciting an incantation in Latin as he wove a long linen scarf that had once belonged to Mairwen's mother, into a complex knot with their hands clasped together at its core. The priest went on explaining the symbolism of the knot tying the two together but Jeff barely heard a word of it, his attention was riveted on Mairwen.

Her hair flowing down over her shoulders was brushed smooth as silk, glistening the color of buttermilk with a wreath of wild flowers woven into it like a halo trailing a satin ribbon. In her crisp white dress she looked like an angel, Jeff had never seen her so beautiful. Transfixed as he was by her beauty he didn't notice at first that the church had gone quiet, everyone looking at him. "I do," he said, hoping it was the time for it.

He had apparently guessed right as Father Ewan responded by saying, "you may kiss the bride." When Jeff obliged him, the villagers filling the church erupted in cheers and showered them with flower petals as they led everyone out into the sunshine of the street where another celebration would run well into the night. Only when the darkness came and most of te town had had too much to drink to notice could the young couple sneak off to the room in the inn that would be their home from now on.

Eldric held the metal sleeve in place while Jeff wrestled with the piston that would slide inside it. It was a tight fit, but it would have to be. "I think that's about right this time," he ventured. "We can go ahead and attach it now."

The machine was beginning to take shape. Built alongside the forge, it took up a good deal of the space in the forge and Eldric had started to complain. When he asked what it was for, Jeff had called it a new still and initially Eldric had accepted that, but after the boiler was done, the additions didn't look much like the still and Eldric was getting suspicious.

When the part was in place, Jeff noticed that they had been joined by Timothy, carrying several jars. "Arthwyr said you needed some lubricants, so I brought you these. One of them ought to be right."

"Thank you, Timothy," Jeff accepted the jars and tested each one for its viscosity before selecting the thickest. He began smearing the greasy stuff on the piston liberally.

"Where is Arthwyr, anyway?" Eldric asked, with a touch of annoyance.

"Where is he ever, these days?" Timothy answered. "He's at the inn, chatting with Gwenhwyver.

"I don't even know why I asked." Eldric said, shaking his head, and went back to the task at hand. "How does it look?"

"It looks just fine," Jeff said as he worked the piston through its motion. Satisfied, he wiped his hands clean, as well as any excess from the machine. "Thank you, Timothy. You've come to the rescue again. Now, as long as I have you, there is another thing I want to discuss." He led the bespectacled man out into the street as he went on. "Come, I'll walk back to the inn with you."

"Is there something else you need?" Timothy asked as they made their way up the road.

"I want to do something nice for Father Ewan and I thought you might want to be involved," Jeff explained.

"Father Ewan has always looked after me," Timothy volunteered, "So, of course I'll help. Just tell me what you want."

"How are you coming with your letters?" asked Jeff.

"Very well, thank you." Timothy beamed proudly, "I know them all, and I can write them. We're working on the sounds and reading now."

"Perfect!" Jeff handed Timothy a rolled paper. "I want you to go and tell him you want to practice by copying the bible. Start with the Lord's Prayer and copy it exactly. Can you do that?"

"Yes." Timothy agreed. "I can do that."

"Good." Jeff encouraged, "Take your time and be careful. When you finish, meet me at the inn."

Scroll in hand, Timothy waited for Jeff to disarm the door to the shed. He had no idea what Jeff had in mind, only the expectation that it would be revolutionary. In the shelter, was a machine, topped by a screw from a cider press. Jeff opened a box divided into little compartments, each filled with rectangular bits of metal, and began placing them on the frame atop the machine.

"It's a little tricky," Jeff said, "working right to left. You'll see why when it's all done." Jeff carefully arranged the pieces in place, corresponding to the page Timothy had copied until he had a mirror image of the paper. He used a roller to apply ink, then placed a piece of paper on the press. With a twist of the screw, the paper contacted the print-face. A second twist brought it back and Jeff removed a perfectly printed page.

"There!" he proclaimed triumphantly. "You see, it has to be backwards on the plate to be forwards on the paper." He used his hands to illustrate as he spoke showing right and left coming together. Timothy nodded understanding, thinking it made sense once you saw it.

"Now, you try it," Jeff invited Timothy. He handed over the roller and inserted the next sheet of paper into the holder. Timothy did as he had seen Jeff do and was rewarded with another perfect copy. He grinned with satisfaction and thrust another sheet of paper into the holder. They repeated the process until they had exhausted their supply of paper and returned to town with a stack of identical pages.

They found the priest in the sanctuary. Jeff presented him with one of the pages. "Timothy wanted to show you his handy work," boasted Jeff.

Father Ewan held the perfectly printed copy in his hands and looked with wonder. "Timothy?" he gasped, recognizing the passage as the one Timothy had copied earlier. "You did this today? How? And so quickly!"

"Then you don't want to see the rest of these. They were all done today." Jeff handed over the rest of the stack. "It's my present to you, our present really. They were done on a printing press and, given enough paper we could have done a hundred."

"I don't know what to say," the priest was clearly moved, both by the gesture and by the beauty of the gift.

"You don't have to say anything. I'm in your debt for all that you've done for me since I arrived. This is a small payment toward that debt." Jeff explained. "I need to make a lot more paper before we really get started, but I wanted to try it out right away. Eventually, with a lot of help from Timothy here, I want to print some complete Bibles for you."

"There is no debt." Father Ewan admonished the younger man, "But your generosity is greatly appreciated."

The minstrel strolled down the road, picking out chords on his lute. He was working on a new song and the tune was coming along nicely, all he needed was a story to tell with it and he hoped to find that in the next town. With the tops of a few buildings visible over the next rise, he passed a farm. The traveling entertainer left the road to approach the farmer who was working the field.

The farmer was a big man, fully a head taller than the musician with the look of a man who was well acquainted with drink, though his eyes were clear and he had no telltale scent of alcohol today. He worked the field with four others, obviously his sons, who ranged from a full-grown man to a boy of ten or twelve with flaming red hair.

The minstrel let the instrument slide around to his back and stepped up to the farmer with hand outstretched. "Well met good sir," he greeted the big man, "I'm Taliesin, a humble minstrel." He was anything but humble, but that never stopped him. "Is this the village of Llewellynn?"

The farmer straightened and shook the man's hand, then leaned on his hoe. "Cynwrig, I'm called, and yes this is Llewellynn." Cynwrig was, as always, a man of few words. His answers were polite, but brief.

"Is it true this village fought off an invasion by the Irish?" The minstrel sought to confirm the rumors that had brought him

"It's true we had some trouble with the Irish." The response was curt.

"And?" the musician did his best to coax the story from the big man.

"And we're not expecting any more." Cynwrig took up his hoe once more in a gesture that said the conversation was over.

Taliesin persisted. "Care to talk about it?" If the stories were true, this man must certainly been in the thick of it.

This time the farmer didn't even look up. "Not really."

Taliesin reluctantly accepted that this man wouldn't be much help. He took up his lute again and continued on his way, in search of an inn where people's tongues invariably loosened. If necessary, he would contribute to the loosening.

Cynwrig went back to working his field with his sons as he had been doing ever since the day of the attack. He had no real memory of the fight. He remembered the deafening roar of the cannon and the ringing in his ears that followed. He remembered the smoke that enveloped him and a greater haze, the haze of rage, after that he remembered nothing. Others told him how he had waded into the enemy with his terrible scythe, cutting and slashing, stabbing and hacking one after another.

When the battle was over, there were the bodies and an awareness that he was responsible and it scared him. That he had a temper was not news to him. What was news was the potential level of violence he was capable of when that temper was fully unleashed. He vowed that he could not allow that temper to ever be visited on his family or friends, to ever be that out of control. When the village began its celebration of their victory, Cynwrig went home to his family and hadn't been inside the inn since.

Taliesin entered the inn and took a moment for his vision to adjust to the light indoors. He spotted Burkellyn serving a patron and approached him. "You must be the proprietor of this fine establishment. Please, allow me to introduce myself." He began brashly, "I am Taliesin, musician, minstrel, troubadour, entertainer extraordinaire." He did not add, shameless self-promoter, but that seemed clear. "I am at your service. For the small price of lodging and a meal, I shall keep your patrons happy and, more importantly, thirsty." He finished by doffing his hat and bowing deeply.

"Seems a fair bargain." Burkellyn acknowledged. Jeff provided all the entertainment he and his guests needed, but a new voice would still be welcome, besides, feeding a minstrel was the best advertising you could buy. At the moment, it was the only kind. "Make yourself comfortable I'll have something for you in a few."

Taliesin hung his lute on a peg by the corner and sat at the nearest table. Biding his time, he acquainted himself with his surroundings. The inn was decorated with all manner of weaponry, shields, spears, battle axes, bronze breast plates, copper helmets. There was enough equipment mounted there to field a small army, all of them deadly, but simple and utilitarian, save one. Above the mantle of the open fireplace, hung a sword, a study in elegance, its polished blade and fine detail made it a work of art.

The evening trade not yet having arrived, the inn was empty but for the minstrel and one other. At the table opposite him sat a man looking into his empty cup. It was, apparently, not his first.

A pretty blonde girl brought a small cup of liquor and set it on the table in front of Taliesin. He smiled thanks to the girl and lifted the cup. "Thank you darling," he spoke in voice that carried across the room, "but it would seem that your ale tankards have shrunk."

Mairwen laughed good-naturedly. "I'll bring you ale if you'd rather, but I thought you might like to try this." She explained, "It's called whiskey and it's a specialty here.

Taliesin sipped the amber liquid and felt it warm him as he watched the girl retreat to the kitchen area. The man at the next table leaned toward him. "Good, isn't it?"

"Interesting indeed," replied the minstrel.

"It is intoxicating." observed the man. Siorus had been known to stop by the inn for a taste on occasion ever since he was old enough to put a coin on the table. When the battle had ended, he, like much of the town, had come to the inn to celebrate, not that he had much to do with the battle's outcome. The party ran late into the night, but for the fisherman, it never ended. He spent much of his time at the inn, and what time he did spend at home, was mostly spent in a drunken stupor. Finally, his wife had enough and kicked him out. He responded by getting drunk.

"I can see you enjoy the finer things in life, my friend." Taliesin pulled a chair up to his table for the man, "Would you care to join me in another?"

Siorus eagerly took the seat while waving Mairwen over for a refill. "Much obliged sir," he thanked the musician, "Don't mind if I do."

Taliesin gestured to the weaponry adorning the walls and commented. "Seems an awful lot of arms for such a nice quiet little town, doesn't it?"

Siorus looked up at a battle axe on the wall. After seeing them every day since the battle, he no longer noticed them. "They're not ours." he countered. They were interrupted briefly while Mairwen refilled the seaman's cup. Siorus took a big gulp of the liquor before adding, "They belonged to the Irish."

Taliesin took a sip of his own liquor hoping it might encourage Siorus to do the same, not that he needed much encouragement, but it never hurt, and the looser the man's tongue the better. "Tell me about that day with the Irish," he prodded, "Who was the hero that day?"

"Lot's of heroes," Siorus mused. "The whole village really." He looked around at all the weapons as he thought back to that morning. "Cynwrig for one I suppose."

"Cynwrig?" asked the minstrel

"Big guy," Siorus explained, "runs the farm on the way into town. A real mean drunk he is, and I ought to know. We raised many a tankard together here over the years. Anyway, he had this big scythe with the blade turned up and he wielded it like a man possessed, cutting down the raiders one after the other, maybe a hundred all by himself."

"I met the man," Taliesin put in his own perspective, "He's certainly big enough, but he seemed a quiet type. Hard to believe he could do all that."

"Don't think he believed it himself." Siorus observed, "but until you face the situation who knows what anybody is capable of. I mean, who would have thought any of us would be out there standing up to an army like that in the first place. Certainly not me." He drained his cup and put it down on the table hard, collected his thoughts and continued. "Wouldn't have happened either if it wasn't for Arthwyr."

"How is that?" Taliesin spurred Siorus on while he poured some of his whiskey into Taliesin's cup, lest he interrupt the narration looking for more.

"We had learned about the Irishmen, that they were coming, and we were getting ready to run into the hills like any sane man would do, but Arthwyr wouldn't have it," the old salt recounted . "Said he'd fight them off even if he had to do it alone."

"Sounds like a very brave man," Taliesin offered.

"Brave, yes, or foolhardy," Siorus agreed, "But a man? Hardly. Arthwyr is a lad, the blacksmith's apprentice, he's strong but young. Still, he has more backbone than a dozen men. He convinced us to stand, and he was right." Siorus looked up to the sword over the fireplace, gleaming in the light. A fine detailed scroll-work etching ran the length of the blade adding a sparkle. "Then, just before the fighting starts, he shows up with that. Never seen anything like it, and he says he found it lodged in the stones of the old abandoned armory. Like it was put there for him to find."

The evening crowd was building in the inn and they were momentarily distracted by a group of men entering. One young man wearing a brightly colored plaid flannel shirt carrying a guitar hesitated when he saw the lute hanging from his usual peg. He stashed the guitar on a shelf in the kitchen area instead and feeling the warmth of the cooking fire, removed the wool shirt and folded it over the guitar. Under the wool shirt, he wore his Marlins T-shirt.

"Arthwyr must be quite the leader," Taliesin urged Siorus on with his story.

"Indeed, he is." said Siorus proudly. "A natural. Right there at the head of the battle with that sword. Chasing them up the causeway when they were on the run, then, once the wizard stopped their ship from running, it was Arthwyr freed the captives."

The minstrel let that sink in for a minute. When he was sure that he had heard right, he asked for clarification. "The wizard stopped the ship?" He repeated, "What wizard? And how did he stop a ship?"

Siorus looked puzzled for a moment. "Yes! I suppose you don't know about him do you?" He pointed in Jeff's direction as discreetly as he could. "That's him there. The one in the funny clothes. He likes to pretend he's not a wizard, that he's just a minstrel like you. But we all know better."

Taliesin looked up to see a young man wearing a t-shirt emblazoned with the word MARLIN. The minstrel wasn't exactly literate, but he knew the Latin letters and their sounds and he made a note of it. It had a sound, he thought, fitting for a wizard's name.

"He has power over thunder and lightning," the man stated flatly. "He arrived one day last fall, from where, nobody knows. It was a thunderbolt brought him, thing is, there wasn't a storm. His magic doesn't stop there either. He helped a blind man see, taught the fishing boats to find their way home in the fog and, of course he is responsible for the whiskey you're drinking. There's some powerful magic in that."

Siorus paused to finish his liquor. "When the fighting began, he used a hollow tree to send a thunderbolt into the thick of them, dozens of men lay dead in an instant, with another one he struck down the leader and they fled. He started hurling them at the ships and when one was struck, the stern nearly blown off it, it swerved around and Arthwyr jumped aboard to rescue the captives."

Taliesin was amazed by the story, it was wilder than anything he could make up. He considered his source and attributed much to the influence of drink and yet it was great entertainment he was after.

Mairwen brought a bowl of stew for the traveler and laid it on the table. "This should take the edge off your hunger," she said as she served him, "would you like another whiskey, or would an ale be more to your liking?"

Taliesin could feel the liquor warming him already. It was enjoyable, but he demurred, "If I'm to be of any value to you, I think the ale would better serve, but my friend here would like another whiskey I'm sure." He turned to Siorus with gratitude, "You've been a great help to me, "he said, "and I thank you." If he was to continue drinking and be comfortable both, Siorus needed to relieve himself and said so as he rose from the table. In his absence, Taliesin sought confirmation of the incredible tale. "Your friend here has told some amazing stories."

"I'm sure he has," said Mairwen, flashing a smile.

"The minstrel leaned closer and asked in a more hushed tone, "Is there anything at all to the bit about the tree that belched fire and thunder and killed all those men?"

"I'd say so," Mairwen replied haughtily before walking away, "You're sitting on it."

The minstrel looked closely for the first time at the bench he was seated on. It was one of several in the inn that was fashioned by splitting a tree trunk, the rounded bottom showing the original contour with the legs drilled into it. Down the center of the bench, was a black stain of scorched wood.

After finishing his supper, the minstrel alternated between entertaining the crowd and talking with them about their experiences that day. To his amazement, except for some disagreement in the actual numbers involved, they confirmed even the most astonishing details of Siorus's account.

"If it works, does that mean I can finally have my forge back." Eldric kidded Jeff who was busily filling the reservoir of the machine with water and stoking the fire within. "It's been taking up half the place for weeks."

"You could just make the place bigger" Jeff retorted, "Not a bad idea actually."

"It's plenty big enough, especially when it's just me here." said Eldric with a touch of indignation. "You and Arthwyr won't be around here forever, you know."

"Funny that you mention that," said Jeff. He threw a few plugs of iron on the forge and then checked on the new machine. It was beginning to whistle as the water heated toward the boiling point. "You're right about that. For Arthwyr, it's only a matter of time, and probably not much at that, before he moves on. As for me, well, you can ask for my help any time and I won't refuse, but who knows how much I'll be around."

The water in the machine had reached a full boil and the pressure built up, the hissing growing louder. Jeff made a few adjustments and opened a valve allowing the steam to drive the piston back and forth, turning the drive wheel and with it, a pair of belts. The smaller of the two turned a fan which replaced the bellows. It had two speeds, either slow for sustained heat or high for increased heat. Jeff engaged it, intensifying the fire around the iron plugs.

"Eventually you'll find plenty of help from Cormac, I'm sure, but that day is still far off." Jeff continued, raising his voice to be heard over the noise of the machine. "In the mean time, this will be your helper when you have a large job or just a lot of smaller ones. Here, let me show you what it can do."

Jeff took a plug of iron, glowing red from the fire in his tongs and carried it to the machine. He stepped on a pedal that engaged the second belt, turning another wheel as it chugged and belched steam. With each revolution, it raised then lowered a heavy hammer. Jeff held the plug in place as the hammer pounded it. Bang! Bang! Bang! Bang! In rapid succession flattening the bar. He then turned it and repeated the process. Each strike had the effect of a dozen strikes by hand.

Eldric tried his hand with it, adding a second plug and working the two together and then the third. In no time they had completed a job that would otherwise have taken hours. When it was done, Jeff released the pressure and shut the machine down. "You'll still want to do your finishing work by hand," he acknowledged, once the noise had died down, "and for small jobs it's probably more trouble than it's worth, but when you have a lot to do, I think you'll be glad to have it."

"I've got to hand it to you," Eldric said, "You never cease to amaze."

Chapter 10 – The Ballad

From the time the Saxons first gained a foothold on the southern coast of Britain, they had been spreading in all directions through conquest and colonization. Greater and lesser kings carved out their realms from lands once exclusively Celtic and later shared with the Romans.

Aethelgren held sway from his castle at the Western frontier of Saxon territory, as he had since capturing it more than a decade ago. At the time, it was a somewhat remote outpost. Although ,with two hundred of his men living in the farms nearby, he never feared attack. He had spent the years since consolidating his hold on the lands between. In so doing he broadened his support with the lesser nobles throughout the Saxon lands with rewards of estates in the fertile country.

The king was a tall man and despite the years of comfort still lean and athletic. A heavy brow and large hooked nose gave him a hawk-like appearance, his pockmarked face, a reminder of a childhood bout with the fever, barely concealed by a graying beard and hair. He stood on the parapet atop his castle with his younger son Thrydwulf, the image of the older man in his youth. Below them was the castle's enclosure with its wooden palisade. Beyond its walls, spread farms in all directions as far as the eye could see.

"When I die," The king told his son, "Your brother Eadberct will inherit all this."

"I know father." replied Thrydwulf, well aware of the customs regarding firstborns and inheritance.

"Like you, I was a younger son. And like you, my older brother inherited my father's lands. And yet, we stand here today, surveying my kingdom." The king put a hand on his son's shoulder. "Like me, you are destined to be king, Thrydwulf, but to do so, you must go out and conquer."

"Yes, father, we've had this conversation before," the young man responded with just a hint of impatience.

"Indeed we have," said the king. "Now though, we must stop talking and start acting. The infantry you command is among the best I have. That is your legacy. For twelve years, we have been consolidating our hold on the lands we own. To the North and West there are lands just as fertile as these, it's time we look to expand again." Aethelgren gently turned his son to face him. "Prepare your men," he said, "It's time we think about carving out your kingdom."

    Taliesin was feeling very satisfied with himself. Since the introduction of his new song, The Ballad of Llewellynn, he was finding the crowds bigger and more appreciative than ever. He had been zig zagging his way through western Britain and Wales for weeks and his fame was spreading before him. Tonight would find him in the hall of the Saxon king, Aethelgren.
    Aethelgren's castle sat atop a hill between two rivers, not far from where they met. The rivers were shallow there and easily forded, making the location both accessible and easily defended. At the foot of the hill was the settlement, more fortress than village. It was little more than a handful of craft shops that provided for the king's needs, surrounded by a wooden stockade with gates on either side leading down to the river fords.
    After spending the better part of the afternoon touting his appearance, Taliesin headed for the king's castle in the setting sun. Inside the door, he allowed his eyes to become accustomed to the dimmer light. The castle centered around a great hall, crowded tonight with knights, overseers and townspeople, all enjoying the king's hospitality. To the left, a corridor led to private chambers, to the right sat the king's dais and a passage leading to the kitchen and storage areas. Directly across from the door was an enormous round fireplace, large enough for a man to walk inside, fully upright. This time of year, of course, there was no fire. He could see steps spiraling up inside the hearth, leading to the parapet and lookouts above.
    The minstrel looked over the dais appraisingly. Five men sat, fully engrossed in conversation, food and drink. At the center of the table was the king. Dressed in regal finery, there was no doubt as to his identity. To the king's right sat two younger men.

Clearly, they were Aethelgren's sons as they had the same long face and sharp features. At the king's left was a man who looked to be about the king's age, probably a trusted advisor, thought the minstrel. He spoke to the king with only a touch of deference, almost as an equal

The man at the end of the table didn't quite fit in with the rest. He was a big man, nearly a head taller than the rest. His clothes, while not those of the common man, were out of place at the king's table. He was a rough looking sort, with a misshapen nose, as though it had been broken many times.

The entertainer worked his way through the crowd and stood at the center of it, wait for the king's acknowledgment. The ruffian at the end noticed him and stood menacingly, but Taliesin paid him no mind. At last the king did take notice of him "Yes," was all he said.

"I beg your pardon, Sire," the minstrel began, "allow me to introduce myself. My name is Taliesin, minstrel, bard, story teller, entertainer of great renown. If you would be so kind as to provide me with sustenance and a place to lay my head, I will entertain you and your subjects with songs both old and new and stories of heroism and bravery, not the least of which is my own new sensation, The Ballad of Llewellynn. Perhaps you've heard of it."

The kind feigned disinterest at the bard's self promotion. "Go ahead and feed yourself, but go easy on the mead," Aethelgren said, "the last of your ilk drank his fill, then could barely recite his name. I aim to be entertained. See that I am or you may find out just how good my aim is." The others at the table laughed heartily at the king's joke.

Taliesin had his fill of the fare that was available, but heeded the king's warning and passed up on the mead altogether, taking the king at his word. Free food and lodging was just a perk in his line of work, the real profit was in the passing of the hat after the performance, but there was no sense in pressing one's luck, besides a clear head meant a better performance and that generally found its own reward.

When his meal was finished, he took up a position by the huge fireplace where he could be seen by all, and picked out a few chords on his lute to quiet the crowd. He began the performance with an old favorite. Those who knew the words sang right along. Those who didn't sang anyway if they'd had enough to drink. The minstrel performed with all the showmanship he could muster, ever mindful of the king's admonition. He sang and he joked and told stories and played his music so that when his show was near its end, he had them in his hands.

"Thank you all," The musician buttered up the crowd, "For letting me spend a little time here in your hall. Before I go I'd like to tell you about the village of Llewellynn." Taliesin strummed a chord on his lute. "Not far from here, on the western coast of the island, a small town like any other was attacked by bandits from across the Irish Sea." He picked out another chord, "Though there was plenty of time to run as most would do, they chose instead to stand and fight and sent the attackers running. This is their story."

The Ballad of Llewellynn

A fleet set sail from Ireland on a voyage of rape and pillage
    They plagued the coast of Britain, every city, town and village.
Along the Pictish shores they ravaged.
    Down to the coast of Wales they savaged.
While in Britain lay the village of Llewellynn
    its people ever tranquil dwellin'.
Seen from afar across the bay
    The village seemed like easy prey.
The ships debarked along the pier
    to dole out death and pain and fear.
They crept upon them, quiet but steady.
    No idea that the town was ready.

From Trymme there came a rider
    whose red hair couldn't hide her.
To outrun two men she was able

and took refuge in a stable.
Until another came and forced
        a quick escape atop a horse.
Her story had been chilling
        one of rape and fire and killing.
In the village none could stay
        with Irish raiders on the way.

To run and hide the town did choose
        until quoth Arthwyr "I refuse.
I've hated raiders since my birth
        I'll fight them here and show my worth.
While some may say I am not grown
        I'll fight with you or stand alone."
One by one the men felt right
        to join young Arthwyr in the fight.
And decided 'fore the setting sun
        to stand together and fight as one.

Though united now, they needed aid
        to fend off pirates in the raid.
Young Rhydderch ran to wood nearby
        where Owyn's men did heed the cry.
Then as luck would have its sway,
        the hunters' path came cross his way.
Then hurried back, the town to tell
        with able men their ranks would swell.
With eight more men to join the fray
        when weapons clashed at break of day..
To meet his foe did Arthwyr need
        a proper weapon to do the deed.
To Roman ruin he retired
        To ponder that which he required.
Before the evening light could fade
        he unearthed legendary blade.
Encased for centuries in stone

       but when released its steel edge shone.
With sword in hand at end of night
       He'd lead the village in the fight.

Among them all the most defiant
       was Cynwrig, quiet Celtic giant.
His life's blood running coldly,
       he wielded scythe so boldly.
He slashed and hacked and stabbed and bloodied
       until the ground beneath was muddied.
He cut them down as they attacked
       and ever higher bodies stacked.
With scythe his bloody crop he sowed
       and littered bodies in the road.

Wahlgren left the big game hunt
       to take to hiding in a punt.
In search of even larger prey
       to hunt the hunter from the bay.
So he with all his gallant men
       lay in waiting in the fen.
When sounds of battle's thunder rose
       they stood and pulled then loosed their bows.
How much weaker foe attacks
       when there are arrows in their backs.

To keep the day from being tragic
       They called upon a feat of magic.
With thunderbolts and lightning hurlin'
       came the wizard known as Merlin.
When Irish saw the village made
       to block the road a barricade.
Their shields together formation massed
       but Merlin loosed a mighty blast.
Then proved his worth again as charmer
       with dinner plates to serve as armor.

The blacksmith with his steely might
      held the center of the fight.
Into the middle of the clamor
      Eldric swung his awful hammer.
When sounds of metal contact clattered
      both shields of wood and bone were shattered.
The enemy was pounded
      and on their heels were hounded
'til last river bend was rounded
      and victory bell was finally sounded.

The townsmen chased the Irish hoard
      led by Arthwyr and his sword.
The fastest made it to the fleet,
      where they attempted to retreat.
Merlin threw a bolt of thunder,
      sending final boat asunder.
When crew was banished 'neath the waves.
      Arthwyr liberated slaves.
among those captured far and near
      was gentle princess Gwenhwyver.

Abatis chopped and set to fire
      became an Irish funeral pyre.
When that grim task at last was done
      time to unleash and have some fun,
to celebrate amazing feats,
      was food and dancing in the streets.
With ale and wine and spirits distilled,
      their pleasures taken and bellies filled.
Invader banished and battle won
      they feted 'til the morning sun.

    When the song was over, Taliesin bowed deeply and basked in the approval of his audience. "Thank you again," he said as he removed his hat and sent it theatrically on its way around the room. "You're too kind."

"I suppose you want us to believe that fable to be a true story?" accused a voice from the crowd.

"Want you to?" mused the minstrel, "No, not particularly, but I do expect you to."

"And why should we?" asked another voice.

"Because I've been there. I've talked to the people and they all tell the same tale." Taliesin reproved the man, "The ship the Irish left behind is still there with the back end of it looking as though it was bitten off by some great serpent. The inn there is adorned with the weapons taken from the Irish dead." The hat had come full circle and the musician bounced it in his hand testing the weight of the donations. "Of course, I don't expect you to take my word for it all," he challenged them before taking his leave, "Go and see for yourself." With a final flourish he strode off.

Aethelgren turned to his advisor with concern. "I don't like the sound of this, villages standing up to attackers, I don't like it at all." Osfrid had ridden by the king's side since his very first campaign. They fought alike and they thought alike and Aethelgren frequently used him as a sounding board.

"This little village must be crushed before the idea spreads." Osfrid observed. "Otherwise Celts throughout the western lands may think they can stand up to us as well." He thought about the details of the song for a bit and added, "It seems this Arthwyr is at the core of it. This sort of thing can usually be traced to a leader. There have even been rumors lately that he may be the son of Pendragon."

The king glared at the ruffian at the end of his table. The henchman tried to make himself small, a task he was ill equipped for. "Waffa, I thought we'd heard the last of Pendragon," The king thundered. "Why am I hearing now about a son that still lives?"

"The castle was searched thoroughly," the ruffian spluttered nervously. The king was not known for forgiveness, especially in matters of failure. "Surely, this Arthwyr is an impostor."

"Whether he is a young Pendragon or not is unimportant," Osfrid weighed in, much to Waffa's comfort, "Peasant armies are like snakes, once you cut off the head, there isn't much to worry about."

"Agreed," grunted Aethelgren, "Waffa, do not fail me again. Go and finish the job with this Arthwyr." Waffa stood and bowed his acknowledgement to the king and turned to look for his cohorts. "Wait," the king had a second thought, "Don't kill him, at least not yet, bring him here. I want to see if it really is Uther Pendragon's son, also the song mentioned a princess. She is probably just a farm girl, but I've found a man can always be counted on to speak when there is a woman involved, and I mean to find out what is going on."

"What about the wizard?" Waffa asked.

"Pfft!" The King's face reddened. "A charlatan. Surely you're not afraid of some impostor claiming to be a conjuror. Now go, before my patience is at an end."

"Very well, m'lord." Waffa wasted no time finding his men and getting on his way lest the king's mood worsen.

When the last of the patrons, a trio of unsavory looking characters, finally left the inn, Jeff hung the guitar on its peg and helped Mairwen with the cleaning up. She was alone since Gwenhwyver, who had been helping out, disappeared out the door with Arthwyr as she did most nights. Tonight she could have used the help.

It had been a long hot day followed by a rowdy night and the inn was a shambles so, when Jeff stepped out to dump a bucket of filthy wash water, he stopped for a minute to catch a breath of fresh air. He saw Arthwyr and Gwenhwyver in the shadows, their foreheads together, talking in hushed tones. They had been spending a lot of time together and he wondered what they would do when her father returned. The couple pretended not to see him as he turned down the alley in the moonlight. As he dumped the grey contents of his bucket in the gutter, there was a commotion back out in the street.

He rushed back up to the street toward the sounds of a scuffle between the buildings and found those three men he had noticed earlier. One had a knife to Arthwyr's ribs, and the other two were wrestling with Gwenhwyver who was fighting like a tomcat. He pulled the pistol from his belt and leveled it at the face of the man with the knife. "Let them go!" he shouted.

The man, a rough looking sort, a full head taller than Arthwyr with a misshapen nose. was not easily dissuaded. He just looked at Jeff scornfully, dismissing the gun entirely. "Or you'll do what?" he sneered as the other two lifted Gewnhwyver off her feet and dragged her around the corner.

Using the gun in the heat of battle had been one thing, it had been instinctive, a reflex, but he had hoped that if there ever came a time like this, that the mere sight of the weapon would be enough. The problem was nobody here had ever seen one before, so the man didn't see it as a threat. The big man put more pressure on the knife, prodding Arthwyr to follow the others when Jeff pulled the trigger. The pistol barked its report and the man, struck in the forehead, collapsed in a heap.

Jeff and Arthwyr ran to rescue Gwenhwyver from the others, but it was too late. There was only the sound of horses' hooves clattering away on the cobblestones into the distance.

Mairwen and Burkellynn rushed out of the inn at the sound of the commotion. They were met by the mayor and, soon after, Eldric. Mairwen recognized the body in the street, "He was inside earlier with two others," she said, "I didn't like the looks of them."

"The other two took Gwenhwyver." Arthwyr said, barely able to keep the emotion from his voice. "They got away."

Mairwen considered for a moment, what else she might remember that could be helpful. "They paid with Saxon coins."

"His clothing looks Saxon as well," added Burkellynn. Over the years, identifying people's homes by their clothing had been a sort of game for him.

Jeff stood over the body of the man, shaken by the experience of killing a man in cold blood. "I had no choice," he muttered.

Mairwen put an arm around him and led him back inside. "I'm sure you didn't." She comforted him. "Don't bother yourself. You did well. You saved Arthwyr's life."

Soon nearly the whole town was there, many brought weapons in case there was more violence. When it became clear that the danger was over, most went home. Timothy and Orson removed the body and the others moved back inside the inn. Mairwen brought whiskey for Arthwyr and Jeff to ease their nerves.

Arthwyr's hands shook as he held the cup. "I haven't felt so powerless since I was a child," he shuddered, "In fact, standing there, listening to the horses hooves fading away, not being able to do a thing, it was just like I was three years old again, listening to the Irish raiders riding off after killing my parents." He took another sip of his whiskey, thinking about how similar two of the worst nights in his life had been. Bells went off in his head and he put the cup down, "Wait a minute!" He looked at Eldric and then at Father Ewan. "The Irish come by sea. They don't bring horses with them and they make their escape in boats." He looked back at Father Ewan, glaring at him.

Father Ewan and Eldric looked at each other, Arthwyr's words hung in the air. Eldric broke the silence. "The boy needs to know the truth," he said. "It's time."

The priest nodded assent, "I suppose it is." He composed himself to recount the story. "Your Father's name was Uther Pendragon. He was a king among kings.

"When the Saxons first came here, after the Romans left, some resisted, others fled, but mostly, they waited until their own lands were threatened before they did anything, and by then, they were hopelessly outnumbered." He looked Arthwyr straight in the eye as he spoke, conveying that he was telling the whole story, coming clean on what had been hidden. "Your Father united us. He raised an army throughout western Britain and Wales and led us against the Saxons. We beat them too, defeated them soundly.

"It seemed we might be able to live in peace as the Saxon's looked to expand in other directions, but apparently old King

Aelthergren never forgot us. He sent a couple of his henchmen one night to assassinate your father. You managed to hide so you survived. The rest of the story is as you remember it. The cook found you and brought you to a church, from there you were smuggled to me.

"We thought it best to say that your parents were killed by the raiders because it was plausible and because we thought that if Aethelgren knew you lived, he might come after you. It would seem we were right. We must assume that you were the target tonight, that Gwenhyver was just a bonus, or perhaps, extra protection.

"We have to go get her." Arthwyr insisted. "We can't just let this happen." It was just a short time ago that Arthwyr stood in front of the villagers and showed his backbone in standing up to the Irish invaders. Now he was rallying support for a new cause, not just the rescue of Gwenhwyver but against a new and more dangerous foe, one who was a danger not just to the village, but to all of Celtic Britain. Even Arthwyr himself was different this time, gone was the petulant youth, replaced by a young leader."

"I can't disagree," Caradog allowed, "but going after the Saxons will make taking on the Irish look like child's play."

"But not impossible," Arthwyr persisted, "My father beat them once. They are not invincible."

"No, they are not," Eldric agreed, "Besides, we may not have much choice. If Aethelgren knows Arthwyr is alive, he'll be coming here anyway. We'll end up fighting, either on their terms or on ours. Given that choice, I'd say let's fight on our own terms."

"On our terms, yes," Caradog said. "We should begin preparing our defenses, like we did for the pirates, only this time, we have more warning. We can fortify the entire town."

"If we wait for them to come here, we won't get the girl back," Eldric said, Arthwyr, energetically nodding in agreement. "But more importantly, he'll outnumber us ten to one, or twenty, or worse. If Aethelgren can take us on piecemeal, no amount of fortification will make a difference."

"We certainly can't do it alone," Caradog interjected, "We'd need help. A lot of help."

"Pendragon... my father united the west countries once," Arthwyr suggested. "How many will join us if the Saxon's are coming this way again?"

Jeff decided it was time to weigh in, "Arthwyr's newfound notoriety may have gotten us this far, maybe it can work in our favor as well." he then addressed Arthwyr directly, "You may not like this part though. As much as I want to bring Gwenhwyver back, safe and sound, we cannot rush into this. We need allies. We need arms for everyone, no pitchforks and clubs this time, and as long as that will take some time, we need training. Those who fought in the front line last time, should work with the others every minute possible to improve skills."

Jeff stood from the table and motioned Timothy to come with him, the others continued the discussion 'til dawn. The people of the village quickly agreed to stand together, a decision that seemed to come more easily this time, and went on to plan how to go about it.

Burkellynn took the bronze breastplate down from the now denuded wall. Empty pegs protruded from the plaster and beams where the arms and armor left behind by the Irish had been. He had claimed three items early in a process, including a helmet and shield, that began when Arthwyr reclaimed his sword before the meeting broke up. The young man made no comment or complaint about what might have been had he not relinquished it, recriminations would do no one any good, instead he solemnly brought the elegant weapon down from its perch above the mantle, and left the inn without a word. A few more weapons were removed, appropriated by those who had captured them in the battle and then the floodgates were opened as all those present scrambled to equip themselves for the coming struggle until the walls were bare. These were the last.

Burkellynn laid the helmet and shield on a table and raised the breastplate to his chest to see the fit of it. Made for a much younger man in the prime of his life, it fell short of covering his bulk. It would cover the most vital areas, but left much of him, especially in the mid-section, vulnerable. Still, it was better than nothing. He put his arms through the straps and did his best to secure it.

"You're not thinking about going with them are you?" Mairwen's tone was mocking, but an element of fear came through as well.

"Thinking about it? No," he replied, "I'm going."

"How can you be serious? At your age? Defending the village was one thing, we had no choice, but going off to war is a pursuit for much younger men."

"Gwenhyver was our guest. My guest. We have a responsibility. I thought to myself, 'what if it was my daughter? What if it was you?' I have to go. Every able-bodied man in the village will be going, I couldn't bear to stay behind."

"I doubt the mayor..."

"I said able bodied. The mayor is a fine leader in the town as far as that goes, but he gets out of breath crossing the street. He wouldn't make it past the edge of town. The same is true of Arvel and a few others, but every man who can make the trip will be going. You won't have to wait for us long."

"Wait for you?" Now it was Mairwen's turn at indignation. "You don't think I'm staying behind, do you?"

"Surely, you don't expect to fight..."

"No, not to fight, but to help in the camp, cooking, sewing and eventually, seeing to the wounded. I expect only those women with small children and the elderly will be staying."

"But, the inn?"

"You said yourself that every able-bodied man in town is going. I'm sure that will include travelers as well by the time we leave, so there won't be much business to miss. Besides, our provisions will be needed, what would we sell?"

"I suppose I see your point," The innkeeper accepted begrudgingly.

"I have a new husband to think about as well. I can't very well have him rushing off without me, can I?" Mairwen reminded her father the gently turned him to inspect the restraints of his armor. "Now, let me see. I can let the straps out a little, but it's going to be a tight fit no matter what I do."

And so, each accepted the other's argument, while holding out hope that minds might be changed before it was too late.

Later that morning Jeff and Timothy returned to town, having exhausted the supply of paper on the printing press. They found many of those involved in the discussions of the night before still at the inn, mostly asleep, slumped over in chairs, some, laying on the floor.

CALL TO ARMS

FOR A GENERATION THE SAXON HAS OCCUPIED OUR LANDS, ABUSED OUR WOMEN, TAKEN OUR BELONGINGS AND ENSLAVED OUR PEOPLE.

FOR TOO LONG HAVE WE SUFFERED FROM THEIR OUTRAGES.

THE GREEDY SAXONS ARE ON THE MOVE AGAIN. LANDS ALREADY STOLEN NO LONGER CONTAIN THEM.

YOUNG GWENHWYVER OF TRYMME IS HELD IN THEIR CASTLE.

NOW ARTHWYR, SON OF UTHER PENDRAGON, CALLS UPON ALL MEN OF BRITAIN TO RISE TO MEET THE SAXON FOE, TO RESCUE GWENHWYVER AND WREST OUR LANDS FROM SAXON HANDS AND PUT A STOP TO THEIR ENCROACHMENT.

EVERYONE'S HELP IS NEEDED AND EVERYONE CAN HELP. IF YOU CANNOT FIGHT, THEN SEND YOUR METAL, ALL THAT YOU CAN SPARE, THAT IT CAN BE FORGED AS WEAPONS AND ARMOR TO EQUIP THOSE WITHOUT.

A GREAT CELTIC ARMY GATHERS IN LLEWELLYNN AND THENCE, NORTH AND EAST TO AETHELGREN'S CASTLE.

"Daffyd, see if you can get the fishermen to carry these across the channel to the Welsh coast. Take them up the rivers as far as you can go, when you can't sail any farther, prevail upon any you can to take them into the interior." Jeff handed a large stack over to the fisherman. He handed the others to Cynwrig saying, "The rest of these we should send on horseback to alert the towns and villages in the southwest of Britain. A job for your son Mercher and any others who can ride, take them far and wide, both on land and on the water, BUT," Jeff cautioned them all, "Be careful not to stray into Saxon lands, it would not go well for anyone found distributing these, besides, the Saxons will get wind of it soon enough."

Aethelgren was in a sour mood, had been ever since the minstrel's song had ended. He paced back and forth across the great hall. "They should be back by now," he muttered, surreptitiously looking at the door.

Thrydwulf and Eadbert knew enough to keep their mouths shut when their father was in such a state. They sat, staying to the shadows. Osfrid sat quietly, watching the king, if he was nervous, he didn't betray it. "They should return soon,"he said, "but they are not overdue yet."

The king accepted that and continued his pacing and muttering until they door banged open. Caerlin and Penda had ridden through the night, only stopping once, not far from the village to securely bind and gag their captive came in, carrying a writhing figure which they dropped unceremoniously on the floor. Gwenhwyver could do little more than whimper through the gag.

Aethelgren looked her over with disdain, "If she is supposed to be a princess, I'm not impressed," he pronounced then asked, "Where is Arthwyr?"

Caerlin fidgeted and barely got out, "Waffa had him."

The king straightened and fixed his stare on the man, "and where is Waffa?" he demanded.

The men cowered under the king's scrutiny. Penda finally mustered the courage to respond, "It was the wizard." he said, trying to conceal his fear of the king's wrath, "He struck him down with a bolt of lightning."

"Superstition!" Aethelgren roared, "You're cowards, afraid of your shadows."

Penda bristled at the insult. "That may be," he said, "but Waffa isn't here now is he?"

The king stifled an urge to strike out at the man's temerity, instead, opting to send him away. "Take her away." he ordered. "And see she doesn't escape." The men picked the girl up and carried her off, happy for any excuse to make themselves scarce.

Aethelgren did his best to compose himself and took his seat again at the table, motioning his sons to sit as well. "So, it seems this Arthwyr, whoever he is, survives again."

"If a confrontation is to be inevitable, it may well be better that we get it out of the way sooner, rather than later." Osfrid mused.

The king weighed his advice thoughtfully, "Yes, you are probably right." He said, "Eliminate them and make an example for others in case they've forgotten what it means to resist us."

"We should march our forces there immediately," Eadbert's impetuosity got the better of him. "They should be crushed."

Osfrid was diplomatic, "I admire your courage, Eadbert," he said, "but we will be marching fifty miles through hostile territory to an enemy we know nothing about."

"We have to muster all our forces." Aethelgren decided, "Gather every able bodied man throughout our lands." He then addressed Osfrid directly," Get word to my brothers and the other Saxon kings as well. If this isn't dealt with, it will be a problem for us all. When all our forces are assembled, we'll march to this Llewellynn."

"In the meantime," the king added, "let's not forget about the girl. As long as we have her there is a chance they might do something stupid, like come after her and save us the walk."

Chapter 11 – Call To Arms

Jeff sat on his stool at the inn, mindlessly picking out tunes on his guitar, never settling on any single one. The few patrons paid him little mind and he paid them even less, retreating into his own little world, his unfocused gaze centered on the far wall.

"Evening, my son." The priest's voice snapped him out of his reverie.

"Hello, Father."

"You looked lost in thought."

"Yeah, I guess I was." Jeff pulled the guitar strap over his head and propped the instrument in the corner behind him. "I've been in this quiet little town for less than a year and here we are preparing for battle for the second time. I have to wonder, would you all be going through this if I wasn't here?"

"Confrontation with the Saxon's, I fear, was inevitable." Father Ewan took Jeff's hands into his own and took a seat. "When the Saxons first arrived on this island and began taking land, the Celts thought it would be like the Romans again. Once the fighting with them was over, the Romans just went on with their lives and let us do the same, and they built roads and bridges and water systems and baths. Life wasn't so bad under the Romans.

"The Saxons are another thing altogether. They don't build anything they just take. They expand their boundaries and then they subdue the people within them. They go in cycles, expansion and subjection, expansion and subjection, they are due for a little more expansion about now.

"The Saxons know the land North and West of here as Wales. It's from their word weales, it means property..., slaves. That's what we Celts are to them, a source of labor and in the way."

Jeff had a new perspective on the situation. It wasn't nearly as different from the raiders after all. The Saxons had already taken a third of the island and he knew from history that the rest would surely follow. While that might well be inevitable, it didn't have to happen just yet because if it did, his friends were in danger whether they attacked or not. If that was the case, they may as well fight on their own terms.

"So, sooner or later we fight?"

"It would seem so."

"Then if Arthwyr can raise enough of a force, we'll take the fight to them before they can bring it to us."

"That would seem a wise course."

"Yes. That is, if Arthwyr can raise the force, a very big if for one so young."

"In that, the lad may surprise you. He has proven himself once already, that is important, but even more so, some will come in honor of his father, and others will come because of the sword."

"The sword?" That was an angle he hadn't even considered.

"For generations there have been tales of a sword such as that. That whoever finds it and frees it of the stone is destined to be king. Many believe in it and they will come. Others may not believe so much but will find it enough to make their decision and they will come as well."

Jeff shuddered as he felt a chill run through him. *Arthwyr's sword is the Sword in the Stone?* "I've heard that story, even before I came here, but always considered it more fairy tale than fact."

"Many legends are grounded in reality, at least at some level. What matters is that people will believe it and they will come." Father Ewan rose to his feet. "This fight is not of your doing, but like with the Irish, you may help in shaping its outcome."

The reassurance should have made Jeff feel better, and it would have if he had thought about it, but now all he could think about was what the priest had said about the sword. *Could it really be the sword from the legend? If so, then Arthwyr is KING ARTHUR.* It was hard enough for Jeff to accept that he was living right in the middle of the legend of King Arthur, but to imagine that the brash young apprentice could be Arthur himself. *And what does that make me? Marlin... Merlin? Is it possible? Merlin was the most famous and powerful wizard of all. I'm just a college kid, or I was.* But people had been calling him wizard for months.

The village mobilized for war. Eldric, Arthwyr and Jeff worked in shifts keeping the forge burning around the clock, pounding every available scrap of iron into ax heads and spear points, though they did try to keep the operation of the steam hammer to a minimum if people might be sleeping. There was no attention given to aesthetics, only to strength and utility.

Arvel and Gareth turned out ax handles, spear shafts and shields at an amazing rate. Arvel in particular, found new energy since receiving his glasses. With the return of his vision, he found a joy in contributing that he had lost.

The potter produced scores of the disks Jeff designed for new ceramic armor. They were smaller and lighter than the plates used before and they interlocked for better coverage. As quickly as they could be fired they were turned over to teams of women, who sewed them into linen vests.

Expecting that the Saxon's might return in force at any time, lookouts were stationed on all roads into town around the clock and the bell tower was manned from dawn to dusk, more often than not by Rhydderch. He scanned the horizons with his spyglass, especially to the north and east, the most likely avenues of attack.

Rhydderch sighted the scope along the coast, running northeast and worked his way over the coast road and the woods to the road running due east inland and then finally around to the coast as it ran southwest where he saw motion. There was a group of people coming up the coast road. It was a fairly large group, including several men on horseback, still well beyond his house and farm.

The boy scurried down the ladder and hastily rang the bell then ran up the road to the field where his father was drilling some men in the use of a spear. "Dad!" he yelled as soon as he was close enough, "there're men coming up the road toward our farm."

"How many?" his father demanded.

"I don't know," replied the boy, "a lot."

Cynwrig mustered his men and double timed them down the road toward his farm. At the ridge just beyond the pasture he spread them out in a double file across the road and waited for the approaching group with Jeff, Eldric, Athwyr and others following close behind.

The others halted a dozen yard short of Cynwrig's men. They didn't appear threatening, which was a good thing, since they outnumbered the defenders easily. A lone rider made his way to the front and dismounted. He was tall and broad shouldered, and though his hair was graying at the temples, still very fit. His finely tooled leather armor as well as his stallion, marked him as a man of some stature. "I am Gryffud." He announced himself, "Lord of the western lands from Devon to lands end. These are my men."

Arthwyr threaded his way through the lines to face the newcomer. "Well met, Gryffud." The young man offered his hand. "I am Arthwyr, son of Uther Pendragon," said Arthwyr, still getting used to his pedigree but growing in confidence. He stood erect and greeted the warrior.

Gryffud smiled broadly and clasped Arthwyr's hand in his own, "Yes indeed you are," he laughed, "I fought alongside your father in his battles with the Saxons as did several of my men, and there is no mistaking that you are his son. A messenger brought word that you mean to face the Saxons again. If that's true, we are here to join you."

Arthwyr felt a surge of pride in the recognition and his spirits lifted at the sight of so many men. "You are more than welcome, "he said, "All of you. We've begun training those who've never fought before, but we can certainly use a few more experienced fighters in that endeavor."

Gryffud gave a signal to his men and a wagon edged forward. "The message also mentioned needing metal, so, as we collected men along the way we collected metal as well." The wagon rattled its way up the road, a stout man at the reins, and pulled alongside the leader. "This is Renfrew, my blacksmith. If you plan to put the metal to good use, I thought you might as well have some help."

"It's good to have you," welcomed Arthwyr. "We'll take a few days to get the men as ready as possible while we turn that lot into something more deadly than chamber pots and candlesticks, then we'll be on our way."

The village continued to swell with newcomers arriving from all directions. Cynwrig, Gryffud and the other veterans drilled the men relentlessly in the arts of war, in the process the men fell into groups around leaders chosen either for experience or an obvious ability with their weapons.

The blacksmiths continued pounding out their products. All the metals were sorted. The brass was put aside to be melted down and re-forged together in one single casting. The result was a cannon that would be the pride of any arsenal for the next thousand years or more.

When the gun had finally cooled enough to handle, Jeff admired their work, "I have to admit," he said, "I have a lot more confidence in this one doing us more good than harm than I did the last."

The four men lifted the heavy barrel into place on the carriage Arvel and Gareth had made to Jeff's design. Jeff installed a sighting apparatus, hoping this time that they might be far enough from the enemy that it will be needed.

Jeff decided that it was all in order. "Let's go see what we've got here," he suggested. The four men rolled the gun into the street where Timothy had a team of horses waiting, hitched it up and hauled it to a field on Cynwrig's farm. They arrived in time to see Cynwrig leading his men in a mock battle against forces led by Gryffud.

Gryffud's men attacked furiously, but the defenders steadfastly held their formation. The battle raged for a while, before the commanders called it a draw. "Very good!" Gryffud praised them, "We get better every time. Now, everybody relax for a bit, we'll get one more practice in before the end of day."

The men took a break, many of them just flopping to the ground where they stood, others making the effort to find a more comfortable spot. Rhyderch and two other boys about his age brought water around. The commanders met with their visitors.

"Pretty impressive," Eldric said.

"The men have been working very hard," Cywrig responded.

"I can see that," Arthwyr said. "Do you think they're ready?"

"Ready?" Gryffud deflected, "No, they won't be truly ready for months, but we obviously can't wait that long. They are much better though."

Cynwrig added his own assessment, "This much I know. They'll fight."

"And that says an awful lot," Jeff acknowledged. "Now if you folks don't mind, I need to make use of the field for a few minutes while you have your break." With Eldric and Timothy's help, he muscled the cannon into position and sighted it on a pile of hay some two hundred yards away.

"Now, you folks over here might want to find another spot to sit while this is going on." He directed those in the line of fire. The townspeople were already moving, so they didn't need to be told, but their guests had no idea what they were about to see, and begrudgingly got out of the way.

When the weapon was primed and loaded with an iron ball, Jeff checked once more to be sure it was safe, then ordered, "Ready! Fire!" The gun barked and recoiled, belched smoke and sent up a plume of dirt ten yards beyond the hay and a bit wide and sending those new to the village scrambling while the others just smiled knowingly.

Jeff made adjustments to the sight, the turned the screw lowering the barrel and reset his aim. The next shot missed only by a few feet, the third was dead on as was the fourth.

"That is amazing," remarked Gryffud as Jeff wiped the brass gun-barrel down with a linen cloth.

"It ought to improve the odds a bit," Jeff said.

"It's certainly an improvement over the hollow maple put forward." Eldric put in his two cents.

"It's a little smaller actually," Jeff replied, "But better accuracy and ammunition should more than compensate."

"So, we know this works," Arthwyr weighed in, "And every piece of metal for miles has been turned into a weapon of some kind. The men are probably as ready as they're going to be. Is there anything else that needs to be done before we start out?"

"I think now, the sooner we leave, the better." Eldric said. "We should be on our way tomorrow morning."

"There may still be more men coming," Gryffud suggested.

"There may," Jeff agreed, "but a few men will make better time than we will. They can catch up. We'll be taking the coast road along the channel and up the river beyond, so the fishermen can leapfrog with us bringing supplies in their boats. They can probably bring along a few latecomers as well."

"It's settled then," Arthwyr said, asserting himself just a bit more, "We leave at first light."

Devlin and Meical returned to a town still recovering. A sense of foreboding descended on the merchant as he and his son rolled down the village's main street past buildings still blackened with soot and vacant lots that once held houses. They were met in the street by Ithel, the mayor and the look on his face told them the worst before he spoke a word.

The merchant got down off the wagon. "What happened here?" He asked.

"We were attacked." Ithel explained. "Irish raiders." The mayor related the story of the attack and the destruction the raiders caused, skirting around the issue of Devlin's family.

Devlin let him go on for some time, but finally his impatience overcame him. "What of my family?" he demanded, "my wife and daughter?"

"Bronwen is there." The mayor pointed to a line of fresh new markers in the cemetery behind the chapel. They walked toward the little church, Miecal following behind.

Devlin understood his reluctance to come to the point. "But not Gwenhwyver, then? She's alright?"

"I'm, afraid the news there is not much better. She survived the raid, but was captured. We thought that was the end of her, but then, came word she'd been rescued when the raiders hit Llewellynn the next day and the village fought them off."

"But you said the news was bad?" Said Devlin, bewildered. "That is wonderful news."

"Well, it would be, if it ended there." The mayor continued his narrative, "She didn't feel safe coming back here alone, and who can blame her?" He took down the notice tacked to the church door and showed it to Devlin. "Now she's been kidnapped and held by the Saxon's in Aethelgren's castle."

Devlin was devastated. He stood silent and looked from the paper to Bronwen's marker in the churchyard and then back to the paper again. Feeling his eyes beginning to well up, he reached for a hope, "Do you think they really will try to rescue her?" he asked.

"I don't know, but I do know this, if they do, they will come right up that road." The mayor said, pointing down the coast road toward Llewellynn then turned and pointed back the way Devlin had come, "and when they go on out that one, every man in this village will be with them."

After a brief prayer in the dawn from Father Ewan, Arthwyr climbed atop a wagon and addressed the men. "The Saxon's are coming, they've made that very clear, we can wait for them to come here and take us one by one, or we can stand together and take the fight to them. It will not be easy, make no mistake, but it is the only avenue available to us that does not end with these lands in Saxon hands and our children in chains."

The army broke into a cheer, "Arthwyr! Arthwyr! Arthwyr!" The blacksmith's apprentice stepped back down off the wagon and took his place among his men while Jeff climbed up in his place. The chanting continued but evolved into another "Merlin! Merlin! Merlin!"

Jeff let the cheer die down, rather than try to talk over them. "The Saxons already know of your bravery, and you prove it again with your very presence here today, so that will come as no surprise, but I promise you, when we meet them, we will have a few surprises for them."

Jeff jumped down off the wagon and took his own place in the column and the army started on their way up the coast road, leaving behind only the old and infirm and those women with young children. They marched with high spirits out of town as the sun peeked over the marsh.

Cynrwig led the way. As a commander he could have a horse, but chose to walk instead, giving up the horse for Berwyn to be his eyes and, if need be, his messenger. Beside him was Rhydderch, doing his best to keep up with his father's long strides. He had wheedled and pled to be allowed to come along on what he was sure would be an exciting adventure. His father finally relented on the promise that, when the fighting began, Rhydderch would be well out of the way.

Deinol and Mercher, big men despite their youth, marched as members of Cynwrig's brigade. They were the heavy infantry. Made up of the biggest, most powerful men, they all wore armor, either ceramic or bronze, and carried heavy shields. The weapons they carried were a cross between spear and axe head, mounted on a shaft both stouter and longer than a spear.

Protecting the rear of the column was Gryffud. Among his men were many veterans of past campaigns and the most experienced fighters. Between Cynwrig and Gryffud the rest of the fighters were spread out, interspersed with supply wagons and women, coming along to help in feeding and providing for the needs of the men.

Directly behind Cywrig's men were Jeff and Timothy escorting the cannon. Beside Jeff, of course were Mairwen and Burkellynn. The innkeeper wore a bronze breastplate and copper helmet and carried a shield and battle ax, all courtesy of the Irish raiders. Jeff thought he was getting too old for this, but couldn't find the courage to tell him, apparently nobody else could either.

Arthur, too was offered a horse, but declined the privilege, saying, "If I'm to be a king one day then as a king I'll ride. Today I am but a man with a sword, marching into battle. If my men are to walk then so am I." He and his men guarded the wagons along with Eldric and his.

Rhydderch began the day full of energy. He walked along beside his father, taking three steps for every two of his father's, but, as the day wore on and the road stretched out before them he began to tire. He fell off the pace just a little, but enough that the men in Cynwrig's brigade slowly passed him. When he felt a nudge on his shoulder he looked up to see the muzzle of a horse pulling a wagon. He quickly shuffled out of the way and picked his pace up as best he could, slipping back into the daze of monotony until a pair of unseen hands picked him up by the armpits and lowered him into the wagon where he immediately fell asleep.

Eldric left the boy in the wagon and fell back in beside Jeff. "I think your young friend has gone about as far as he can for one day," he said. The army plodded up the road as it meandered along the coast, sometimes in sight of the water, other times through the woods. At one of its turns inland, Eldric pointed out a group of buildings that could be seen on the waterfront ahead. "That'll be Trymme," he said, "we should be there in an hour."

The three smiths worked their way forward so that they were right alongside Cynwrig when they made the last turn into town and found two men waiting to receive them.

"Welcome to Trymme," greeted a prosperous looking man, "This is Ithel, our mayor, and I am Devlin. Gwenhwyver, the girl at the core of this mission is my daughter. I cannot tell you how grateful I am to each and every one of you for doing this. I am in your debt."

Jeff and Arthwyr stepped forward, hands outstretched, to formally accept the reception. "We came to accept your daughter as one of our own in the time she spent with us," Jeff offered as they introduced themselves, "and the Saxons are a threat to us all."

"Indeed they are," Ithel agreed, motioning them all to continue into town, "The boats arrived some time ago, so we expected your arrival and that you'd be hungry. So please accept our hospitality."

"I have grown very fond of your daughter, sir," Arthwyr said to Devlin as they walked, "besides that, when they took her, they were after me. So this is personal for me as well. I won't rest until she is home safe."

Well young man, it seems we are in this together." Devlin put a welcoming arm over the shoulder of the younger man. "Along with most of the village, I will join your forces. Anything I can do to help I will, as soon as I heard you were really coming, I sent my son north to ask for help from Urien in Rheged, whence we had just returned."

"My thanks, Devlin. Every bit helps."

The band progressed North and East along the river, coalescing more and more into something that could truly be called an army. Arthwyr worked his way from one end of the column to the other, walking with each group in turn, spending time with the men, cementing their bond. At night he met with the leaders around the cook fire, discussing strategies until the embers were cold. He listened more than he spoke, taking in their counsel and learning from their experiences but always putting his own stamp of approval on every decision made.

Jeff came away from these meetings with a new found respect for his friend. Gone was the brash young man, prattling on incessantly and spoiling for a fight. In his place was a careful but confident commander. In a few short months he was transformed as he took on the mantle of the leader.

Gryffud rode along the column and pulled up alongside Arthwyr and Jeff. "Looks like we may have some company," he said pointing out a cloud of dust, rising above the trees across the river.

"They've been shadowing us since the channel narrowed," Jeff acknowledged as the column came to a halt. "Sometimes in sight, sometimes not, but always there. We need to find out who they are." He looked around for a familiar mop of red hair and found it, alongside his brothers not far ahead. "Rhydderch," he called out, "Why don't you go up a tree and see if you can't figure what we have there."

His assistant chose a tall pine with a good view across the water and clambered up it as easily as he would have climbed a ladder. He pulled out the spyglass and scanned the opposite bank for the source of the dust cloud, and found them easily, but took several minutes to observe them before he reported.

"It's a large group," he said for all to hear, "Not as big as ours, but definitely an army. Most of them are on horseback and wearing armor like Gryffud's men."

Below the tree Arthwyr, Jeff and Gryffudd weighed the boy's information while Rhydderch kept up his watch. "I don't think we're in Saxon territory just yet," Jeff said, "But they could be an advance team, sent down river to find us."

"If they are," Gryffud added with a touch of concern, "They are probably looking for a place to cross."

Rhydderch kept the glass on the horsemen across the river who appeared to be conferencing as well. Lone riders came in from different directions, scouts he thought, and addressed a man on a black stallion, a moment later, the man waved them off and they rode out again. The wind picked up somewhat and Rhydderch saw something he hadn't noticed before. The man next to the leader held a banner. "There's a banner!" he called out, "with a dragon, a red dragon."

Gryffud laughed out loud, "It's Cadeyrn!" The others all looked at him uncomprehendingly so he explained, "He's lord in central Wales, and a friend of your father's Arthwyr. He's come to join us."

"That's terrific news!" said Arthur.

"Indeed it is. We've got to get over there." Jeff agreed, then called up to his apprentice, "Rhydderch? Any sign of the boats yet."

The fishing fleet still brought them supplies daily, but since the channel went from open water to narrow river, they were having trouble keeping up. Rhydderch searched the waterway for the boats. "Most of them are still working their way around the last bend, but one should be here soon."

"That'll be Daffyd," said Jeff, "In the meantime, let's get someone out on that point to try to flag them down before they move on." A man took a pennant out to the tip of a promontory and waved it until a group of riders came out to the bank and acknowledged him.

When Daffyd arrived, they offloaded his cargo as quickly as possible, then Jeff, Arthwyr and Gryffud boarded for the crossing. Cadeyrn and his aide met them at the water's edge.

"Gryffud you toothless old goat," Cadeyrn greeted his old friend, "Don't tell me they let you come along."

"That'll be enough of that. I see just as much grey in your beard," Gryffud countered, "Unless you've been using it to clean out the fireplace again." The two men embraced, laughing, then Gryffud stepped back to introduce his companions "Good to see you again, old friend. This is Pendragon's son Arthwyr and the other goes by Jeff, but most know him as Merlin."

Cadeyrn shook Arthwyr's hand,"You favor him," then Jeff's "I've heard about you."

"Thank you for coming," said Arthwyr.

"The Saxon's are a scourge on us all. If we're to fight them sooner or later, it might as well be sooner. I'm getting too old to wait for later." The Welshman stroked his beard. "We've been looking for a place to cross since we spotted your column the other day. It's been a dry spring and the river is very low, so the horses could cross just about anywhere, but there are fifty or so among us on foot, for them the channel is too deep."

"The rest of the boats will be here shortly, so ferrying them all across will be no problem. As to the horsemen though, I have another idea." Arthwyr drew a map in the dirt. "As long as you could cross over at any time, why cross now? I think it might be a good idea to have a presence on both sides."

"Not a bad idea."

"The boats can provide communications and supplies, so you can travel light." Arthwyr continued, taking charge. When the army left Llewellynn Arthwyr was commander in name only, in reality a figure head, but with each step they took toward the Saxons he became more and more the leader. "Also, we are getting close to Saxon country, so, from now on, we need to have scouting patrols out ahead of us at all times."

The scouting party crept through the woods parallel to the road the rest of the army would be coming up on later. At the edge of the wood, the ground sloped away to a field planted with barley on one side and vegetables on the other. Half a dozen men and women bent to the task of digging out the weeds trying to take hold around the growing squash vines, with a man watching over them. At the far end of the field anther identical group did the same.

Wahlgren observed the closest overseer carefully. He was armed with a seax, the sword from which the Saxons derived their name, it was a nasty piece of business, but at the moment it hung harmlessly from his belt. In his hand instead, he held a narrow wooden cane which he used liberally on each of the workers in turn for any imagined infraction or slight, exhorting them to work faster. Despite spending his entire day in the field, no dirt would find its way under his fingernails.

The hunters split into two groups, Wahlgren led two men to the far end of the field while Haydin stayed behind with the other two, then all six slipped into the barley and silently worked their way across it.

The workers struggled their way up the rows scratching away at the weeds, sweat rolling off them. An older woman unconsciously stretched to ease an aching back. The overseer immediately swooped in with his cane. "Back to work you hag," he cursed her as he snapped the cane across her back, "I'll show ye what pain is." But before he could raise the cane again he was hit by an arrow. He stumbled a step and was hit by two more before he hit the ground.

Three men came out of the barley and pounced on the man, making sure he didn't get up. He didn't. At the other end of the field the other Saxon met the same fate. The workers were frozen in horror at the sight of the armed men and the oozing copse in front of them. Wahlgren asked in a low voice, "Are there any more of them?"

Most of the workers were too stunned to speak, but a younger man finally pointed toward a line of shrubs. "Two more there, in another field beyond those bushes."

"Move into the barley, you'll be safe there, but quietly." Wahlgren lead the hunters of to the bushes and disappeared again. Minutes later they were back with another dozen workers.

The workers were all dressed the same, in a one piece shift of the coarsest material, and wore an iron ring about their necks like the collar of a dog. They were unkempt and bedraggled, their hair in knots and their skin dirty. They all stood hunched over so as never took look their masters in the eye. A generation of servitude rendered them cowed and silent, but one man finally stepped forward to speak for the group.

"Who are you?" he asked, "Do you know what you've done? The Saxon's will surely come after you."

"We are Celts like you and we're here to take on the Saxons."

"I admire your courage but it'll take a lot more than six men to do that. Unless you plan to take them on two at a time, they breed faster than that."

Wahlgren chuckled at the thought, "No, we are but the first, a scouting party, the main body of our army will be along shortly."

"My name is Dewi. I was a boy when the Saxons came here and took this farm. My grandfather cleared this field with his own hands and worked it all his life as did my father. For a dozen years now, I've been a slave on my own land." The serf's voice cracked with emotion as he recounted his tale. "If you are to face the Saxons then I will face them with you. I know every blade of grass between here and the castle. I have no weapons but, when the time comes to fight, I'll do so barehanded if need be."

"That won't be necessary. I'm sure we could find you something, but I have a better idea. There are blacksmiths among us and I'm sure those iron collars would make perfect spear points with a little persuasion."

Chapter 12 – The Battle

With Dewi's help, the Army made its way to Aethelgren's castle. He brought Arthwyr, Jeff and Gryffud to a ridge just over a mile from the castle from which they could survey their goal. The castle sat on a point of land, protected on the far side by the Severn River and on the near side by a smaller tributary.

The castle sat atop a hill a hundred yards from the end of the peninsula. A stockade ran down one bank and up the other before it ran across between the rivers, protected by a steep sided ditch broken only by a causeway leading to the north gate. Above the causeway, they could see an encampment in the pasture land.

From the ridge, the main road ran down to a stone bridge arching over the spillway of an earthen dam that held back an irrigation pond formed by a still smaller stream and also fed by a channel that had been dug across the low lands from the tributary. Beyond the bridge, the road divided a field of flax as it ran to a ford and the castle's west gate. Below the spillway, the stream itself provided no real barrier, but the bank on this side was steep and high.

Behind the ridge the road split, to the north ran a narrow track that bypassed the settlement winding its way through a dense wood then opened up to another pasture that sloped down to the stream. Here the banks were all but nonexistent and the stream was easily forded on a long front. The track went on to merge with the road from the castle's North gate then forded the main river channel before curving to the North.

Arthwyr stood among a stand of tall pines on the high point of the ridge where he could observe the castle and its surrounding unnoticed. It looked exactly as he thought it would in an oddly familiar sort of way. It had a commanding view in all directions and made the utmost of its position for defense, and it was overrun with fighting men.

"It's going to be very difficult to attack that. It's a fortress." Arthwyr said shaking his head. He never expected this to be easy but, it was now sinking in, just how hard it might be. "Should we go straight in the main road, or do you think it would be better to go the long way round and attack from the north?"

"Which do you think?" Gryffud turned the question around, glad to see he was looking for counsel.

Arthur weighed the options carefully before responding. "With the river so low, I would say straight in."

Gryffud smiled and nodded, it was a good answer, and well reasoned. "Not bad, but actually, I would have to say neither."

"You're not saying we should cross the main channel, are you?"

"Oh, no! I'm saying we shouldn't attack." Gryffud was a veteran commander and wanted Arthwyr to have the benefit of his experience. "A direct assault against a position like that, with a large force inside would be bloody indeed. A siege would be better, but it would take too long, and Gwenhwyver might suffer from it. I suggest we try to draw them out."

"We'll prepare to defend from right here." the veteran commander surveyed the terrain, sizing it up as a defensive position. "If they don't come out after us, we'll keep raiding his farms until he does." He pointed toward the encamped soldiers. "The men in that field must be eating old Gryffud smiled and nodded, it was a good answer, and well reasoned. "Not bad, but actually, I would have to say neither."

"You're not saying we should cross the main channel, are you?"

"Oh, no! I'm saying we shouldn't attack." Gryffud was a veteran commander and wanted Arthwyr to have the benefit of his experience. "A direct assault against a position like that, with a large force inside would be bloody indeed. A siege would be better, but it would take too long, and Gwenhwyver might suffer from it. I suggest we try to draw them out."

"We'll prepare to defend from right here." the veteran commander surveyed the terrain, sizing it up as a defensive position. "If they don't come out after us, we'll keep raiding his farms until he does." He pointed toward the encamped soldiers.

"The men in that field must be eating old Aethelgren out of house and home. With a force that size, supplies won't last forever, but they may need some persuasion to come out."

"It looks awfully crowded. Why don't they spread out into these fields as well?"

"They're safer there. A few archers in these woods could create havoc and then disappear before the Saxons could saddle a pursuit. Those open fields give them a buffer." The old warrior went silent, gazing at the encamped foe. "On the other hand, they do look a bit too comfortable. Maybe a few arrows in the night would do them good."

The castle was a hive of activity as armies from all over Saxon Britain gathered. The area inside the stockade had filled to overflowing days ago and now the fields beyond the north gate were trampled, their crop a total loss. Inside the castle, the king's mead hall sharing the mid day meal, things were not much better. The hall was packed with the commanders and lesser officers representing each of the allies present.

The king sat at a dais, nervously picking at the carcass of a roasted fowl. There was still no word yet from Loefric and if he waited much longer, the others would eat him out of what kingdom he had. The extra men weren't really necessary, he thought, but an overwhelming force was always preferable and made the victory even sweater when the enemy ran in terror.

To Aethelgren's right sat his older brother Cynbeald. The family resemblance ran strong here. His brother had the same Hawkish visage, minus the facial scars, and with a bit more grey in the beard. Along with his aide Brandt, Cynbeald was first to arrive, giving support to his brother.

Next on the dais was Wybert. His kingdom in the south shared no border with the island's original inhabitants. While this meant he was safe and secure from their encroachment, it also meant he had no opportunity to expand. If new lands were taken in this campaign his supporters could be rewarded either here or by exchanging for lands closer to home.

At the end of the table was Wealdhere. Aethelgren's summons had brought him reluctantly from the East where he had been happily expanding his kingdom. He was the youngest of the Kings present, open to fits of impatience and rage. If Wybert and Aethelgren had not come to his own aid a year ago, there is no doubt he wouldn't be here today. He was the most recent arrival and his complaints had started immediately. They had been rewarded handsomely in their time and now it would be his turn.

The first arrivals had claimed the shade of an orchard just outside of the north gate. As more troops moved in the vegetable fields filled in as well. By the time Wealdhere's men arrived all that was left was a pasture that straddled the trail that skirted the castle's environs. Devoid of shade in the summer heat and dotted liberally with the droppings of the recently departed dairy herd it was an inhospitable home to flies, far from the gates and the shops they protected.

At the other end of the dais, were Aethelgren's two sons. Thrydwulf, as the youngest, sat at the end with Eadberct to his right. Eadberct was the nominal commander of the king's bodyguard, the only warriors permitted inside the walls while armed. He looked as his brother would after a life of comfort, his body softer, his face fuller, his armor burnished to a high gloss, every stud and clasp shining.

Eadberct found the prospect of conflict exciting, his own military experience being limited to the occasional ceremony and to security of the walls and gates. A man had neglected to declare a hatchet at the gate one time, when it was discovered by the guards he had been beaten mercilessly. It never happened again.

The anticipation of conflict was not the only thing keeping Eadberct on the edge of his seat, there was also the promise of reward. New lands and wealth were not terribly important to him, he stood to inherit his father's kingdom one day after all. The prize he coveted was seated between him and his father.

Gwenhwyver sat forlornly with her head bowed. She didn't eat or drink or participate in any conversation. She was merely there on display, dressed in a burgundy gown the king had

had made to showcase her beauty. She stifled a sob, denying them that small victory.

Aethelgren had offered the girl out as prize to whoever most distinguished themself in the coming conflict. With his father as sole judge, Eadberct had no doubt that she would be his when all was said and done. He imagined her by his side as a dutiful wife, perhaps not willingly at first but certain she would come around in time.

At the end of the table Wealdhere eyed the girl as well. He was a warrior. His men were well acquainted with battle. If the outcome of the battle was not enough to justify his claim to the prize, then a little intimidation should do the rest.

A fading bruise on her cheek peeking out from under her golden hair and the way she cowered when Aethelgren raised a hand to summon a servant spoke to her obedience. Wealdhere would gladly complete that training. He also imagined their future together, the look of fear in her eyes as he bent her to his will, her humiliation as he sought his pleasure, the feeling of power as she cried out for mercy. He was eager to get underway.

"How much longer do you plan on waiting for Loefric?" Wealdhere prodded his host. "My men are restless, eager to be on our way before they begin to smell as bad as the pasture in which they camp."

Aethelgren had been weighing this very question as they ate. The Mercians should have been here by now. He sent the girl away and got down to business. "I had hoped to have word at least by now," he said. "I will give him one more day, after that, it will be several days march before we meet the enemy, they may well be able to catch up."

"One day," echoed Wealdhere accepting the king's decision. He turned to his aide, Garrick, seated at a smaller table behind him, "Have the men ready to march on a moment's notice." When Garrick left the hall to ready his men, his counterpart's in the other armies and their lieutenants did the same.

With the subordinates out of the hall, it became quiet enough for the commanders to get together and discuss their route of advance, the likely places of resistance and tactics to use depending upon what kind of opposition they meet. The discussions continued, heated at times until they were interrupted when a scout burst in.

"There is a large force on the river road." The man rushed into the room letting the heavy oaken door slam shut behind him. He approached the dais and went down on one knee before continuing with his report. "I had been sent south toward Aquae Salis. I turned west to meet my captain at a crossroads along the river. I arrived just in time to see the last of his party killed in an ambush. My way back was blocked, so I doubled back to the west and then south and spotted their main column. Unfortunately this route took a long time, and I'm afraid there isn't much time. If they are not already approaching, they will certainly do so tomorrow."

Aethelgren stood as he usually did when he was under pressure. "You've done well," he told the scout, "Go to the kitchen and get yourself something to eat and I'll see that you are rewarded." When the soldier was gone, the king addressed his guests. "Well, gentlemen, it seems our foes have saved us from a long walk. Put all the men on alert, if they don't attack tonight, we'll go after them in the morning."

Try as he might, Jeff couldn't sleep. The full moon, high in the sky told him the dawn was still hours away. He looked over at Mairwen, marveling at how pretty she was in the moon glow. Careful not to wake her, go got up and walked through the silent camp.

The main camp was set behind the ridge, out of sight of the castle, but no other effort was made to hide their presence. Campfires dotted the area. Men sat around them, talking hushed tones and passing round the sharpening stones, honing every edge and point. On the other side of the ridge, Gryffud had set his own fire where he could keep an eye on the Saxons while he and the commanders could toss around ideas for the battle that was sure to come in the morning.

As Jeff approached the campfire, he noticed one face conspicuously missing. At the edge of the tree line, he spotted Arthwyr standing alone. His friend's gaze was locked on the distant castle until he turned at Jeff's approach. "We'll get her back," Jeff said.

"Yes, I believe we will, but…"

"But what?"

Arthwyr took a few steps toward the ridge so that he could see the camp area. "All these people, hundreds of them," he said. "They're here risking their lives. Doubtless, many of them will lose it. And for what? For one life I care about? I'll do anything for Gwenhwyver. But them, why should their lives be at risk? I asked them all to come here and because of that, tomorrow some of them will be dead."

"It's a heavy load to carry on one set of shoulders." Jeff put a hand on Arthwyr's shoulder. "It's true they came when you called. But they didn't just come because you did, or even to rescue Gwenhwyver. They were waiting for the call, for a leader. The wanted an excuse to face the Saxons and they needed someone to rally behind. They've been waiting for you all your life."

"For me?" Arthwyr shrugged Jeff's hand off. "All I want is to get Gwenhwyver back. I'm just a kid. What if I'm not a good leader? I could get them all killed."

"That's one reason you'll be a good leader, because you care about them." Jeff held Arthwyr by both his shoulders so he could look straight into his eyes. "Centuries from now, this island will have seen scores of kings come and go. Most of them will be forgotten by all by the most avid historian, but not all. One king will be remembered above all the others, his stories told in even the farthest land, the legendary King Arthwyr."

"Thank you, Marlin. Those are kind words. But you don't know that, you can't."

"That's the strangest part of all, Arthwyr. There is so much here I don't know about, but this I do. Fifteen hundred years from now, they will be telling stories about you. Some will be true, others, the purest fiction. Some will even mention your wizard,

Merlin." Jeff gave a theatrical bow that. "One thing they will all have in common is that King Arthur will be remembered as a king who did what was right. Now try to get some rest and I think I'll do the same."

Rhydderch was up before dawn. He looked forward to a day without walking. He had chosen his tree in the last light of day with an unobstructed view of the castle and its approaches. In the predawn darkness he made his way up slowly, carefully, picking his way through the branches. He wanted to be in position so that when the first light of the morning broke, he would know whether the enemy was stirring.

When the black of night turned to grey, Rhydderch could make out the camp on the road behind him. He looked on up the road to the ridge where his father's men straddled it and down to the bridge. Spaced out about fifty feet apart, in an arc surrounding each end of the bridge, were four piles of stones. Each pile was about waist high and even now, a few men were bringing in more.

The predawn light increased to the point where he could make out the castle itself and the fields beyond it. Rhydderch took out the spyglass and observed the enemy. The high stockade walls of the compound hid well any activity within, but in the fields to the north, he could see the encampments coming to life.

On the ground below waited Bryn, ready to relay Rhydderch's report to the commanders. "Go tell my father, the Saxons are up." He spoke loud enough to be heard below, but careful that his voice did not carry.

"Are they coming?" Bryn betrayed a hint of nervousness in her reply.

"Not yet. It's too early to tell."

Bryn ran along the ridge to Cynwrig's position. He stood with Arthwyr looking for signs of movement from the Saxons. Whether they were up early or just couldn't sleep, she couldn't tell. She passed on the information and returned to the tree. Arthwyr took the message in stride, "Alright then, let's get into positions," he said, rousing the men, "If they're up, we're up." He then turned back to Bryn, "Make sure all the commanders have gotten the word, then let me know if there are any new movements." The young girl ran off with a nod.

Back in the camp, Jeff gave Mairwen a long hug. Neither could find any words to say that didn't betray the danger of what the day likely had in store. He held up a brave front, trying not to convey his own apprehension. "Try not to worry," he said, but his reassurance did little to ease her tension.

"You make that sound easy." Mairwen's eyes welled up, but she held back the tears.

"I know it's not," Jeff wiped a tear away from the corner of her eye. "But there's an old expression that hasn't yet been invented, 'the die is cast'. There is no turning back now." He kissed her tenderly and walked away quickly, taking longer would only make it harder to go.

Mairwen stood watching him walk up the hill to join the other commanders and a tear finally made its way down her cheek. "He's right, you know," said her father's voice behind her. "You shouldn't worry yourself about him. He knows how to watch out for himself. He's very resourceful."

"But then I have to worry about you, too." Seeing her father preparing for battle was an even bigger shock, Burkellynn carried a battle ax and wore a bronze breastplate both of which had been liberated from the Irish. He was still struggling with the straps on the armor. "Here let me help you with that." She said, turning her father around. The leather straps were sodden with morning dew and even she had some trouble getting them tight enough.

The innkeeper sensed that she was fiddling with the restraints in the hope that she might delay him enough to miss the battle altogether, so he turned. "That'll do fine. We'll both be fine. I'll be in reserve, so I should be safe unless things really get out of hand, and if that's the case then we were doomed anyway, even if we stayed home." He kissed his daughter on the cheek, fought back a tear of his own and followed Jeff to the battle.

The world brightened bit by bit, enabling Rhydderch to see well enough to pick out details that had been hidden in the shadows. The ridgeline dropped off after the road crossed it, bit continued out to a rocky promontory that jutted into the bend in the river. There, under heavy camouflage of sapling branches, Rhydderch could see the shine of the brass cannon, placed where it would be safe and yet it could be brought to bear on either crossing point and most of the fields beyond.

From his vantage point high in the tree, the boy could see a few of Gryffud's men, spread through the forest along its winding trail. He trained his spyglass across the river to the camp of the enemy and watched them form up just as his own men were doing, then as the units came together, they began to march. The gate to the stockade swung open and a procession emerged. Lines of soldiers marched sharply and fell into a battle line forming across the lower island.

"They are coming!" he called down to Bryn. "They're forming up on the island and they are definitely coming!" Bryn ran off to spread the word. Arthwyr, Eldric, Owyn, Cynwrig, Devlin and Jeff congregated at the edge of the line, making last minute details when she came by.

Jeff stepped away from the group and placed a stoneware jug on the ground. In it he placed a thin strip of wood with a paper cylinder three inches long at one end which trailed a fuse. The bottle served as a stand, keeping the paper cylinder head pointing skyward protruding from its mouth. When he crouched down with a taper and lit the fuse, the bottle rocket hissed a gout of sparks, soared into the air and exploded with a bang, telling anyone within two miles that the battle was on.

Things began to move more quickly now. Latecomers rushed to join their positions Arthwyr and Cywrig's men formed up with their shields overlapping making a wall that looked impregnable. Daffyd and the other fishermen had beached their crafts and now came up to join in, accompanied by a young man.

"Father!"

Devlin swung about at the sound. "You made it!" he extolled. Father and son threw their arms around each other. "Did you reach Urien? Is he coming?"

Meical shook his head, bowing. "No. Urien has Saxon problems of his own, but he did pledge that he would keep those in the north too busy to come here."

Arthur shrugged off his disappointment. "We could have used Urien, that's too bad, but I can't say I'll miss those Saxons." The troops were all in position and the enemy's intent was clear, so he signaled the slingers to move forward.

Eadberct rode proudly beside his father as they led the first of the troops through the gate. Perched atop a fine black stallion, its hair gleaming in the morning sun, the mane and tail combed and braided, the young prince felt the very model of a military officer. His leather and bronze armor was polished and buffed to a high gloss, every buckle and clasp glistened. Behind him, his men marched in absolute precision, their uniforms fresh, their posture rigid, they made him proud to be their commander.

The column forded the stream to the lower island and took up a position on a bit of high ground from which they could observe what would soon be a battle ground. Eadberct's men took up station in front of their commander. Their primary function was the protection of the king.

A few paces behind the last of Eadberct's men was Thrydwulf. His chestnut stallion was massive, powerful and ill tempered. Thrydwulf's armor showed signs of wear and scars of battle as did that of his men. They moved as a unit, their posture more relaxed, their strides were the long easy paces that shortened a march. The only metal they carried which truly shone was along the edges of their blades. They were all business and their business was killing.

Behind Thrydwulf came Osfrid and then Cynebeald and finally Wealdhere. Together they formed a line of battle that stretched across the island from river to river. Only Wybert was absent. He and his men remained at the ready in their field above the north gate.

Eadberct looked up and down the lines of Saxon troops and then across the river to the ridge where their foes were gathering. "They look hardly worth the trouble, father," he jibed.

"Never underestimate your enemy, son" Aethelgren thought that today he might finally get through to the boy, a sense of what war was really about. A lesson his younger brother had grasped before he could ride. "There will be more beyond the ridge."

Eadberct started at the rebuke. He hoped to impress his father that he understood more than the king seemed to realize. "Then is this the best line of attack?" he asked. "After all, we will be vulnerable when we cross the bridge. Wouldn't it be better to take the bypass road where the ford is wider?"

"Good," The king was quick with the compliment after the reproof. "I'm glad to see you're thinking. The crossing would be much easier there, but then the road becomes a narrow track through a very dense wood. It's a perfect ambush point. Either way we will have to go through a choke point, so we have a choice, a mile of woods or fifty feet of bridge."

"I see your point," the prince considered how the enemy might use the terrain in light of his father's analysis. "Might they all just wait for us in the woods then?"

"I'm sure there will be men in there," Aethelgren agreed, "but they didn't come all this way to hide in the woods. In any case, Wybert will take the ford to secure our flank, then once we take the ridge, if they run to the woods they will be surrounded." The parched grass, brown in the summer heat caught his eye. "If we have to, we can burn them out."

Gwenhwyver sat alone in her cold dark room dressed in the burgundy gown. The room was a stark contrast to the finery she wore. The stone walls were unadorned and windowless, a single flickering oil lamp, the only illumination. The only furniture was an assortment of crates and kegs and a pile of straw for a bed. She waited with dread, the return of the Saxon king.

The Saxons were expecting a battle today, she had surmised that much, and when it was over, she would be given away. That the prospect was not good was not in question. The only question was just how bad it would be. She didn't think she would end up with Cynebeald or Thrydwulf, they both seemed indifferent, Eadberct wouldn't be so terrible she thought, even if he was a fool, he seemed harmless enough, but the notion of being taken off by the East Saxon king sent chills through her body. He was cruel and cold but even worse, it meant being taken far away. As long as she was here, she felt there was at least some possibility of rescue or escape, but once she was taken to far off Londunum, all hope would be lost.

Aethelgren continued his son's tutelage, discussing troop movements and other strategies while their forces took their positions. Cynebeald and Wealdhere joined them on the hill to coordinate the attack.

As the last of Wealdhere's troops filled out the line, some two dozen young men streamed down the hill across the river and ran over the bridge. They split into groups, each centered around one of the piles of stones and began loading a stone into the pocket of a sling, then whipping it around their heads and flinging it at the Saxons. The fire was sporadic and though deadly should one find its target, largely ineffectual, easily deflected by shield, but it did get their attention.

"Should we have the archers eliminate them, father?" Eadberct was incensed by the effrontery of the slingers.

"Not yet," his father nodded to Wealdhere who, in turn waved a command to his cavalry lieutenant. "At this distance against a dispersed target like that, a volley would be a waste of arrows."

Forty horsemen under Wealdhere's command thundered down on the slingers, whooping and hollering as they rode. A few slingers whipped off another shot as the riders bore down on them, then they ran over the bridge to the stone piles on the other side.

The horsemen pulled up short of the bridge and circled, sling stones landing in their midst and others whipping past.

Under the cover of the cavalry charge, Aethelgren's archers moved forward. They split into two groups and took up station on either side of the road. The slingers across the stream launched their missiles at the new target until a few well placed bow shots put two of them on the ground. The remaining slingers, helping the wounded, moved out of range of the deadly arrows.

The bridge was secure. The slingers were out of range. So, Aethelgren ordered the attack to begin. Osfrid had the honor of leading followed by Cynebeald. "Shouldn't Thrydwulf have the honor of meeting the enemy first?" Eadberct asked his father.

"If the victory is easy, there will be little honor in it," the king leaned closer to keep his counsel private," and many more to come for your brother as we move west. If it is bloody, as I expect, the honor will be hardly worth the losses. And if the first wave is unsuccessful the honors will be to your brother as he runs to their recue." He straightened and pointed toward the bridge as he went on to explain the tactics of his plan, as if that was the subject all along. "This is the point of danger," he turned in his saddle to wave to the guard at the gate, "if these Celts are smart, they will attack before our main force can be across. The archers will discourage that, but in case that isn't sufficient, I have a little surprise for them."

The stockade gate swung open and a dozen soldiers emerged pushing a catapult. The war engine was of Roman design, left behind when the empire pulled out of the island and discovered by the next invaders and maintained like a prized antique. After some difficulty crossing the stream despite the low water, they fell in line between Thrydwulf and Osfrid. The heavily armed and armored infantry marched down the road and over the bridge.

At the far side of the span, Cynebeald's men turned right and formed a new battle line protecting the approach and Osfrid's men began to do the same to the left. The catapult was pushed to a position on the bank of the stream to one side of the bridge and its crew began the process of cranking back and loading it. It was capable of launching hundred pound boulders and smashing down castle walls when needed, but today the bowl would be filled with dozens of two to three pound stones and bricks.

The heavy infantry stood shoulder to shoulder, shields overlapping, swords at the ready. The two commanders' forces extending the line further and Thrydwulf's men moved up to guard their flank along the stream. Still there was no response from the Celts at the top of the hill. "I find it hard to believe they've come all this way to throw a few stones," Aethelgren commented. "Soon we will have too many men across to be stopped. They should have attacked by now."

"Perhaps they lack the courage." Eadberct suggested.

"Do not doubt their courage as individuals," the king insisted, "But it may be that whoever is in command over there lacks the fortitude to commit the lives of others." He barked out a command and an aide waved a banner. In the fields above the north gate Wybert urged his men forward. "It's time we secure the flank. Wybert's men will hold the ford in case they decide to go around us once we are committed here."

"Wealdhere's men will be our reserve. Should the enemy flank us they can easily shift to Wybert's aid and if not, they will join the main force and lead the pursuit once they break." This would also put them in position to claim the best lands once they reach Celtic territory and the old king knew that would appeal to Wealdhere's greed.

Eadberct was quick to pick up on the fact that only his men were now without a role. He couldn't see his father awarding him the prize of Gwenhwyver if he didn't participate. He allowed his annoyance to creep into his voice. "What about my men father? Are we to just stand here, looking good?"

Aethelgren turned a shade of red even his son rarely saw. "When I am gone you will be king," he bellowed. "Learn one thing now if you learn anything. You are not some gallant Lieutenant proving his heroism on a field of honor. If your army is victorious, but you are killed you have lost. Your men have a job to do, and that is to protect their king!" The king turned his back on his son and signaled the horsemen to move up through the infantry.

"There're more of them coming up the other road," Rhydderch shouted, no longer concerned how far his voice carried, their presence was clearly no longer a secret. Jeff placed another rocket in his jug/launcher. As the second rocket rose into the air it arced upstream and exploded high over the bypass road. From the treetop, Rhydderch could see Gryffud's men emerge from the woods to face the new threat.

Jeff, Daffyd and Timothy pulled away the branches concealing the cannon and prepared to fire. Timothy took a linen bag with a pre-measured charge of powder and stuffed it down the barrel. Daffyd followed that with an iron cannon ball and rammed it securely into place. Jeff thrust a wire into the touch hole pricking open the bag and then primed the hole with powder.

From the Saxon line, the horsemen made their way to the bridge. The foot soldiers crossing stepped aside making way for the horsemen to pass through. Jeff sighted the cannon carefully and looked back to Arthwyr and Cynwrig who both nodded readiness. When the first of the riders emerged though the lines, Jeff lowered a smoldering ember to the powder and fired.

The Saxons shuddered at the horrendous sound, horses panicked and reared. The ball struck the catapult at the base of the arm, shattering it. With the release of the tension, the arm sprang back at the men twisting the reel. Splinters from the timbers flew in every direction, impaling those nearby.

In a copse of trees downstream, Wahlgren hid with his hunters and bowmen from every town along the way. In his hand he held four strings. Jeff's cannon blast was his signal to reel them in. He gently pulled in the slack and saw them rise as the tension increased. They ran down into the stream bed and then across the ground to the piles of stones. The hunter took a single strand in his right hand and yanked it.

Inside the waist high pile of stones, the end of the string was tied to an iron file which was held tight to a flint. At Wahlgren's tug, the flint showered sparks that ignited a stoneware jug filled with powder. Hundreds of baseball sized stones were hurled by the blast to devastating effect, especially among the king's archers at the rear of the pack. The hunter repeated the action again and again and again, with each explosion the Saxon panic increased along with the death toll

At the base of the bluff, well hidden by the laurel bushes there, Eldric waited with his men. Having supplied the files for the deadly mines, he insisted on the honor of setting some of them off. Seconds after the first detonation, he tugged at strings of his own, setting off the stone piles on their own side of the river

The explosions surrounded the Saxons, acrid smoke filled the air, choking them, stinging eyes. Stones tore through bodies close to the explosions and rained down on those farther away. Horses threw their riders and trampled foot soldiers, their screams adding to the terror, bodies were thrown over the bridge rail, down to the stream below.

Across the stream, the Saxons facing the Celtic onslaught had no time for panic, no matter how terrifying the explosions or their aftermath. A sword point at your throat will always take precedence. But in the rear, things were different. Those archers not killed in the blast fled in terror, followed closely by the foot soldiers on the approach to the bridge.

Thrydwulf saw them turn and spat in disgust. "Cowards! Afraid of a charletan's parlor tricks."

His aide leaned toward him and said quietly, for the two men, alone, "Those parlor tricks just killed a hundred of our men."

"Then we'd better put a stop to him quickly," Thrydwulf countered. He shouted out a command to his men. "Kill any man who tries to flee!" He drew his own sword and took down the first archer he could reach. His men were seasoned fighters all. Their training took over, surmounting their fears. Faced with death in either direction, the soldiers turned again and headed for the bridge.

Daffyd swabbed out the cannon and Timothy pushed in another charge to reload. This time, instead of a ball, they used canister. Marble sized iron pellets filled a tin can that was just strong enough to hold them together until they left the gun's barrel, they then spread like shotgun shot. Jeff concentrated his fire on the rear of the pack.

Cynwrig led the charge down the hillside, with Arthwyr close behind, their men's shouts drowning out all but the explosions themselves. Eldric and his men emerged from the laurels to come in hard against the right flank and Owyn and his woodsmen did the same on the left.

The attackers slammed into a Saxon army that was in complete disarray. No semblance of formation still existed, many of the Saxon fighters were unaware even that they were being attacked until it was too late, but many others were professionals and they regrouped to face the screaming Celts.

Cynrwig's men met head on with the best fighters the Saxons had to offer, who, despite their losses, kept their heads and met the onslaught with their swords. The long shafted halberds that Cynwrig and his men carried kept the Saxons off guard. They stood shoulder to shoulder, keeping their tight formation like a giant porcupine advancing on the Saxon line. The short Saxon seax was no match.

Arthwyr's sword slashed right and left as he waded into Osfrid's men. Taking every advantage from the disorientation caused so far he and his men kept their foes off balance. Though the Saxons still far outnumbered the Celts in the battle, their broken formation and separation by the bridge meant that Arthwyr and his men faced them as if theirs was the larger force. No sooner would Saxon meet Celt, shield to shield and weapon to weapon, than an unseen blade from the left or right or even the rear would cut the Saxon down. His sword edge bloodied, the young smith penetrated the enemy deeply. He found no enjoyment in taking enemy lives, but knew they gave him no choice.

The Saxon bridge head was surrounded and being pushed back regardless of their still superior numbers. On the bridge there was confusion as some men pushed through the mass of bodies to get to the front and others worked just as desperately to flee. From the trees upstream, Wahlgren's archers unleashed their arrows, picking the remaining horsemen first as targets and the cannon fired as quickly as Jeff and Timothy could reload.

Devlin and Burkellynn moved up to the ridge line when the others moved down to the bridge. Devlin led the reserve force, and it was his job to plug any holes that developed as the fight progressed. On the long walk from Trymme he and Burkellynn had become fast friends, as fathers of girls, they found a good deal of common ground. Burkellynn tried to put himself in his friend's shoes, had it been Mairwen that was taken, he wasn't sure he could have held up nearly as well.

"Burkellynn! Devlin! The stream bed!" Rhydderch shouted from the treetop. Some of the Saxons across the river had broken away from the pack and sought to bypass the bridge by crossing the gully further downstream.

Devlin led the charge with an overhand wave. Made up of the oldest, youngest and the weakest of the fighters and those who had joined most recently and therefore had no chance to train, the reserve force was held back with good reason. They were to be committed only in emergency. They streamed down the hill and met the Saxons as they scrambled up out of the ravine. Standing on solid ground to fight men who still needed their sword hands for balance climbing the steep slope more than compensated for any shortcomings. The Saxons at the bottom reversed direction, glad to have the streambed between them.

Gryffud led his men out of the woods and down the plain to the ford to meet Wybert. For every two men in his line, Wybert had three. "Tighten up the line," he ordered. The men closed ranks until they were shoulder to shoulder and moved on. When a hundred yards separated the two armies Gryffud called a halt, but the Saxons kept coming.

Every other man in Gryffud's command carried a rocket like those Jeff used as signals but instead of a jug to send the rockets aloft, they used a bipod that would send the missiles just a few feet off the ground. Each rocket carrier was paired with a man carrying a coal from the night's fire.

Wybert's men splashed through the ankle deep water of the ford and climbed the bank beyond and then, as one, they increased their pace. Gryffud waited until they were fifty yards away and coming fast to yell, "Fire!" In a fury of smoke and shrieking fire, the rockets arced into the oncoming Saxon hoard and exploded in their midst in a deafening cacophony. There were some minor injuries, but what the missiles really sowed was confusion and fear.

Obscured by the smoke, Gryffud's men attacked immediately. They crashed into the now broken line with a savage ferocity. Axes cleaved flesh and rent shields. Disarray was a great equalizer but the Saxons reformed their line and their superior numbers pushed Gryffud back toward the woods. The Celts fought heroically losing ground, slowly but inexorably. Behind the enemy line, their commander rode up and down, exhorting his men back into formation to press their advantage.

Aethelgren' mood grew fouler by the minute, as his battle plan withered. He gave the order for Thrydwulf to move ahead. The Saxon's best troops moved confidently into the fray. When he reached the bridge, Thrydwulf turned to his top commander, "Take your men across, but don't try to go straight ahead. On your right flank, you'll be facing woodsmen's axes instead of swords or spears. They're the weak spot in the line."

As the men went ahead, the young prince turned his attention to the chaos on the bridge itself. Before he could hope to put enough pressure on the enemy to break their line, he first had to get them over the bridge and past the deadly blasts of the cannon. The task was made more difficult still by a hideous tangle of the dead bodies of men and horses. "You men," he ordered, "Get that horse's carcass over the side." He stood at the crest of the span, directing traffic, pushing his men into the melee as quickly as possible. Already, the surge began to have its effect, pushing the Celts back.

Thrydwulf took one of his captains aside. "Get down into the streambed and join up with the men there. Take them downstream around the bend. The bank there is lower and more easily climbed. You should be able to reopen that flank there.

From his vantage point on the promontory, Jeff watched the battle progress with alarm. The little cannon was becoming dangerously hot. That was just as well because the canister was all gone and only a handful of cannonballs remained. While the effects of his charges and the cannon had initially been devastating, the Saxons had recovered. Eventually they would move enough men over the bridge to break through.

"Timothy, "Daffyd yelled, pointing down the stream bed. "They're trying to get around us. We've got to get them before they get around the bend." He pushed the gun around to bear on the offending party, but there wouldn't be time.

The situation was desperate, but Jeff had one last trick up his sleeve. Below the cannon, hidden in the laurels was one more Celt. With a brown bandana on her head lest her bright red hair betray her, Bryn held the last string. "Now Bryn! Pull it now!" Jeff shouted.

Bryn reeled in the slack on the twine that led to the last, and largest of the black powder charges. A whiskey keg of powder was wedged into the spot where the arch of the bridge met the spillway of the dam. The explosion blew the span off its base, taking forty men with it. Stones from the bridge were hurled into the backs of the Saxons fighting the Celts, killing or maiming dozens more.

The blast went into the dam with equal effect, tearing a breach out of it as wide as the stream itself. A wall of water surged down the streambed. The men seeking to flank the Celts were swept along until they were well out into the Severn.

Beyond the distraction and disorientation of the fireworks, there was another effect. After the roar of so many explosions at point blank range and over the ringing of swords and axes and the screams of men, the Saxon army didn't hear the pounding of hooves or the exhortations of their commander as Wybert tried to warn them and turn some of them to face the oncoming rush of Welsh cavalry.

Cadeyrn and his horsemen had worked their way around the castle as far as the by-pass road. When the second signal rocket went up they crossed the main channel of the Severn then followed Wybert's men across the island at a distance and went into a gallop at the sound of the fireworks. Now they charged right into the backs of the unsuspecting Saxons.

Caught between the anvil of Gryffud's infantry and the hammer of the charging horsemen the Saxons were slaughtered. A few escaped and managed to run upstream or into the woods, most never knew what happened.

With their ranks diminished and no new reinforcements over the bridge, the Saxons at the forefront were outnumbered. The Celts, no longer fearing a flanking attack committed every man to the fight. Their foes were soon surrounded and defeated but now they were cut off from the Castle and the rest of its defenders. Arthwyr called out to Burkellynn. "Bring up the ladders and lay them across the opening in the bridge." The ladders had been made to scale the palisade once they were ready to attack the castle itself. At twenty feet, they would easily span the gap. "And lay the bodies of the Saxon dead to fill between the rungs. They may be of some use after all."

When Thrydwulf's men saw what the Celts were doing, they streamed back to the bridge to stop them. This time the bottle neck would work in their favor. The met the men coming over fiercely, pushing them back onto the ladder where footing would be as much a problem as the fight itself.

With the flank secured, Gryffud and Cadeyrn moved on to join the main battle. They found a spot where the ditch was easily crossed. Gryffud attacked the rear of the forces at the bridge. Many of the Saxons had already had enough and were streaming away in droves. They were ignored. The horsemen charged headlong into those still fighting. Cadeyrn brought his men alongside to face the still uncommitted reserves.

On the bluff overlooking the battlefield the last of the canisters had been expended so Jeff reloaded with an iron ball. He watched Cadeyrn's cavalry tear into the rear of the Saxons at the bridge so he moved on to other targets down range. Wealdhere's men wheeled to attack the horsemen but hesitated when Gryffud's men climbed out of the creek bed and turned again to confront the infantry first.

The cannon roared once again and the cannon ball spouted dirt from the field between the two lines and skipped along like a stone thrown across a pond. It touched down again a dozen yards in front of the East Saxon line then went through half a dozen men like a bowling ball through pins on an alley.

After watching the carnage at the bridge, this was all many of them needed. Nearly a third of the line turned on their heels and began running, others hesitated at Gryffud's advance. When another round struck the line further down, killing three, the line melted altogether.

Aethelgren had been crossing back and forth between horror and rage, saw the exodus and shouted to Wealdhere. "Where are they going?" The horse fidgeted under him, sensing his anger and he spat on the ground. "They haven't even faced the enemy yet! Cowards! They're leaving without a fight! Stop them!"

Wealdhere wasn't about to take the abuse. He brought his own horse around and faced Aethelgren. "I probably couldn't stop them if I tried, but I won't. I came here to share in your victory and its spoils not your slaughter. This battle is over." The younger man spurred his horse and rode off after his men, not to halt them, but to join them.

The Saxons at the bridge were surrounded and now had no more hope of rescue. Beaten and bloodied, their will was broken, the situation could not be more desperate, they began laying down their arms.

Gryffud wheeled his men to face the king and advanced in the hope of ending the battle once and for all. Cadeyrn's cavalry joined them on the left. Aethelgren reigned in his horse and commanded "Open the gates!" and led his bodyguard back into their stronghold.

Cynebeald watched the two kings ride off with distaste. He wasn't sure who was more disgusted with, Aethelgren for bringing this on in the first place, or Wealdhere for abandoning the men. His own forces were caught in the vice at the bridge and Wealdhere left them in the lurch as much as he had Aethelgren's. He finally decided it didn't matter, they were both beneath his contempt. He spurred his horse and rode off.

The gates slammed shut as the last of Eadbercts men ran to the safety inside, chased by the jeers and taunts of Gryffud and his men. Arthwyr and Cynwrig met Cadeyrn coming over the bridge the other way.

The last of the Saxons had either laid down their arms or fled and the victors went wild cheering and congratulating each other. Arthwyr cut the celebration short. "We've done well here! But we have not finished." Gryffud and Cynwrig gestured to the men to calm down. "The Saxon army is beaten, but we came to rescue Gwenhwyver and she is still captive. We cannot rest until the castle is taken and she is safe."

Chapter 13 – The Castle

Cadeyrn and his cavalry retraced their path back around the castle to ford the Severn and guard against the king's escape. As bad as it was for Gwenhwyver to be held in the castle it would be worse if they got away and went deeper into Saxon territory.

Gryffud held the road from the north gate. Eldric's men stopped off in the woods to select and cut a tree to be used as a battering ram and joined Gryffud. The rest of the army gathered at the main gate. The cannon was brought up the road and positioned on the river bank, right across the ford from the gate.

Devlin wasn't sure which was making him sweat more, worry for his daughter or the heat of the sun. For Burkellynn, it was the sun. So much had happened and it was only midday. He tugged again at the leather straps of the breastplate. They seemed too tight, having dried in the summer heat. Perhaps the leather had shrunk.

On the sound of the cannon's first roar, Eldric and his men began pounding at the north gate with the ram. The two gates gave way within seconds of each other. The two forces streamed into the enclosure ready for the fight to resume, only to find it empty. Most of the king's body guard had fled into the castle, those that didn't had left altogether at the first shot.

Inside the compound the leaders met to discuss the next move while men went through the shops in search of any defenders that might be hiding there. Some of the shops were empty, the shopkeepers having left with the defenders. None of them hid any soldiers

"The castle keep will be more difficult." Gryffud looked up at the stone structure atop the hill that dominated the compound. It was an imposing sight. "And then the doorway is the only way in. It'll be the bridge all over again, only we'll be the ones squeezing through the narrow gap. We can do it, I'm sure, but it won't be easy."

"We can get the cannon up the hill, I'm sure, "said Jeff, gauging the steep incline, "But the archers will be a problem."

A woman came out of the bakery carrying a basket of sweet cakes, cookies and tarts. She walked up to the men as they were discussing strategy and started handing out her treats. "Bless you all," she said, "thank you so much." When she came to Arthwyr she stopped.

"Arthwyr?" The old woman threw her arms around the young man who didn't know how to react. "Is it really you Arthwyr? We've been hearing rumors, but I couldn't believe they were true." Holding him by the shoulders, she looked him over from head to toe. "It is you," she decided, "You look just like your father." She rummaged through the basket and pulled out an apple tart and gave it to Arthwyr.

The woman did seem vaguely familiar, but he couldn't imagine how that could be. Arthwyr took a bite from the sweet. It was wonderful. Perhaps because it was so out of place and unexpected, coming in the middle of this day, but he could not remember eating anything that tasted so good. And then he did. He remembered happy times as a child, of sneaking out to get treats like this. "You do know me, don't you?"

"Yes! Since you were a little boy."

"I lived here?"

"Yes." the baker pointed toward the keep. "Up there actually."

"I remember sneaking down here to see you." Memories came flooding back and he had an idea. "Gentlemen!" he called out to his commanders, "There may be another way in."

The bakery was nestled into the side of the hill crowned by the castle keep. At the rear of the bakery Arthwyr entered a cool storage room that was dug right into the hillside. He moved some containers of lard out of the way and opened a panel revealing a passage. The tunnel was crisscrossed with cobwebs and infested with who knows what kind of vermin, but was open and seemed intact.

Arthwyr led the way on his hands and knees up the tunnel with a dozen of his best men, along with Devlin and Burkellynn.

Rhydderch followed behind them, ready to scurry back down and let the others know when they were in place. Most carried oil lamps to see by, but Arthwyr used a torch as much to burn away cobwebs and scare off any inhabitants of this dark place as to see by.

The passage led upwards, sometimes at a steep angle as it led to the basements of the castle atop the hill. Arthwyr could barely imagine a child of the age he had been, negotiating this tunnel alone. At least, though he would have done it fully erect.

Crouched over, the men worked their way up the narrow incline, waddling like so many ducks. Burkellynn thought this was a job for a much younger man, but wanted to be along to lend moral support to his friend Devlin. He kept pace the best he could, considering he was scraping the walls on both sides, his armor felt tighter than ever across his chest, and something must have bitten him, because his whole left arm felt funny. He pushed on without a word.

Finally, he reached a doorway similar to the one they came through in the bakery. Arthwyr pushed against the panel covering the exit, but it wouldn't budge. He handed the torch to Devlin, and tried again, putting his weight behind it. There was a grating sound from the other side and the door opened a crack. Arthwyr peered through the opening, but he couldn't see a thing, only blackness.

Confident the Saxons weren't waiting for them on the other side, he shoved the door again as hard as he could. This time it swung wide, the grating sound was accompanied by a loud thump and a chorus of rattles. Quickly, Arthwyr re-closed the panel and listened, expecting sounds of alarm, but none came.

Opening the panel again, Arthwyr entered, lighting the room with his torch. They were in a store room in the castle's basement. Scattered about the floor were a number of small kegs, the source of all the noise. One was filled with oil but, with the harvest only two months away, the rest were empty. He was glad it wasn't November or they'd never have force the door open.

As the assault team emerged from the tunnel, word was

passed down to Rhydderch, "They are in position!"

Jeff worked his way up the hill to the castle keep carrying a jug filled with gunpowder. The cannon sat unused at the bottom of the hill. They had reasoned that while they could drag it up the hill with some effort, the recoil would send it back down, much to the misfortune of anyone unlucky enough to be at the bottom when it arrived.

He expected a hail of arrows at any time. Wahlgren and his archers were there to return fire when it came in the hopes of suppressing it. When he made it to the door without misfortune, he laid the charge against the door and took cover. Gryffud's and Arthur's men would lead the charge with swords and axes, Cynwrig's halberds were too cumbersome for the close quarters. The men lined along the stone walls of the keep, pressed closely and waited for the door to blow.

Aethelgren ran around the great hall ordering men about, preparing to defend against the assault that he knew was imminent. Men were carrying anything heavy that they could find and barricading the door. A pile of furnishings, crates and food barrels mounded behind the massive oak door.

"Get some archers up on the parapet." He ordered his son who didn't seem to be doing anything.

Eadberct had done about all there was to do, given what there was to work with. "There are no archers," he explained. "None that made it back here, anyway."

The king was desperate, looking for any way he might avoid the wrath of the horde at the gate. Then it came to him, he had a ticket out. The girl. He could still bargain her for his life. He was running for the stairs to bring her up when the door blew apart.

Arthwyr extinguished the torch and the lamps were put aside before they ventured out of the storeroom. He opened the door a crack and peered out to be sure no one was outside it. There were two storerooms on this level off a short corridor and a stair case that led up to the private chambers, they would search this level first and then move on up to the upper floor.

As soon as Arthwyr was in the corridor, he understood why all the noise they had made hadn't aroused anyone's curiosity, from the noises coming down the stairs, it was bedlam up above. Quietly they began their search.

The Saxons had returned, so the battle must be over. They would be coming for her soon. Gwenhwyver could hear sounds, some far away and muffled, others closer by. It hadn't been very long so things must have gone well. She couldn't hear what anyone was saying, but from the volume, it was a raucous celebration.

A string of noises came from the other storeroom across the hall. Somebody rummaging around knocked a bunch of things over. They are probably drunk. Perhaps, she thought, if she could make an escape, she might be able to make use of the confusion and get away.

She looked around the room for anything she might use for a weapon. The barrels were too heavy, she could barely lift them and the crates were even worse. The lamp was the best she could do. She blew out the flickering flame and the room went dark as a cave. Holding the lamp above her head, she hid behind the door and waited for it to open.

She didn't have long to wait, the door opened slowly, the man trying to find her in the dark crept in. The moment he was clear of the door, she brought the lamp down hard on his head. The armored figure fell to his knees, dazed by the blow, but recovered and straightened. Gwenhwyuver wasted no time, she rushed out the door right into the grasp of another man. She struggled to break free, but his grip was firm though oddly gentle.

"Take it easy, Gwenhwyver." The voice was soft, not wanting to be overheard by the wrong people, and reassuring. "It's me. It's alright." It was her father.

Gwenhwyver fell into her father's arms, tears streaming down her face. "Father! How did you get here?"

"I had a lot of help," Devlin explained. "Apparently you have a lot of very good friends, particularly the one you just gave such a headache."

In the shadows of the room, Gwenhwyver could finally make out the face of the man she had hit with the lamp. It was Arthwyr. "Arthwyr!" She squealed, throwing her arms around his neck. "Are you all right?"

"I'll be alright," Arthwyr shook the cobwebs out, "I'm glad for my helmet." The young couple embraced wordlessly until a thunderous explosion shook the building. "We have to go! Devlin, take her into the other storeroom and bar the door. Open it for no one but me. If anyone else does come to the door, take her down the tunnel."

Devlin brought his daughter into the other room as Arthwyr led the rest of the men up the stairs and met Aethelgren coming the other way. The Saxon king wheeled at the sight of them and fled up the steps with Arthwyr on his heels.

The corridor opened on the great room where a battle for the doorway was underway. Aethelgren skirted the fighting and ran for the huge fireplace with Arthwyr and Burkellynn in pursuit while the others attacked those defending the doorway from the rear.

In the fireplace, the Saxon king took the steps two at a time up to the parapet. When the stairs opened onto the balcony, Aethelgren sought his escape, looking for a place where he might make a jump, finding none. Even if he did manage to land without breaking a leg from this height, he would tumble all the way down the hill to the mob waiting below.

Burkellynn tried to keep up with Arthur with limited success. When the king ducked into the massive fireplace he thought they had him trapped but when he reached it himself and saw the stairs leading up he understood. Gasping for breath, he began his ascent. The stairs curved up and around the inside of the chimney to a landing, then there was a door out onto the parapet or a series of iron rungs climbing straight up to the chimney top. He hoped they had taken the door.

The innkeeper huffed his way up the stairs when, just before the doorway, he felt a sharp pain piercing his heart. His last thought was that, for all the trouble, his armor had failed him. The moment the door was blown, Celtic troops stormed through the breach. Eadberct's men resisted at first, but once Arthwyr's men attacked them from behind as well the fight went out of them and the parade force was overwhelmed quickly.

When Jeff entered the great hall the fighting was over and the celebration begun. Gryffud led a small detachment in a search for any hidden resisters. "Where is Arthwyr?" He asked a fighter from Arthwyr's unit.

"Last I saw of him he was heading toward the fireplace."

Jeff didn't like the sound of that. He checked the primer charge of his pistol and went after the youth. He bounded up the stairs, slowing at the sight of the body at the landing. His heart sank when he saw it was Burkellynn. The man was the closest he had to a father in this world and now, with his marriage to Mairwen, had become one in fact. He took a moment to look over the innkeeper's body but found no sign of injury, nor did he find any sign of life, but he couldn't dwell there. With a heavy heart, he moved on.

When Arthwyr emerged onto the parapet, sword in hand, the King drew his own and strode across the stone balcony. "You must be the young Pendragon I keep hearing about." Aethelgren swished his blade left and right, testing its balance. "Your battle here is won and yet you risk your life."

"I like to finish what I start."

"The lesson here is one young puppies seem reluctant to learn, and I am eager to teach it." The two men circled, looking for their opening. "My battle here is lost, but you offer me a chance to take some victory from it." The Saxon took a step to the right, windmilled his blade, and in one motion, attacked. The clash of blades rang out as Aethelgren pressed his furious assault. Arthwyr fended him off desperately, feeling the jarring impact with each blow he deflected. The Saxon blade swished through the air an inch from Arthwyr's face, but missing, giving him the opportunity to go on the offensive.

    Aethelgren's experience came through as he backpedaled while parrying Arthwyr's best attempts, then sidestepped and advanced again. Now Arthwyr blocked first one blow, then another and locked blades with the older man on the third. The pair struggled in a test of strength and wills. Aethelgren stomped a heavy boot down, intending to smash Arthwyr's foot. Arthwyr had just lifted it to correct his stance and the blow glanced off without damage.

    Aethelgren lunged forward again, testing Arthwyr's defenses with practiced, precise strokes. When Arthwyr launched a counter attack, the king caught Arthwyr's blade on his own, moved in closer and butted his helmeted head into Arthwyr's. Arthwyr gave him an elbow to the jaw to break them apart again.

    The Saxon was the bigger man by several inches and outweighed Arthwyr handily, but youth and years as a blacksmith gave Arthwyr the edge. As the King bore down with his weight on the sword blade, he withdrew a dagger he had hidden, tucked behind his back, but Arthwyr was pushing off before he could plunge it home.

    The king brought his blade around in a wide arc aimed at Arthwyr's neck which the younger man ducked easily, but the Saxon was ready for that. He smashed the pommel of his sword into the side of Arthwyr's face with a powerful back hand stroke. The coppery taste of blood in Arthwyr's mouth told him he had to end this soon. He was younger and stronger but while he had been fighting the Saxon army at the bridge, the king had been sitting effortlessly astride his horse.

    Aethelgren came slashing in with another series of blows that pushed Arthwyr back until he was against the wall and their blades locked again, lower this time, across their chests. With greater leverage, Arthwyr was able to throw the king off and send him to the end of the balcony, off balance.

    Arthwyr saw his opportunity and rushed in to take advantage, but in his haste, he stumbled on the flagstones and went down, catching himself on the pommel of his sword. Grinning at the youth's brashness, Aethelgren reacted swiftly with an overhand arc aimed at the younger man's neck, but no sooner did he step forward to deliver the blow, than Arthwyr, sliding forward on one knee, thrust the still upturned sword up under the lip of the kin's breastplate in the move he had practiced so many times in the old roman barracks. He drove the point deep, through muscle and organs until it struck bone at the rear of the ribcage.

The old King's face registered surprise, then pain, and finally panic as Arthwyr's weapon ran him through. His own sword clattered across the stones while his blood ran hot and sticky over Arthur's hand to the floor. His eyes fluttered, his knees buckled and he was dead.

Jeff arrived as the old king collapsed to the floor. Arthwyr wiped his sword blade and hands on the king's tunic then stepped back and steadied himself against the stone wall. He was exhausted both physically and emotionally.

"Are you alright?" Jeff asked, the concern clear in his voice.

Arthwyr, still working hard to control his breathing, simply bobbed his head.

Jeff propped his last rocket against the stone balustrade. Found some dried moss in the wall to use as tinder, then emptied the flash pan of his pistol over it and struck the flint, instantly flaring it into flame. Gingerly, he picked up the moss and offered it to Arthwyr. "Would you like to do the honor?" Arthwyr took the moss and lit the fuse, sending the rocket soaring skyward, the signal to all outside the walls that the battle was won.

Rhydderch went to the cellar and found Devlin and Gwenhyver. They all reached the great room about the same time as Cadeyrn. With each new arrival the cheers surged anew. When Arthwyr and Jeff emerged from the hearth the roar reached new heights. Arthwyr waited for their enthusiasm to wane, then announced, "Aethelgren is no more!" The crowd responded with whoops and hollers, cheers and stomping feet. "The Saxon menace in this part of Britain is at its end."

The celebrations went on undiminished until Gryffud and his men came out from the kitchen with a captive. "We found this hiding in a barrel of flour." The crowd bellowed and reeled with laughter at the sight of Eadberct. His finely polished leather armor was completely dusted and his face and hair were powdered white. With his hands bound behind him, he was prodded forward at the point of a sword to the delight of the jeering Celts.

"What are we to do with this one?" Gryffud demanded from the crowd.

The mob responded with more jeers and taunts and the occasional anonymous "hang him." Eadberct became even more nervous until Gwenhwyver spoke out. "He can have my old room." The crowd showed their appreciation of that irony with another round of laughter.

"That would be fitting," Arthwyr agreed. "We'll hold him while we see if any other Saxon lord wants to pay his ransom, if not, we'll put him to work in the fields."

The celebration would go on well into the night, but it held no attraction for Jeff so, after a few congratulations, he got help loading Burkellynn's body onto a wagon, hitched the cannon's horses to it and headed for the camp. The mood at the camp was tempered by the harsh realities of the fight. When the battle had moved on to the castle those left behind saw to the casualties at the bridge and the ford. Still, the signal that all was over was welcomed with both joy and relief.

Mairwen spotted Jeff as soon as he crested the ridge and ran to meet him on the road, he ran into her arms, leaving the wagon behind. She threw her arms around him and showered him with kisses. "I was so worried," she said, holding him desperately. "I'm so glad you're alright."

Jeff stood, looking into her bright blue eyes, trying to find the words. Before he could say anything, she knew something was wrong. His face, normally a mirror on his sunny disposition, belied the news. "What is it?" she asked. Still unable to speak, he led her to the wagon and her father's body.

Mairwen clung to Jeff, tears rolling down her cheeks, "He promised," she sniffed. "He said he was just going to be in reserve unless thing turned badly. He promised he wouldn't be in any real danger."

"He kept his promise." Jeff gave her as much comfort as he could. "The Saxons didn't kill him."

"But? Then how?"

"I looked him over when I found him," Jeff explained, "There wasn't a mark on him. It looks like his heart just gave out." It was small comfort, but comfort nonetheless.

"We have to take him home." Mairwen insisted, "We can't leave him here, so far away."

"I think we can do that," Jeff allowed. He looked around until he spotted Bryn, not far away. "Bryn!" He called out, "See if you can find Daffyd for me, we're going to need a ride."

Burkellynn's body was wrapped in a sheet and loaded onto Daffyd's boat for the journey back to Llewellynn. They tacked their way down river, using the current when it helped and the wind when they could. The little craft entered the open water of the channel as the sun began to set. They sailed on through the night, taking turns guiding the boat by the light of the moon.

Daffyd took over the tiller in the early morning, in time to navigate the narrow approaches to their home harbor. The moment their sail entered the river mouth, it had been spotted. By the time they rounded the last bend, a crowd had already gathered in spite of the hour.

In the cool of the morning, Jeff wore his wool flannel shirt. The bright plaid patter stood out on the deck of the sailboat like a flag making it clear to the crowd ashore that this was no routine supply mission. As Daffyd maneuvered the craft into the dock, Jeff threw a line to those waiting and the boat was quickly tied fast.

With Father Ewan at his side, Caradog spoke for the town. "What news do you bring?"

Jeff stepped ashore, then casually helped Mairwen do the same, allowing the suspense to build before he spoke. "The battle is won!" He let the appreciative roar of the crowd subside before he added, "Aethelgren is dead and Gwenhwyver is safe. The castle is taken."

Caradog and Father Ewan did what they could to help Jeff and Daffyd as they unloaded their cargo. The townspeople's jubilation ebbed as they realized, one by one that it was a body they carried, bringing home the reality that victory comes at a price. Jeff found Bryggyd's ashen face in the crowd and set her at ease. "Eldric is fine," he told her "He'll probably be the first one home in a few days."

Others inquired about their own loved ones, but Jeff could only respond to each in the same way, by apologizing for his ignorance. Their quick and early departure had meant that he just didn't know.

They carried Burkellyn's body to the inn and laid him out on a table. Jeff loaded the maple benches that had once been a cannon onto the cart and delivered them to Arvel. He gave the carpenter specific and detailed instructions and made his way to the forge. He took off the wide leather belt he had worn every day since his arrival in Llewellynn, removed the buckle and took a chisel to it.

The men of the village had still not returned, were probably at least another day away, but the funeral for Burkellynn could not wait. Jeff knew how much loved the innkeeper had been throughout the town and it pained him to know so many friends would miss it. But it was unavoidable in an era without refrigeration or embalming and so it began almost as soon as Arvel delivered the coffin.

The maple benches had been split into planks and joined to make the box with the lid over two inches thick. Arvel sealed the wood inside the box and out with several coats of varnish and buffed it to a high gloss shine. At the head of the lid he had inlaid Jeff's Smith and Wesson belt buckle for ornamentation and varnished that over as well. It was splendid, but it was heavy.

With no pallbearers available the coffin sat on the cart at the altar while Father Ewan performed the service. Any Latin that Jeff might have been able to decipher went right past him, requiring far more concentration than he was capable of at the moment. Kneeling at the altar with Mairwen by his side his only thought, how they had been in this very spot such a short time ago for their wedding. How happy a day that had been and how sorrowful this.

After the mass, the entire village followed as the cart was rolled up the road out of town and then hauled to the top of the hill on which Jeff was found almost a year ago and sang a hymn while the beloved innkeeper was laid to rest.

Late the following day, Eldric returned at the head of a grand parade, leading the triumphant army home. The men held their heads high as they strode into town, eager to see the loved ones left behind and Eldric was no exception. He found Bryggid and the baby and rushed over to embrace them.

"Welcome back" said Jeff, proffering his hand once the blacksmith looked like he was willing to take his eyes off his wife. "I see Arthwyr isn't with you."

"And don't expect him either." Eldric held his son up over his head and then brought him down in a gentle bear hug. "He, Gryffud and Cadeyrn are heading north to Rheged to give Urien a hand with his own Saxon problem, but even when that is done, he'll probably settle in his old family home at the castle."

"I can't say I'm surprised at that." Eldric continued the walk home, leaving Jeff behind to greet others as they came by. Some were wounded, though still in high spirits. Those who could, walked, the rest rode in the supply wagons.

"Wizard!" Jeff craned his neck until he spotted the familiar mop of red hair. Rhydderch ran along, weaving his way through the marching townsmen to greet his mentor.

"Rhydderch! Good to see you home!" Jeff welcomed the boy, "I suspect that this little town won't be needing the services of a wizard much anymore, while those of an innkeeper will be in high demand." Ryhdderch was crushed. Being a wizard's apprentice made him feel special in ways he had never imagined and he wasn't near ready to let that go. The disappointment was written across his young freckled face. "However, if you'll come by the inn and help out for a little while every day, I'll be happy to continue your education.

Epilogue

ST&C Labs
Present day

And... it's gone!" Harry Stevens announced triumphantly. The center of the plaza where the monument had been was now an empty hole in the ground. The scientists whooped with glee at their success.

"It worked!"

"Oh my god, Jeff, did you see that?" Tom could barely contain himself, "We've made history." He looked to see his friend's reaction to the groundbreaking experiment. "Jeff?" Tom scanned the area around them to see where his friend had gone. He hadn't noticed him moving in the excitement. "Jeff? Has anybody seen my friend Jeff?"

"He was right there," said Chris. The team looked around for any sign of the visitor but found none.

Tom was in a panic looking for his friend. He could see the parking lot from the plaza and since they were here after hours, the only cars parked there were their own and an old MGB. He ran inside to check the stairwell lab and bathrooms, all to no avail. He walked forlornly back onto the plaza, "He's not here."

"Do you think maybe he got too close?"

"He was behind me," Steve discounted that possibility.

"From my angle, it looked as though there might have been a reflection." David's words hung there while it sank in. The young American was gone and he was probably caught in the beam.

The police arrived fifteen minutes after Harry Stevens' call reporting the incident. They ran the video tape back and forth several times and ,while Jeff was off camera, there appeared to be no sign of foul play. The detectives were somewhat incredulous when the scientists described the experiment and what it was purported to do, but separated, their stories were identical. Whether they bought the idea of time travel or not, it seemed clear that what had happened was a tragic accident and nothing more.

Through the registration papers in the MG, the police were able to provide Harry with a phone number to contact Jeff's aunt and uncle in London and in turn, Jeff's parents in Connecticut. After the two most difficult phone calls in his life, he went home and spent a sleepless night thinking about what might h vvave happened.

At nine o'clock Harry started the day, as always with a meeting. "The first thing we need to do, is analyze the data. We need to work out just what happened." Around the room heads bobbed in agreement. "Bill, any idea how far back we sent him?"

"The machine was cranked up pretty high." Bill took a deep breath and took a shot at it. "A thousand years at least, maybe more, then we have to figure what adding the boy's mass does to the calculation."

"OK. Let's get on it. Go over everything, in the meantime, Tom and I will be out in the plaza. If we are right about what is going on, that monument still exists and we ought to be able to find it. It may be buried under new soil and it will be eroded, but it ought to be there." Harry Stevens and his son left the others to their work and moved outside to the plaza.

The pavers that made up the plaza were unmoved except at the center where the monument had been, there, all that remained was an empty crater. Tom spread out a tarp alongside the work area so that dirt that was removed could later be sifted if that proved important. They went to work using hand tools, not wanting to overlook anything, and first enlarged the hole before going deeper.

They had only removed a few inches of dirt when Harry struck something hard. He brushed away the dirt to reveal the grainy surface of the squared edge of a large object. "Whatever it is, it's not our monument. It's made of wood and it's very old!" They brushed away more dirt and got an idea of the size of the thing, nearly two feet wide and six feet long.

"Do you think it could be a coffin?" Tom Worried. "Maybe Jeff was killed..."

"It's possible the machine could have killed him," Harry mused, "But it didn't put him in a box."

"What if someone found him and decided he should have a proper burial?" Tom insisted.

"I guess that's what we need to find out," said Harry, smoothing away more dirt off the finely grained surface, "I think we need to call in an expert."

As a scientist, Harry understood completely the importance of expertise in a delicate situation. He called the British museum and was eventually connected to an archaeologist working in Stonehenge, a professor Spencer, who said he could be over that day. For two days a team from the museum worked at the site, unearthing whatever it was that was buried there.

Late in the afternoon of the second day the archaeologist came into the lab and confirmed Harry's greatest fear. "Mr Stevens?"

Harry came over and shook the man's hand "Professor, how is it going out there?" he asked.

"Yes! Well I thought you would like to know," The archaeologist reported. " We've removed the wooden box and I have to tell you your suspicions were correct. It is indeed a coffin." Tom was listening in across the room. The news was devastating. "But it doesn't appear to be your missing lad though. It's an older man, probably near forty, been there since the early middle ages it would seem, wearing bronze armor." That was welcome news for all in the room, even if it didn't solve the larger problem. "We've sent samples along to the lab for Carbon 14 and other dating techniques, so we'll have a definitive date but it will take some time. When I have more information, I'll call you with the update."

"Thank you Dr. Spencer. That period is consistent with what we were expecting." Harry walked the man to the door. "I look forward to hearing from you again. An accurate date would be a great help to us."

In the two weeks since the experiment, the team had gone

over the data exhaustively. But in order to properly assess the power and wavelength settings, they needed to know just how far back in time the monument and Jeff had gone. The carbon dating that would provide that would not be back for another two weeks. So they turned their attention to fine tuning the machine itself while they waited for the results.

Harry was working busily at his desk, getting up to date with administrative work when the phone rang. "Stevens." He answered as he always did at work.

"This is Professor Spenser at the museum."

Harry was a little surprised at the call. He didn't expect any word until the dating was done. "Yes Professor, what can I do for you?"

"There's been a development that puts some doubt on the authenticity of the site." Disappointment was evident in the voice. "We've been looking mostly at the body and burial artifacts so far and they've been consistent, early middle ages I'm sure, but yesterday one of my team moved on to the coffin itself. It's marvelously preserved, which could be a problem in itself, but there is one thing in particular."

"On the lid we found an inlaid bronze plate. The surface was very corroded, again consistent with age, and any markings on it are indecipherable but when we removed it we found an inscription very clearly engraved on the back."

"Were you able to translate it?" Harry's interest peaked at the thought of clear documentation.

"Well' I'm afraid that's the problem, we didn't have to." The professor explained, "It was in English, modern English. I'm afraid the artifacts could not have been in that location for more than a few hundred years, but probably not more than a few decades."

Harry was confounded and disappointed. The body was apparently part of some elaborate hoax. Memories of the Piltdown Man came to mind. "I'm sorry to hear that, Professor. I assure you I had no idea. Is there any clue who might have been responsible? What did the inscription say?"

The archaeologist read the inscription, "It said, 'I'm OK! Jeff Warren." There was no date.

Acknowledgements

Thanks to the Mythbusters, Adam Savage and Jamie Hyneman, who proved possible Jeff's contribution to the effort in Chapter 8. Now, if they can only get me past Chapter 1, we'd really have something.

14011124R00137

Made in the USA
Charleston, SC
15 August 2012